PACK LOREN:

KING'S BOUNTY

by

Howard Night

A DARK UNIVERSE COLLECTION

King's Bounty is a collection of three novellas:
Kings Hunt,
Kings Ransom,
Kings Court
by
Howard Night

Howard Night can be contacted at HowardNight.com

ISBN 10: 0985560312
ISBN 13: 978-0-9855603-1-7

Cover art by
Natiq Jalil
http://artofnatiq.com/

This work is set in the Dark Universe: Interregnum, a shared science fiction setting in the space opera genre. Characters, settings and concepts have been created and contributed by authors from across the country. This work includes references to these copy written concepts and characters with the permissions of the various creators.

Khalid Cassad, Ziara, and Samake
appear with the permission of Milton Davis
http://www.mvmediaatl.com/

Galvin Onted, Quaznians, Jemsa Overmind, Wars of the Blade concept and Norlans
appear with the permission of Ronald Jones
https://www.facebook.com/ronald.jones.1481

Euphrates and related concepts
appear with the permission of Penelope Flynn
http://www.penelopeflynn.com/

The Marajeshi, Averator and Sublimator concepts
appear with the permission of DaVaun Sanders
http://davaunsanders.com/

The Taj Pirates concept
appears with the permission of Marc Peterson
mdpeterson27@gmail.com

all other references, concepts and characters created and copywritten by author Howard Night
http://www.howardnight.com/

FOR THE INDEPENDENTS

THE FALL

About twenty-three cycles ago the most powerful worlds under the control of the empire got together in secret to figure out how to beat the top dog; the Cassads. Most people will tell you that was the beginning of their fall but really…it was the Blade. The Blade did to the Cassads what it did to most; cut them up and bled them numb.

The New Regime got bolder after that. The known began falling faster and the Cassads couldn't feel the reigns slipping through their cold fingers… couldn't hear the scores of worlds crying for liberation for the buzzing in their ears.

Now the Known is in chaos and the Cassads last worlds are under siege.

It's a good time to be a merc…

46TH TASK UNIT
EXO-RANGER

PACK LOREN:

Kings Hunt

by

Howard Night

A DARK UNIVERSE NOVELLA

CHAPTER ONE:

The INDO Bar

"Just a piece of fek dive bar, Pack," my pops once told me. "They're the same everywhere in the known." He'd just pulled me and Drez out of "Jags", the local hole in the wall back in Buckets Hollow. I remember how terrified we were when he popped up in front of us at that filthy corner table where we were sitting and freaking out because we couldn't pay our tab.

"Look at you now…" he'd said more annoyed and disappointed than anything else. Ten Arcadian cycles, an eye, an arm and All knows how many "piece of fek" dive bars later and I understand why. We were young and looking to get in on all the action the adults were hiding in that little after hours spot but Pops told us better. There's nothing in these dark little watering holes worth wasting anyone's time.

Of course…here I am…again.

Third bar on this world, the seventh straight night here and I'm beginning to think the intel I bought ain't worth fek. The only thing I'm finding is the same thing my old man told me to expect; nothing.

The *Last Ship Out* is what remains of a nearly five hundred year old gunboat and sits down deep in the lower levels of Passieun City; third biggest port city here on Indo. Ownership and the name has changed dozens of times since it was first dragged into the old city and opened but since then it's pretty much always been a dive bar. It's a big space but dark, even to those with optic upgrades. Most places like this fill the air with the standard privacy invasion counter measures. So the booths, the alcoves and the far corners of the room remain cloaked in shadow. The bar is lit up, of course, as well as the tables in the center of the floor. The servers are illuminated by little balls of light that orbit their bodies to allow the patrons to see them coming. Wouldn't do to have one of them walk up unnoticed and hear something they shouldn't.

One makes her way back around to my table. Most places still use live servers because they can offer more than a droid or bot. She asks me if I want another drink, hoping that the ink I'm sipping on will get me chambered up enough to zip her some cred. But I'm not interested in binding with some wage slave when it might cost me finding my mark.

I flash two fingers at her, ordering another ink. Got to be careful with that though; "gunks" are the most ridiculous looking addicts.

The big door at the end of the bar collapses open and lets in a gust of cool air that doesn't smell of alcohol or burnt sugar. Only for a pulse beat, though; a small group of Indo workers shuffle in bringing the funk of a hard day's work with them. They work salvage out in the dead plains where the electromagnetic field is still up on this world. A hold over from the *Wars of the Blade*, an area about a quarter of the planet is a tech dead zone. Thousands of war ships fell to this planet's surface during a particularly nasty battle. Usually the wrecks would have been long since plundered but somebody forgot to turn off the EMF over that one fourth of the planet and whatever's generated it is still running ten cycles later. Conventional salvage can't be done even with the best faradon gear but the wrecks are way too valuable to be left out there. So, by hand, the Indo workers work the dead plains, dragging the debris clear of the EMF and manually picking the wrecks clean.

Hazardous work, I don't envy them even with the big coin they're pulling in.

The Indo workers find a quiet corner of the bar and turn it into a loud one. Servers come rushing up to take advantage of the coin in their pockets and the hard worked salvagers are eager to give it. I watch the negotiations for a bit, growing more restless. By the time a few of the group disappear into the dark recesses of the private booths I'm ready to leave myself. Seven straight nights and seven straight no shows means that…whoa now.

He's big, like I expected, as most of them are, but older than I would have thought. There's more gray in his spikey stubble than black now. Even so he moves with a grace that I would never have noticed if I didn't already know what he was. The clothes on his back are pretty commonplace and don't mark him as being from anywhere in particular.

But they're roomy enough to hide a good sized weapon.

Maybe two.

He crosses the room at an odd angle, as if he's so tired he doesn't notice where he's going, then he catches himself and cuts back across the room.

Nice.

Without giving himself away he's just gotten a good look at everyone in the bar. And he wouldn't have bothered if he didn't have military grade optics so he knows what everyone in the bar is packing. That includes me.

Anything more serious than a bladed weapon would have set off all the bells and whistles of his security gear. Course there's plenty of ways to beat military grade optics. Next gen military grade camo, for one, would deny him a peek at what you've got. If you've got the coin the upgrade will even make him think he's seeing an unarmed man.

I do not have the coin.

There's a sweet V.I. hacking matrix that will render his optics unable to read specific weapon signatures but you have to know exactly his optical manufacturer. Now I know where this guy got his originals but I really doubt he's still using those.

No, I have to beat his optics the only way left to me; I have to actually be unarmed.

But not too unarmed. A small blade won't look as out of place as being completely unarmed in a pit like this would look suspicious and I don't want him looking at me any longer than he looks at anybody else. I slump in my seat to shorten my long twenty decimeter frame. I'm nowhere near as tall as this guy but Arcadians grow pretty big so I tend to stand out just a bit. Right now we're the two biggest guys in the bar and I'm hoping that doesn't draw his eye.

Surprisingly he takes a seat in the well-lit center of the room, with his back to the door. He's either not worried about who's coming in behind him, which I doubt, or he's got it covered somehow. Either way I settle in and begin my recon.

Two fingers again call the server over with another ink. I just want to look like another beat up Indo scavenger dulling away the day's pain. But I watch him, try and figure out exactly how he's armed and what allies, if any, he has. He's probably got one of the servers or even the owner on his payroll to keep him updated on newcomers. Hopefully the fact that I've been coming here for over a week will give me enough of a pass that they won't bring it up to him.

To my surprise though he says nothing to the server other than to order a drink and turn down her extra services. Can't tell if they're communicating sub-vocally… doubt the servers here have that kind of gear. Still, he hasn't shown me or anyone else in the bar the slightest bit of interest. Could be he's sure that he's far enough off the grid that he's got nobody looking for him here.

Not a bad assumption given the state of the known right now. It's total chaos across damn near a hundred systems. Long standing "second tier" galactic powers are vying for control of what was once the Cassad Empire and vultures are swooping in to glean the pickings of the once proud house.

Vultures like me.

The big guy takes a long swig, drains his cup in one downing then signals the server to bring him another. He doesn't look like he's expecting anyone to join him so I can wait until he gets good and "nice" before I move in. Not really sure if that'll make him more or less dangerous though.

There comes a ruckus from the far end of the room. A brief argument between two indo workers ends with one of them on the floor and the other laughing his ass off. I feign mild interest in the fight but my mark snaps his head in the other direction. Caught off guard I realize too late my mistake as I look to see what startled him.

It was a ruse and my backwater ass fell for it! My eyes jump back to him and the smug bastard is staring right at me. He's wearing a nasty "I got ya" smile and with one hand he beckons me over.

I had better do as he says 'cause with his other he's leveling one mean looking gun at me from under his table.

Buckin' Royal Guard…if I live through this I'll never underestimate them again.

CHAPTER TWO:

COMMERCE

I don't hesitate to get up but I take my time. Not sure if he'll fire off that heater here in the bar. Can't risk it; body armor I'm wearing is good enough for the minor weapons fire that the stick up scabs outside in the lower city are packin' but not for much more. Can't see it clearly but it looks to have a decent enough power cell, which means it's energy based and more than he'll need to make most of me a memory. So I get the buck up and with my hands in the clear I make my way over to his table.

He gestures to the server and she slides a second chair over to his table. She's nervous, I can see, so I know she's the one who tipped him. Won't underestimate the wage slaves again either.

I try and adjust the chair to my advantage as I sit but with a quick tap of that gun to the underside of the table he lets me know he's on to me. The old guy grins, tight lipped and wide, spreading out that prickly stubble which sticks out like the quills of a scared daggerback. The surprise I felt from his getting the drop on me pales in comparison to the shock I get when he first opens his mouth.

"The infamous Pack Loren," he says. "…of the legendary 46th."

What the buck? How does he know who I am? Evidently the surprise on my face is apparent because the bastard laughs.

"What? Didn't think I could I.D. you that quick?" his voice is smooth, deep and slides out of his throat in that pompous Median belt accent.

"The Infamous?" I ask. "Legendary?" Sure, my old unit was pretty well known back in Arcadian space but why would anyone from the larger worlds have heard of us.

"Of course, Loren. You most of all" and his mouth stretches into an even wider grin, lips parting, showing his ink stained teeth. "You are Loren, right? The file I have details the loss of that eye and arm. Both regrown, I see, not replaced; my optics can tell. It's the corticolin bands just beneath the skin that give you away. So, you're Sgt. Pack Loren of Arcadias 46th Task Unit, who held their own against the Giaks and the Junns when the rest of that bit of space fell into chaos."

Hoofer-Fek. Nobody ever took notice of Arcadia and no one but Arcadians cared when the Giaks and the Junns tried to invade. What's he playing at?

"The *Wars of the Blade* raged all over," I say. "But our little piece of it never seemed to matter much to the rest of the known."

Somehow that smile grows even wider. "Maybe the hubheads didn't pay too much attention, but when human soldiers from small worlds take down ten foot tall Giaks in unpowered combat…well, anybody who might have to eventually deal with that is gonna take notice."

I don't say anything to that. Can't tell if he's just glossing my finish or if he's speaking level. No reason for him to lie but the "admiration" has got to be fek.

With a sigh he leans back in his chair, seeming to relax a bit, but still keeping that gun on me. "And then there's you, Pack Loren…"

"I came here…" I try to cut him off but he just talks over me.

"…first a war criminal…"

"So say the Junns." I snap.

"…then a traitor…"

"I don't need a…"

"…an avenger…"

"I've got coin to…"

"Then last I heard, Loren, you turned on your own unit" and with that his smile vanishes. There's the look of deadly intent I'd expected to see in the eyes of one of the Royal Guard.

I should just try and deal, after all that's why I tracked this bastard to the outer territories, to the Desolate Perimeter. But I can't help it; his little tirade on my personal history has me way off my game.

Which wasn't all that good to begin with.

"That's a lot of info on me. How long have you known I've been looking for you?"

After another swig of his freshly filled cup he answers. "Just about as long as it took me to order a drink."

"And you got all my stats just like that?"

"Oh no. I meant it when I said you and the 46th were infamous. Anybody in the merc game has looked up your unit ever since they started popping up throughout the known as hired soldiers."

That was true. Without a war most of my old unit had turned to being paid soldiers ever since we lost Arcadia. The memory bites hard…We lost Arcadia…

His eyes shine a bit as he watches my reaction. "I do wonder why you've been taking out your old crew. Maybe the betrayal of Arcadia wasn't your decision?"

I grind my teeth and somehow I remember why I'm here in the first place. "I'm looking to make a purchase" I say.

His eyebrows rise. "You think I'm selling something?"

"You've something I want to buy."

"If you're thinking of hiring me out…I don't guard anyone or anything but myself these days."

Now I feel like I got some footing. "That's right; you were dismissed."

Those eyes flare for a moment then soften as the big man suddenly laughs. "Perhaps," he says with understanding in his voice. "rumors and data bits are not to be trusted to tell the whole story."

"Perhaps."

"Then what does the 'infamous for perhaps no good reason' Pack Loren need to purchase from a 'Dismissed' Guardsman of the First House of Denir?"

I had hoped to make this offer from a position of strength rather than sitting with gun aimed at my poker. Really, I have got to get better at plan making.

"I would like to buy your armor." I say flatly.

"My armor? My battle Armor?"

"No sir," I explain. "Your Royal Dress armor."

For a long pulse beat I watch as his mind races trying to figure my angle. Not to worry, he'll never figure out what I'm…

"You're after Cassad."

Fek.

His palm slaps the table with such a clap that I thought the gun had gone off. Damn, I had underestimated him again.

"You've got to be kidding me, Loren" I wish he'd stop blurting my name out loud. "Cassad's Royal Guard are nothing like the Denir Royal Guard."

But he says it with just a bit of hesitation. Probably 'cause they were alike. The House of Denir was a Cassad house long ago, but the Royal Guard had been protecting the Cassads for longer than that. There were some very important similarities, such as the Royal dress armor.

"I'm sure you don't need it anymore." With that I very carefully reach into the folds of the Indo jacket I have on and pull free the small but brightly colored data card hidden within. As carefully as I can I place it on the table.

"If I even still have it…" He says as he picks up the data chip and examines it. "Well, look at that."

He still had it. The only question was; would he part with it? "Not much I know," I say indicating the chip.

"Not much," he agrees. "but QED certified Old Reg currency…damn you make it tempting."

I'll bet.

"And you have this with you here?" he asks with a tightness in his voice.

"I can get it to you as fast as you can get me the armor."

I watch what remains of the old Royal Guard wage war with the disgruntled and betrayed man he's become. The Denir had summarily dismissed their Royal Guard at some point during the last decade. A purge that had been a bit bloody according to…rumors and data bits. Still, the man had once been indoctrinated into one of the most fanatical military arms in the known. Getting his armor from him isn't going to be easy.

"Deal" he says abruptly.

Buck me… "Deal?"

"Yea. Surprised? Do you know what the Cassads did to us? To the Guard?" he asks leaning back into the chair. His faces grows dark and his eyes stare at nothing. "We were…pillars…no…we were golden shields of light…protecting to the Lords of the universe. And we did not do it for prestige or crukin' coin!" he grows quiet for a pulse beat then adds in almost a whisper, "it was for love…"

There's a "click" and I know he's reset the safety on his weapon. He looks at me again trying to figure me out a bit more.

"What is this for you, Loren? The credits they're offering for

Cassad is a symbolic gesture. No one expects him to be caught… killed maybe… in a planetary assault. But Cassad can't be captured and brought to trial. Your attempt for that ridiculous bounty is practically suicide. You want to die? Or…maybe you blame the Cassads for what happened to Arcadia."

"You said we had a deal. Where do we make the exchange?"

The big man lets out a big nasty hot breath and then cracks his neck. "You can bring the qed here."

"No. I may be slow, but I reboot quick. You OWN this bar."

He almost snickers. "On my honor I'll deal with you fairly, Loren. You bring that coin here and all is legit; I'll give you my armor."

"The entire set," I insist. "Intact and complete."

"On my honor.

CHAPTER THREE:

HONOR

It's raining by the time I make my way back down to bar, not that any rain drops actually make it down this far to the lower levels of the city. Instead there're several man made "waterfall" conduits conducting the water down to the reclamation plants below. The walls of the building units run slick with drain water and there's a steady falling mist that drenches everything else sitting outside for extended periods.

Never the less I stop before I go in, considering this madness one last time. Without the need for a cover I came back to the bar in my flight suit, field jacket and virtual visor. It helps a bit against the sudden cold wetness.

On his "honor" he'd said. Don't trust honor…not one bit. Soldiers put their lives on the line for it in one battle, then in the next you discover they never had it at all. Of course the Royal Guard were a different animal. Most of them were born into the Guard, living for their Houses like most live for their god. But those fanatics were all dead, either killed in the purge or dead by their own hand when they found themselves out in the real known.

But this particular gentleman was indoctrinated through their regular armed forces. Still a fanatic but not as religious about those he guarded. Hopefully that works to keep him honest about this deal.

Before I can decide to enter the front is lit up in brilliant blue light. The entrance opens and out comes the Ex-Denirian Royal Guard flanked by a few well-armed employees.

"Were you having second thoughts?" he asks.

I take my time answering, letting him watch me look over his small army. My Virtual Visor covers my face from just above my eyebrows to just below my nose. With it on all he can see of my eyes are the two glowing holographic representations; ghostly, triangular patches of white light with no pupils, but they open and close in sync with my real ones. The visor also highlights some of the tech his squad is toting. One of them reads really high in the EM spectrum… might be a bogey… or maybe borged up. "No. Just wondering about the honor of the Royal Guard."

He snorts derisively. "You don't seem to have my qed."

"You don't seem to have my armor."

With another one of those nasty breaths the big man nods to one of his crew, who in turn walks back into the bar only to return a pulse beat later followed a huge, self-motivated crate. The Royal Guard opens the front of the crate and low and behold there sits his dress armor as shiny and polished as the last day he wore it. It's a pretty close match for the design the Cassad Royal Guard use. The armor gets passed down from Guard to apprentice I think so his set could be a few centuries old. He's taken care of it…and that worries me.

"Now how about you show me whatever it is you've got hidden under that holocloak."

He's good alright. Carefully I reach into my jacket and retrieve a small two ended remote. It's a simple little device, well-worn with chipped and faded white enamel, that has two buttons that can be set to trigger multiple devices of various manufacture and function. I slide it around in my hand and depress the narrow ended side.

Right next to me the ground shimmers and distorts until a pretty hefty cargo container can be seen hovering just off the ground. I reach down with one hand and pop the opening to reveal about two hundred and fifty thousand Old Regime Credits, all Q.E.D. certified and neatly stacked. It's nearly the sum total of everything I have left and it took me some time to get.

"Do you mind if I verify?" the Ex-Guardsman asks. I pull my own scanner from my belt.

"If you don't mind."

We step past each other without outward signs of worry or mistrust and I try to appear totally focused on my own scans as I have my back to him. I do notice however that the hired guns in his small little group are constantly peering about, no doubt looking for anything or anyone else I might have cloaked and waiting in front of this bar.

My scan completes first and I'll be damned…the old bastard just might be dealing fair. So I turn and wait for him to finish. Seems that after the purge the big guy has decided to check and then double check anybody he's dealing with. He scans every single qed.

"Looks good" he nods slowly but doesn't look satisfied. It's not the money… The QED certification, given by the Brython Currency Exchange, meant that the seven big wigs of the New Regime would still recognize the currency. So it was good practically from one end of the known to the other despite the war on the Cassads.

"Then I'll just be on my way."

"Just a second." He says and his little army produces a ton of small arms.

I flash a grim smile. "You're not reneging on our deal now are you?" Something's off. His little gang of makeshift guardians look a bit unsure of themselves. They weren't expecting this it seems. What's the old guy thinking?

"I did a bit more research on you, Loren. Just trying to get past all the rumor and innuendo."

I drop the smile and ask again, "Are. You. Reneging?"

"Just wondering what your plan is for my old armor."

"Thought you had that figured out."

"More like," he hesitates and now I can see the proud face of the old Royal Guardsman peeking through. "How many of Cassad's Royal Guard are going to die in your attempt to bring him in?"

What the… his buckin' honor! How do I handle this? Uhh… "Not so many as you probably want."

His face goes blank. "As I want?"

"I know about the part they played in the dismissal of your Guard."

He stares hard, no doubt running every optical scan of me as he can trying to see if I'm lying. But I'm wearing my Visor now, so this time he won't get anything and he'll have to judge for himself.

I jump back in before he can challenge my play. "Look, I'm not your payback for whatever it was they did. I'm going after Cassad and I need him alive, so I'm not risking going in chambered up to kill."

His face draws tight as he studies me for a moment, then he looks back at the crate full of currency. "This a Doppler switch?"

"Yup." I say. As long as I'm in range of the crate I can blow it. Once I'm clear and gone…the switch deactivates. They're pretty common place so I'm sure he's not worried about it.

"Fine. Go." And just like that the deal is done. But I don't like the way he looks like he's still thinking.

I'm back to the port when I know the deal is going bad. It wasn't hard to find the three tracers he'd placed on the crate though I was surprised that he'd put none on the armor itself. Probably didn't want to compromise it I guess. What worries me isn't the crate; it's the little group of moles he has spread out at the port.

They're easy to spot; you can't turn failed salvage workers into clandestine spies. Edgy and looking over everybody traveling with cargo through the terminal, they evidently don't know I can holo-cloak the armors crate as easily as I did the credits. Looks like they're looking over everyone wearing anything like my visor. So I stow mine in my jacket next to my gun.

As I walk right past his ragged looking sentinels I wonder what happened that made the old guy change his mind. Maybe it was concern for Cassad's Royal Guard. Maybe he figured out I made up that part about them having something to do with the purge of his unit.

I reach the hangar where my ship is docked and find a little welcoming committee. Looks like at least one of his hired hands has got a decent brain; must've looked through the registry and took a guess at which ship was mine. There are seven of them, all armed but only three look like they're any good in a fight. I walk right up to them.

"This your ship?" I ask.

"Who are you?" the leader of the gang asks. He's little and holds his chin high with a clear chip on his shoulder.

"I'm Tagget, the Engineer you asked for."

He looks me up and down. "Where's your equipment?" he challenges.

"Uh…" I shake the tool belt I have sitting quite plainly on my hip. "Right here. Thought you weren't gonna be here. But you can show me where the problem is."

"I ain't the owner, backbirth!" he snaps and a few of his boys laugh.

"So…" I continue. "…you can't show me where the rad leak is?"

"Rad leak?" he asks and I point to the warning, flashing brightly on the holo terminal at the hangar hatchway.

"s'what I'm here for."

"Where's the owner?" he demands even as he and his guys step away from the hangar hatchway, one of them even bothering to shield his crotch.

I shrug my shoulders. "I don't know…salvage run? What's the problem? The leak getting' by the dampenin' wall?"

Again he snaps, "I don't know! I ain't the rustin' port authority. Go fix it!"

I just shrug my shoulders again and step through the group of retreating thugs while trying to hide the growing smile on my face.

THUNK!

"Wha'd on styx is 'dis?" croaks the tallest of the thugs. I turn about and see him kicking a slightly wavering patch of air. The others all grow very interested in what nearly tripped their buddy.

Fek. The cloaked crate should've been closer on my heels but the damn power cell must be low. Would've switched to my own equipment but once I cleared out the tracers I saw no reason to give up the old guard's container.

"Hey. Didn't that guy the boss wanted have a…"

"GET H…" WHAM!

I take out the leader first with the hydro-spanner on my tool belt, despite his being the furthest from me. He drops like a Targo indigul and his crew fall into discord even faster than I'd have hoped. Of the rest, only two pull out handguns, both projectile weapons, which makes it better odds than usual. But as I pull my own NOK 37 handgun they rush me instead of retreat, actually providing cover for the armed buckheads. What on styx is he paying these fools?

I pop the gunmen with the clearest line of sight first but have to backpedal to avoid the wild swing of a long curved blade that sinks right through the floor almost as if it was a holo. A Kendo blade? Where'd this fool get a *Wars of the Blade* weapon?

He's surprised he can't pull the blade free so I know it's not his. While he's yanking at it he gets two in his back from his panicky buddy.

Duck another swing from a stun baton. The Royal Guard must not be too deep in cred if he can't afford thugs with better weapons…

Duck.

Shoot.

…or who are smarter. Don't think anyone of them thought to call for backup. Good thing I shot the leader first.

Block.

Shoot.

Got the second gunman with that one. He drops and I get another one trying to recover his weapon. The last two are smarter than the rest or at least they wise up in time 'cause they're off and running. Don't know how long I have before they collect themselves and call the Guard to let him know where I'm berthed so I can't dawdle.

Still, no sense in leaving behind perfectly good weaponry…but the two handguns are Barron Inc. pieces of crap. Should've figured. The blade is fine though and I slide it up out of the floor with ease. Long time since I've seen a blade with a Kendo edge. It's pretty unremarkable; dao shaped…but no identifying marks or wrappings…no world colors. Might be older than the Blade then? The guy welding it was just a thug though, the blade never even whistled as he swung it. Wielding it requires a learned touch or you'll just end up getting it stuck in whatever you hack at. Idiot couldn't have known what he had, blade like this could bought him a small ship. Wonder how he came by it? Buck it…I don't have all day.

Through the hatch with my new armor in tow I step onto the hangar deck which sits cliff-side overlooking the white plains. The dark cloudy sky has just a hint of the approaching dawn so the silhouette of the far off Stony Mountains is just starting to emerge from the blackness. My ships running lights illuminate the hangar bay as I approach.

The hangar registry reads my ships name as: *Calypso's Lie*. Anybody close enough to read the emblem on her side would find it too burned and charred from rough entry to make out, but her real name is *WarChild*.

I found her in the Targothian Graveyard, floating deep in the smashed up flotsam, somehow, miraculously still intact despite the conditions there. She's a Mutt…M.U.T.T., a Multi-purpose Utility Troop Transport. A holdover from the first space wars during the Great Age of Discovery. I'm not sure what duty she saw back then but I had to paint her new name over the faded original 'cause I couldn't sand it off. Some kind of animal glyph I think. Would've left her there to continue to sink deeper into the graveyard but I recognized the cete-armor. It looked like a wild animal then, spikey where impacts hadn't chipped off the new growth but the whole of it had withstood the pounding like a champ. So I claimed her and took the better part of two cycles rebuilding her, keeping her hidden from the raider gangs that worked the graveyard, spending almost every last bit of my coin to get her up and running.

I added the wings. Been in too many rough drops where an EMP or EMF strips away all power to not know that you'd better have decent mechanical hardware back up for your powered tech. I rebuilt three Tarkanian EMT engines and jammed two of them into the jet housings, keeping the third for a spare. Then I lucked into some Element G for the grav-well which meant I could do something few could; cross most of the known on my own without having to hitch a ride or even use a gate.

Of course I keep most of this a secret as much as possible. Ship like this is worth its weight in lifetimes. I've had to protect *WarChild* as much as she's protected me.

Her rear cargo hatch opens at my approach and I ascend into her belly with my new gear in tow. She's got a nice sized cargo bay which is mostly empty right now. Just some light ore that I can't unload cause it's overpriced and my, currently down, eight-leg walker.

I stow the armor beneath the floor of the bay in a pirates hold and then make my way up to the command deck. With the grav-well off line the footing in the ship is a little precarious as *WarChild* is constructed with the decks curving around the ships gravity center. Not a problem but it's a hassle when I'm trying to keep her specs of the grid.

WarChild was originally designed for a three man command crew at minimum or a wartime crew of about seventeen. She can transport seventy conventional soldiers or up to twenty heavy armored personnel. It wasn't hard for me to convert her to be piloted by one man but her command deck still holds three stations. I really don't see the point in wasting the time on changing it; Ops and Tactical are still slaved to Primary. Besides the configuration is almost exactly the same as the Hawkbats I used to fly in the *Blade*.

I'm just strapping myself into the Primary control seat when my proximity alarm warns of pedestrian traffic. I check the ground feed and see the old Royal Guard, in full assault armor striding into the hangar with a bit more of his better armed employees in tow.

"LOREN! Power down your ship or I'll scuttle it right here!"

Ships sensors highlight why he even thinks that's possible. One of his men is leveling a pretty nasty piece of hardware at my ship; an armor piercing High Yield Explosive launcher. I try and gauge where he's aiming. It looks enough like he's targeting the cete-armor parts of the ship that I'll risk it.

A quick subvocal command and *WarChild's* external speakers come online. "Thought we had deal?" I say. "Thought we both made out."

His men spread out around the hangar, ridiculously trying to surround my ship. Some are trying to find the cockpit, but *WarChild's* canopy is now safe behind a two meter thick cete-armor shield.

"Deal's off Loren! I want the armor back! I cannot dishonor my fellow Guardsmen"

"Funny, I see your honor didn't get you to bring back the coin I dropped you."

"You power down and we'll work something out! You try to launch and I'll gut that ship… and then you!"

I check the angle on that HYE launcher again. Hmm…pretty sure. He'll likely target one of the engine housings.

"LOREN! Last warning!" The old guard is pointing his own weapon at my ship. His battle armor doesn't look at all like the fighting armor of the Cassad Royal Guard. A couple of hundred cycles makes all the difference. Not sure he's got the fire power to do any real damage but he's more likely to know what he can hit to keep me on the ground. Even as I'm thinking I'm pulled down into the Primary Control seat as the grav-well powers up.

"Sorry, but all deals are final!" I say.

"You can't think your little plan is gonna work now anyway, Loren! Not when I let them know you've got my armor."

He's bluffing. No way he'll come anywhere close to contacting the Cassad Royal Guard. They might not have actually had anything to do with his Guards purge but sure as styx ends they'll try and take his ass of the board if they learn where he is now. The Denir and the Cassads are not exactly allies at the moment.

Still…there's a risk. Don't want to have to kill the old guy but he's putting himself in my path. I can't help but to admire him for his sense of honor, as late in the game as it is. Damn it…

I start the launch and take her up…slow.

"FIRE!" I hear him order. There are two bright flashes; I missed seeing the other HYE launcher, and then two big explosions. *Warchild* hardly even shakes as her cete-armor absorbs the blasts and reflects a ton of it back down into the hangar. I cut the hangar feed a moment too late and see the Royal Guard burned out of his armor.

I wonder if anyone'll give him the last rights he probably deserves. Wonder if there's anyone who'll honor his memory at all.

CHAPTER FOUR:

DREAMTIME

I'm just about done pulling the Royal Guards dress armor apart when *Warchild* alerts me that we've arrived at Hampton's Gate. With a groan I stand up from my work stool and take a look at how much I've done. The fancy purple and gold armor hangs in the workshop bay like a macabre marionette, its innards open and exposed. It was harder to open than I thought it would be but somehow it still didn't take very long.

I trudge up to the Command deck and check the ships status. We're just coming up on the first of the outer markers, close enough to the gate that a check of the long range scanner is warranted. Not much traffic coming in from this angle, which is good…which is planned.

The trip here took a bit longer than it should have because I put a deep, long dogleg in my flight course; needed to come into the gate from a vector that would match the course direction and time stamps in my fake log in case they're inspecting. Never know who's in charge of the jump gates these days with the Cassads falling off the map. The Junns took control of the gate at Cannius when the Giaks drove the Cassads out of the "Quad". The Protectorate Gate was nearly destroyed in the uprising at Sennal. The Amber Gate is being fought over right now by the Quaznians and the Norlans… don't know if that's been settled. The three big Gates; Scion, Alpha, and Maren are too big and too close to the heavily settled areas to be controlled. Still, with almost half the jump gates in jeopardy I've got to move quick. Can't be on the wrong side of the known when one critical to what I'm trying to get done is blocked; I'm on a tight timetable.

Hampton's Gate is a good sized gate that'll get me close to my destination with some time to spare. It's showing nominal traffic along my vector. Still a bit too far out for me to read what the ship types are so I subvocalize a command to the ships Computer Ops Program to notify me as soon as transponder beacons are recognized.

Hopefully I can get through the gate without much problem. The long way to Cassad space would blow my timetable.

I tread back down to the workshop to get back to work on the armor, stopping along the way at my weapons locker. Going to have to test how well the old guard's gear holds up in a firefight.

My boots ring loudly on the deck plates. Wind screams across my armor pulling me toward a ragged, gaping star filled black hole. The entire side of the ship has been breached and is open to space. The launch bay is voiding air, equipment… ships… and men. We hit a null mine; a cloaked mine designed to breech capital ships, Giak design.

They'll be coming soon.

The wind dies. The bay is a vacuum now. I still hear the harsh ring of my boots on the deck vibrating through my armor as I race toward the breech. The rest of my Fire Team, what's left, races at my back.

No matter how hard we run we won't get there in time.

I see the bodies of flight deck personnel, having been blown out of the bay, flying away from the ship, some burned and charred.

I draw my Lance. My team pull their rifles.

We won't get there in time.

I don't want to take another step but it ain't up me.

I don't want to…see… but that don't matter.

The ship is listing. The null mine was one of three that we hit. The stars outside the breech spin as the ship slides off course.

A bright blue light fills the bay as the great western hemisphere of Arcadia rolls into view through the breech.

I want to stop.

I don't want to see it again.

I'm running, my heart beating hard in my chest in horrible anticipation. I want to turn away, I want to close my eyes but I can't.

I'm dreaming.

A.C.M. Training; Arcadian Combat Memory Training was the ADFs answer to the sudden blitzkrieg of the *Wars of the Blade*. It was pretty effective; a soldier like me could learn from the experiences snatched, post mortem, from the minds of veterans who fell in the opening conflicts. What took months of hazardous combat to ingrain could be implanted in just a few safe one hour sessions. The training helped me to survive my tour with the 46th.

But… they never told us about the side effects. Forcing your mind to dream through an entire memory bucks up your head something wicked. There's Rem Jam, for one, or Black Sleep syndrome. But most suffer from Loop Dreams.

After enough training, you start dreaming memories. At first it's the combat memories but soon you start dreaming your own memories… the most intense ones, which of course are usually the bad ones. Secondly, because it's a memory you can't change what happens. You can look around a bit more, maybe see something you didn't notice consciously before, but the memory plays itself out just like it happened in life; no selective perspective… no lying to yourself.

And third; you're lucid during the whole thing but unable to wake. Combat training needed to access your consciousness in order for you to gain the experience in real time. So now I dream, while wide awake, the most horrible things I've ever seen.

The entire rear port deck has been blown away. We're in high orbit over Arcadia and I can see almost the entire western hemisphere. Deep beautiful blue seas… verdant green forests…a jewel of a world. I wish I could say it was the last image I have of Arcadia.

It had been so long since I'd been home…

Shadows fill the breech… big shadows.

…Deep blue seas…

The shadows fly through the breech; their landing footfalls pound the deck plates so hard I can feel it through my armor.

…Verdant green forests…

My Tact-net flashes warnings of enemy weaponry at me.

Here it comes; a flash of light in high orbit that I see out of the corner of my eye. I glance once, sparing only that while I raise my Lance to fire on the enemy. Then another…

…down below on Arcadia.

It's only a wink of light. An impact on the southern continent, Embrezia. Only a wink of light.

I don't want to watch this.

Not again.

The C.O.P. pings me. It's enough of an electrical jolt to wake my sleeping body and pop my trapped consciousness free.

The chains holding the old guard's dress armor upright rattle as I shudder awake and I drop the small Cassad built rifle I'd been using to test it. Fell asleep trying to finish working on the old guard's gear. I'm soaked with sweat that I didn't work up during the project.

I hate dreaming.

Another ping. Time to get to control.

CHAPTER FIVE:

HAMPTON'S GATE

The space around Hampton's Gate is filled with ports, arrays and of course; traffic. Every gate is a hot spot for commerce. Ships making the jump are either going to or coming from halfway across the known most times. There are over five hundred major interstellar ports sitting in orbit of Hampton's, all offering all kinds of services to the weary travelers. And because this gate is one of the closest to the edge of the unexplored space there are a ton of settler convoys and scientific expeditions from just about every corner of the known. The G-Det is lit up like firefly mating season from all the traffic and each little bit of light in its holographic display has a corresponding transponder tag.

If there were any hostiles or even groups that I personally flagged then the G-Det would be pinging something crazy but it looks clear. Could be something on the other side of the gate but they're not likely to try and make the trip around; Hampton's is too big.

The gate itself is one of a unique pair, unlike the other gates in the known. Hampton's Gate is older than the Age of Discovery and was first found by Measure Hampton, a Cassad schooled physicist from some backwater world. She guessed at its existence when its sister was discovered in the inner realm. Bold as a bica she figured out how to access it and on her own, traversed the damn thing in a bucket of a ship to open up a whole other section of the galaxy and increase the size of the known by almost half.

The old broad, I think of her as old but I don't really know what her age was when she made the trip… the old broad must have had serious adrenal to even approach a rotating singularity let alone take her ship through it.

Hampton's Gate, here on the perimeter is a massive black "ring", a spinning, rotating singularity that's holds a wormhole open from here to the Dark Ring; an identical rotating black ring sitting in the inner realm. Doesn't really look much like a "black" ring; it's an open circular band of hot glowing gas that faces you no matter what angle you approach it from. The wormhole sits dead center and when you're close enough you can actually see the other side.

My comm-board lights up. A not so clear, pale blue, holographic image of an attractive woman appears above the old console. "Welcome, *Quiet Storm*, to Hampton's Gate. Please transmit your ships registry."

Good to know my new transponder is working. The fake Laplace plate cost me a bit but wouldn't work at all if I couldn't hide my real plate in the gravity well of the g-rock dead center of the ship. I transmit my credentials and wait. The greeting was automated and with the traffic at the gate there's gonna be a wait. I spend the time looking through the list of transponder signals broadcasting in the area while ignoring the constant stream of calls from traders, service stations and supply depots advertising their businesses.

There's quite a few of Cassad-space convoys coming through the gate now, no doubt trying to escape the tide of bloodlust running rampant through the inner systems. Without the Cassads' mighty Ziaran military to protect them, the inner realm is open to plunder. Only a few of them are still holding their own, but that won't last too long. One long convoy, just coming through the gate, is being protected by a Ziaran battleship that looks like it's on it last leg. Must have been a styx ride gettin' out of there.

Probably going to be just as bad going in.

I count seven different Cassad space convoys. Two Phaestus frigate convoys, five convoys out of Ngola that look makeshift and desperate. And there's one very well to do colonization convoy decked out with all the trimmings. Those ships are new and their transponders aren't registered, if they even have Laplace plates at all for a G-det to pick up. Looks like someone got their act together before the revolutionaries got too deep into the inner realm. There are probably even more exiting but the gate distorts every radiating field so I'm only getting a clear picture of what's happening on a small area of this side of Hampton's.

My comm-board lights up again. "*Quiet Storm*, please transmit your ships log, manifest and crew roster."

Not good. Could be standard now, what with the increased traffic, but it could also be bad news. I transmit the faked log along with the manifest of cargo I don't have hidden and my phony crew roster without delay.

Quickly I run through the rest of the ships showing up on my G-Det, searching for any that might also just be arriving from Rox822, which my fake log lists as my last port of call. I don't think there are any here. There shouldn't be any here; Rox is a good ways farther away than Indo and my timetable had me beating any possible registered traffic coming from there by good margin.

An hour passes before I hear back from the Gate Authority. All the while I run through my options.

Hampton's Gate is too big for the Gate Authority to police in any effective way. Ships "Jump the Gate" all the time. But those ships either are desperate, have the speed to beat pursuit or have friends on the other side to beat the Gate Authority there.

I'm not desperate. Not yet. *WarChild* still has her own grav-unit with a fat hunk of Element G. I can reach the inner realm on my own without the gate but that would take the better half of a cycle and the use of another gate. I don't have that kind of time.

Warchild is fast. She can hang with almost any ship her class or that has the firepower that she carries. But she's got no acceleration. If I wanted to jump the gate I should've starting pouring on the juice long before Hampton's was even visible. If I try it now I won't make it through before I'm targeted by half a dozen ships. *WarChild's* armor can take some serious hits but if a system fails, like guidance or an engine, I could get caught or worse, fall into Hampton's event horizon and get "spaghettied" around the ring.

And last time I checked I don't have any friends… of any kind.

"*Quiet Storm*," this time the holograph is a young man, live not automated. That means trouble. "Captain Sivad, please adjust your heading and set sail to these coordinates."

I don't need to check the numbers; I already know that they want to me to fall in line for inspection. They're directing me toward a high traffic station with several ports and likely plenty of staff. "Sure thing G.A., but do you mind telling me why I'm being diverted from the gate?"

The hesitation on the kids face is all I need to know it's bad. "Routine inspection, *Quiet Storm*. Please shut down your engines once you're in the pipe and open your nevron link."

Fek.

I adjust my heading but I'm just buying time. The kid looked apprehensive but not too charged up. That faked log cost me too much buckin' money for them to have found something wrong there.

If it's the log I'll kill Sticky.

Maybe they just think I'm running some contraband, which is par for the course these days. Might just be a shakedown…might be something more.

I check the G-Det again. No other ships are moving toward my position, but some are falling into line for inspection. They'll be in position to target me if I comply. Still, it doesn't look like an ambush.

It just feels like one.

Fek! I need to get through this gate! I drop *WarChild* into line with the inspection station.

"*Quiet Storm*, please open your nevron link."

"Roger that, G.A.; nevron link open," I say, for all the good it will do them.

Only takes them a few pulse beats. "*Quiet Storm*, we're having trouble accessing your ships command systems. Please stand by."

The advantage to having out of date, hodge-podge systems is that you'll always have an excuse for something not working right. No way they'll be able to connect to *WarChild's* command systems, especially since I never networked them. It'll look suspicious but not too out of place for ships out on the perimeter. Now, if they think I'm merely carrying contraband then they'll tell me to dock it manually. But if somehow the old guard got word out on me then they'll send ships.

"*Quiet Storm*, we cannot establish a connection" the kid says without any further anxiety in his voice. "Prepare to dock manually"

I bring *WarChild* right up to the dock and moor the ship without so much as a bump; don't want to give the Gate Authority reason to be overly aggressive. The port is big enough that the docking chamber could accommodate several ships her size, but because they couldn't gain remote control of her they had me line up *WarChild's* rear hatch with their secondary docking ring. No problem, I make my way down to the cargo bay to greet them.

They're pounding on the rear hatch when I get there. Apparently my docking controls are out of date too. So I pop the seal and lower the hatch for them myself.

The G.A. came with a bit of force. There's one female in standard Gate Authority dress, carrying a data board, smiling and looking very officious and then there about ten others behind her; two in mech exos, the rest hiding arms… and no smiles.

"Greetings, Captain Sivad, to G.A. station Tortiv. Your automated review is done. Are your ship and crew ready for physical inspection?" The inspectors' manner is a bit of a contrast from the muscle standing behind her. Plus she's a looker; tall, lean and a good enough face job that I can't see the scars. They're disorganized… you don't run the muscle in right next to the distraction. That tells me that whoever's in charge of this facility didn't set up the inspection. Could be good news… or bad.

Hmm…what's the… oh yea, "*Quiet Storm*'s a tight ship. We're always ready for inspection, Mrs.?"

"Ms., Captain. I'm Chief Donna Kirk. This is my inspection team." She says with a wave toward the muscle. She's good; hardly winces at all when she looks back at them. The exo gear the two dech-techs have strapped on are basic work units. But these've been racked; the power boosted and the response time doubled or tripled with incompatible servo units. Kinda gearing Pops taught me and Drez how to do for fun as kids. On our own we learned the hard way not to upgrade the power of an exo without reinforcing the frame.

"Well, let's get on with it. I don't want to be delayed too long."

"Of course, Captain." And she starts up the ramp with the muscle. I put on my best confused face and hold my hand up.

"Hold. You're not going to inspect without the proper gear?"

Now her look is genuinely confused. I see the muscle behind her get suspicious and fidgety.

"I'm sorry?"

"Well, as it states in my log; my crew is down with Rox-pox; nasty bug… highly infectious. Standard sterilization and air filters kill it just fine but you're gonna be inspecting the cargo hatches, engine accesses and the command deck. Can't be too sure that the scrubbers got to those areas."

"Rox-Pox?" asks the thick necked, pocked faced "inspector" standing on the ramp right behind Chief Kirk. He's wearing a tech vest with no under shirt, showing off his biceps which are pretty impressive if not stock and trade for a deck-tech.

“Yup. My Chief Engineer decided to get in some cheap binding while we waited for our cargo to get to port. Must have picked it up then.”

“Do you mean Rozier’s?” Kirk asks a little fearful, nearly dropping her data board. She should be upset. Rozier’s or “Rox-Pox” hits women harder than men. You wanna see someone age two rotations in a week? Check out the Rozier’s ward anywhere on the perimeter. Of course it’s entirely treatable, but it requires a shipment of the inoculant or military grade nano-bodies. Neither of which the G.A. should have.

Or so my info tells me.

“What equipment do we need?” Biceps asks.

I have no idea. “Standard Bio-hazard wear. Standby testing terminal… the usual. You guys did read the log?”

Kirk is half-way down the boarding ramp. “I…I’ll have to…report this to my superiors…”

“Hold up, Donna!” Biceps has been eyeing me. “How do we know he ain’t full of hoodoo?” and he takes a few steps up the ramp.

Pathetic; he’s trying to test me and he’s giving away all of their intentions. If they just wanted to shake me down then they would play it cool and try and wait me out. But if they want to…TAKE my ship then they want to jump in here now.

But their disorganized approach must mean that they don’t have approval…or worse.

“Look,” I say. “The cargo hold and most of the ship is just fine, I’m sure. Come on up.”

Biceps actually takes a few steps up the ramp. The rest of the muscle is split with half backing up and the other half is moving toward the ramp. The Chief inspector is caught in between, on the ramp, her eyes wide.

“I should go check their log” she offers.

Biceps spits. “Fine! You,” he points a huge finger at me. “You come out of there so we can…inspect…your…ah…you!”

Biceps looks like he wants to pull a weapon, which I have no doubt he and his tiny little army have.

I slide my finger over the top side button of my remote.

Just then the bay alarm sounds. At the far end of the room a pair of doors open. Out walks a small group of men who look more the type to be running a Gate Authority inspection station.

"Hayland? Kirk? What on styx is this?" He looks young but as he gets closer I can see the streaks of gray in his hair and the washed out color of his eyes. Unlike his chief, he's had real cellular repair work done, most likely to keep up physically rather than for the cosmetic side of it. With this crew of muscle-heads I can see why.

Kirk puts on her best smile and strides straight up to him. "Director Pile, we found some inaccuracies in this ships log and we…"

"And you what?" he snaps. "Thought I wouldn't know that ship was pulled into my station?" he brushes past her, knocking her data board from her hands. The man strides up the ramp right into Biceps face.

"Hayland?" he says through clenched teeth.

Biceps doesn't answer at first, he just looks over the rest of his buddies. I've seen this look before; he's checking their positions…about to go for broke. I turn the remote over in my hand until the button on the other side is under my thumb.

"You let that little…" Director Pile starts.

Biceps pulls the pulse gun he's been hiding from under his jacket screaming wildly at the same time. I thumb the remote and the small hologram wrapped around the kendo blade disappears. There's a piercing, yet musical whistle that drowns out his little battle cry as I swing the blade. So loud was the whistle that everyone in the bay, those about to draw their weapons and those about to get shot, all stop and look, almost in time to see me return the blade to the holographic camo I drew it from.

Those biceps aren't as impressive when severed and lying on my ramp. Still…there's enough strength in that arm to squeeze the trigger two times, firing pulses out into the bay above his crews heads.

The Director and his staff pulled their own weapons. I raise my hands as innocently as I can while the Director himself puts me square in his sights. Luckily there isn't a firefight. Kirk and her little shake down crew don't seem to want that kind of heat.

Of course that doesn't help me at all.

CHAPTER SIX:

GATE JUMPING

Here it comes.

"My crew found some very interesting discrepancies when we boarded your ship, Mr. Sivad."

Fek. Had I known I'd be held up using this alias so long I'd have made up one that sounded a little less buckin' ridiculous.

I'm sitting in the Tortiv's Visiting Crew lounge, which may not sound like I'm in their brig but there's no real difference. Director Pile's decision that would be, but it's the extent of his appreciation for keeping his head from being blown off.

"I'm not sure what you mean" I say. *WarChild* is in lockdown mode. That means that the Command Deck, Grav-Well, Infirmary and any of the ships access ports are sealed. Those hatches and plates are also part of *Warchild's* cete-armor body. Doubt this station has anything that can cut through it. And *WarChild's* systems are, for the most part, incompatible with theirs so they're not hacking in.

"Well, your crew for one. We can't find any of them" Director Pile is looking at me pretty hard. Probably can't figure me out. I could be anybody with almost any motivation for going through Hampton's Gate. But I saved his ass and that's got him wondering.

"Crew is in medical quarantine. Can't be accessed until the Pox is out of their system."

"Right. That would be Roziers?"

"Like it states in my log."

"Yea. Well, I've checked with Rox822 and they're not reporting any Roziers outbreak." He's watching my reaction.

I'm not much of a poker player unless I'm actually holding all the cards. So I've just got to have faith in the fake log package I bought. Roziers is supposed to be a problem on Rox.

"That a fact?"

"That's a fact" he says with an almost pitying air, as if he's caught me in a lie.

"I did wonder how my engineer caught it. Seeing how the port we landed on was the only port on Rox… without a Roziers clinic." I mirror his pitying look right back at him.

He smiles. "So, your crew can't use the comms? Let us know they're alright?"

"Roziers requires a quarter cycle deep sleep session so the virus doesn't tear the body up while they recover. My Ops officer was supposed to be up now but the sickness must have advanced to where he decided to freeze himself."

Pile purses his lips in doubt. "So I have to wait three months to verify your story?"

"Actually my Engineer will be up in only a few earning rotations but what's to verify? We're just going through the gate. Why the fuss?"

Pile looks at me for a pulse beat before answering. "The Inner Realm is in turmoil right now. The New Regime Coalition, the Cassads and a whole bunch of smaller war powers are grabbing what they can. We are monitoring gate traffic especially hard right now."

"Traffic coming out sure, but going in?"

"Going in even more so. We know citizens of the oba worlds are heading out here to escape the *blood tide*. But there are dozens of worlds out here looking to claim a bit of a stake back there as well; sending in mercs, weapons and supplies to whoever they can make a deal with."

"…*Quiet Storm*'s not a supply ship." I almost forgot the buckin' fake name again.

"Not a big ship but you could carry specialized hardware easily enough. I recognized the cete-armor. Your ship could drop gear or men right onto the Cassad homeworld itself."

I laugh. "With our systems winking out the way they do we're lucky each landing isn't our last. You're kidding me right?"

"You've just seen what the fall of the empire is doing to us even here. You think I'm kidding?" Pile leans back in his chair and continues to consider me. He could keep me here for the three weeks I lied about but something's off. He's in a hurry.

"With everything that's going on why are you trying to head into the Inner Realm then? Not the safest place for lone ships" he asks.

"You've read our log, Director; been a long tour out here on the perimeter, now we're going home."

He looks at me again then looks down. He's hard to read but that's supposed to be a sign of someone who's about to lie. "We're seeing some bad activity on the other side of the gate. You're gonna have to go another route."

And with that I'm escorted back to my ship.

My cargo bay is a mess. They dug into everything they could but they did not find the pirate hatches and they were not able to breech any of the areas on lockdown. They kept me in the lock up for so long that the battery in the holo-emitter failed. The Kendo blade juts up out of the bay plating right where it landed after I relieved Biceps of his namesake. Apparently no one here knows how to pull one free once it's been embedded.

I even find my remote in the vent where I dropped it before they took me into custody. Somebody went through my tool box though…looks like they grabbed my good set of calibrators.

Fek.

Takes me nearly a full wake cycle to square everything away; they actually pulled my walker off its rack to search it for contraband. I finally get the damn thing to hang straight when a very chastened looking Chief Kirk climbs *WarChild*'s ramp.

"Captain Sivad? The Director wants to know when you will be ready to shove off. You haven't answered our calls."

"Somebody wrecked the comm line." I snap. "Can't access the comms."

She waits a bit longer while I stow away the lift-jack. Then she clears her throat. "It's just that we need the bay to continue inspecting…"

"Soon as I put my ship back together." With Pile flagging my ship, *WarChild* will be tracked as far as their sensors extend. That's a good ways. No station around Hampton's will service her and every Gate Authority police ship will be set to fire on me if I make a gate approach. And they'll probably send a tracking ship after me until I jump. That means I'll have to leave Hampton's space, change transponders and then return to make a "run". Something that will cost me time and most likely buck my schedule.

So I take my time, using the excuse of securing the ship to check the G-det and get a look at the situation around the gate. There are Dogon ships stuck at another Gate Authority port but the ships of the Khem are already on their way to the edge of Hampton's gravity well where they'll be able to jump to wherever they're going. They've got real money so I figure they must've paid off somebody.

My comm board lights up but it shows no incoming transmissions. Looks like the Gate Authority is transmitting coded messages… a lot of them.

They don't have "entangled" comms but my systems aren't good enough to break their encryption anyway. I doubt all this chatter is about me but that doesn't mean it's not trouble. I study the G-Det for a bit longer then run a passive scan on everything the gate isn't disrupting but I don't see anything worth worrying about. I take a quick walk back down to the cargo bay.

Chief Kirk is still in the Authority bay. She has a distant look in her eyes that tells me she's on a virtual line, either communicating with someone or just looking in on a transmission feed.

As casual as I can I walk down my boarding ramp and cross the bay to her. She doesn't notice me until I practically on top of her.

"Oh! Uh…"

"We're ready to make way."

"I…yes of course…" she stammers enough for me to start to worry.

"Everything alright?"

"You…" she plays with her data pad and in a pulse beat I see a green light flash on the bay status indicators set about the moorings. *Warchild*'s been released.

"You can leave immediately, Captain" she says over her shoulder as she hurries from the bay. No sooner has she disappeared through the bay doors when klaxons sounds and the indicator lights switch to bright red and pulsing. My remote is in my hand and I'm hauling ass back to my ship but there's no pursuit, no armed guard…whatever's happening, it ain't about me.

"STATION ALERT! SENIOR OFFICERS REPORT TO THE ANCILAR OFFICE. PREPARE FOR INCOMING HOSTILE CRAFT!!"

I slam the ramp controls and run like a treader for the command deck. The whole room is alive with warnings on nearly every holographic display.

It takes a pulse beat to squint through the mess in the G-det but then I see it clearly enough. A squad of fighter craft just came through the gate, guns blazing. Looks like they're targeting the Cassad ships. I pull up the comm-net; got to be something on there.

"There is no escape from the blood tide!" The holo lights up with the image of a man in fatigues and a beret. On his chest he bears the latest insignia that the so-called "Revolutionaries" are using; a Coalition patch.

Wonder how long you have to be in power before you're no longer considered a revolutionary?

I fire up the twin engines and more warnings sound. The alert must have reset the status of the dock release. *Warchild* is still locked to the bay hatch. It'll be fine…the magnetic lock is connected only to her cete-armor.

There's a nasty whine as she begins to pull away from the station that only stops when their docking clamps snap. Every ship in the area is pulling away from the gate so I set my heading directly for it.

It's risky; a bad hit from enemy fire can send a ship into the event horizon. But the revolutionaries are so concerned with the Ziaran ships that they'll ignore my transponder until it's too late.

Warchild is a fast ship, when she gets up to speed, but it takes a while. The engines burn pushing her through the procession of escaping ships and into firestorm of convoy ships under fire.

I have to take manual control as we get in close. The down side to hodge-podge systems is that you can't rely on the automated systems in combat.

Close enough now to worry about debris. I close the forward blast shield over the canopy and go to navigating off of the virtual holo display. Millions of kilometers close to hundreds of thousands and quickly to thousands and the space begins to get tight relatively speaking. We pass over one besieged convoy and then another. I'm thinking we're gonna go through without a hitch until my comm board pings.

"*Quiet Storm*, this is Prelate Gaston of the First Coalition Expeditionary Force. Reverse your course! Hampton's Gate is now under the control of the Coalition of Free Worlds."

He goes on to say that all gate traffic must be approved by the New

Regimes Coalition. I laugh. In over a thousand years no one has been able to really control Hampton's Gate. The G.A.s control is marginal at best and only because the Cassads used a multicultural, multisystem task force to govern it. What makes the New Regime think they can do that when it they haven't even defeated the Cassads in twenty two years?

WarChild is gaining some speed now. Hopefully it'll be enough to shoot past the rebels on the other side.

Proximity alarms ring out; looks like the New Regimes Expeditionary Force is sending a little attention my way. Two Tyco fighters; Cassad design…probably Giak built… they're good ships but they lack the fire power to stop me from making the gate. Still it wouldn't be smart to let them know that too soon, they might send more at me.

WarChild is made to fight in the nastiest of the nasties. She carries an impressive weapons package…most of which doesn't work worth a damn right now…and her main body in composed of cete crystal, one of the toughest materials in the known. She can take a beating. I charge the top mounted pulse cannon. It should be enough to keep them off me.

The pulse cannon opens up on the Tycos with nice accuracy. The leader's engines go dead in the first salvo and the second pulls off to avoid the same fate. *WarChild* shrugs off their return fire like a champ.

Again the Command Deck lights up with warning holos but it's just the proximity to the event horizon. I'm so close now that I can see the weird fishbowl eye of the wormhole showing the other side of Hampton's Gate. The G-Det is drawing a blank at this range but I'm sure there's a nice Coalition force sitting there waiting in ambush. Luckily for me they're expecting haggard refugees or docile cargo haulers.

Back to the auto systems for the trip through the wormhole; if the ship isn't lined up and traveling exactly perpendicular to the gate then she'll be pulled into the event horizon. The computer makes the adjustments to our course and I see that there wasn't much space between my ship and the gate to spare.

WarChild drops into Hampton's and the perimeter fades and shrinks behind us. Ahead the Inner Realm blooms, opening like a weird black flower as we pull away from the Dark Ring.

"This gate is under the control of the Coalition. Stand your vessel down…"

Yea, yea. The New Regime has its little fleet spread out around the gate in pretty standard formation. Looks like Gun-boats mostly…probably a battle cruiser and a capital ship on the other side of the Dark Ring, maybe more. But like I said; it's near impossible to control traffic on a gate this big. The dispersal of their fleet has them spread out too thin and most of their ships are in holding patterns around the various Gate Authority stations on this side. They're what's important. I just have to get *WarChild* past them and out of the Dark Rings gravity well where I can pop the G-rock and jump the ship away. There's only one ship close enough and moving at the right angle to cause me any trouble.

When it's apparent that I'm not stopping they open fire.

The area is lit with particle fire, showing me their Commander's inexperience. His fleet is too close to the gate for particle targeting to be reliable. And indeed the gunboats targeting is awful at this range. If I were intent on doing them damage and if I had some decent offensive weaponry I could probably take out the ship. Never the less I've got places to be.

I pour on the speed. More enemy fire crosses my flight path from aft. Looks like a couple of the Tychos followed me through the wormhole. My ship shudders a bit and the holo tells me that the pulse cannon is down.

Fek. Just got that fixed!

No way to fire back. I alter course enough that the Tychos will have to drag their route too close to the gate to fire effectively. Unfortunately the new course lines me up nicely in the gunboats sights.

Another barrage of particle fire and this time *Warchild* is hit hard enough to shake me in my seat despite the grav-wells inertial safeties. The holo lights flare with even more warnings but I ignore them and change course again. The gunboat tracks me, trying to force me into the reinforcements I'm sure are on the way. Can't let them corner me. Taking fire from one gunboat is better than getting hit by two…

Warchild swings hard into the path of the New Regime ship. G-Det tells me it's a Cutlass class, Meridian; Cassad built. Good ship. The particle fire opens up again and *Warchild* can't help but take fire. Again the warning icons in the holo spin frantically but the cete-armor holds true until I'm past the gunboat and out of weapons range. Then the ship gives a horrible shutter.

BUCK! The starboard side engine blew…I check the holo and see the auto systems already attempting to compensate by slowing us down. Can't do that!

I jigger the power distribution and fire the port engine to max. Then I check G-Det… the Tychos are pulling back; they're not sure I'm toothless and don't want to pursue without back up. The gunboat is faster but she's got to correct her course before she can come after me and that gives me time.

But not much. With only one engine running, the gunboat'll be able to catch up and could be back in effective range in a little over five hours. *Warchild* can't make a jump until we're completely out of the gates gravity well which'll take almost two days at my current speed and acceleration…which is crap.

I hop out of the primary control seat then head for the workshop and my mech gear. Can't risk troubleshooting the problem, I'll have to swap out the entire starboard engine with the spare. Never pulled an engine in under five hours while pushing C…but there's a first time for everything.

I crack open the suit locker and begin hauling out the EVO-wear.

Then I stop and take a breath

Halfway there.

CHAPTER SEVEN:

INNER TURMOIL

The gunboat and a few of its friends got close enough to fire just outside the edge of their effective range before I got the back-up engine to spark. They were still able to gain a bit but I made it outside the Dark Ring's gravity well and jumped with no problem.

First jump and I repaired the pulse cannon but couldn't fix the buckin' swivel mount. It'll only fire inside a very tight fifteen degree field now. So I point the thing aft as I'm more likely to be running than attacking. Wish I had more time to get it working properly but I don't.

Fourth jump and I finally finish with the Royal Guard's armor. Back's aching and my neck is cramping from squatting in front of its open innards for so long but it was worth it. Finally something I plan actually goes the way it's supposed to. I hit the scrubber and take nap; Grav-well will be up for the eighth and last jump by the time I get up.

The stars wink out and pop back into view in different positions. I always marvel at how fast…what the buck?

The G-det shows nothing, but the damn thing always takes a pulse beat to catch up. What I'm seeing on the V-hud is from the weak visual feed. What I'm seeing is incoming.

I slap the manual control override and throw *WarChild* into an off kilter spin pulling her out of the path of what looks like a small freighter. We're not even past the freighter when another ship…a Cassad fighter cartwheels at us, spewing rads and out of control.

I pull *WarChild* up thinking we're not gonna be able to avoid it but somehow we miss colliding by what must be only meters. What on styx…

The G-det finally flares to life and fills with overlapping tiny points of light. The whole buckin' field is filled with ships! What the buck did I jump into? I plotted the jump for well outside Orun's kup-belt… well outside the anywhere where there should have been any traffic leaving the Cassad home star. But it looks like I jumped *WarChild* right into the middle of a skirmish.

Staring at the G-det nearly gets me into another collision. Damn lucky…I know better than to get distracted when I override the autopilot. Even luckier still *WarChild* hasn't been targeted by either side of this conflict. I chance another look at the G-det, trying to determine how on styx I'm getting out of this mess.

The first ships that the G-det is able to I.D. are the dead ones, as always. They're easier because their defenses are offline and they usually aren't moving as fast as the others so the G-Det gets a better look at them. Cassad ship...Cassad ship…looks like it's a major skirmish…

Or… or something else.

Very little weapons fire. And as my comms come online, suddenly there's lots of comm traffic; distress calls.

I pull *WarChild* out of the path of another ship, more hunk of debris than space vessel now; it's a Cassad light cruiser damn near split in half. Behind that an even bigger ship, battle cruiser…holed by some kind of internal explosion maybe. And it gets worse.

There are ship I.D.s popping up on the G-Det now that aren't dead. Denir ships, Marajeshi fighters, Junn Ships…a few Giak ships and the list goes on. They aren't attacking each other, which is odd 'cause the Giaks are currently at war with the Junns. Instead all the capable ships seemed to be engaged in rescue operations. So who attacked them?

I lean forward and tap the icon of one of the ships transmitting a distress call. At once a pale gold holographic image of a woman, the ship's captain maybe, pops up.

"This is the Planetary Commonwealth ship the *Confident Seven*, we are currently under attack by Rebel forces and require assistance…"

Without listening to the rest I tap another ships icon.

"…the *Lagrange Miner*, we are being boarded by Afan pirates…"

"…engines are dead. They're slaughtering the passengers! Please help us!"

"…the damn Stompers are pulling our ship apart! They're not letting us launch the escape pods! Oh no…"

Twisting in primary I draw the G-Det holo closer. The ships I thought were running rescue ops are actually pirating the ships. The Giaks are stripping ships down with the crew still alive inside, the Junns are running down fleeing ships like a pack of sulu, and the Denir are just riddling weakened ships with small arms fire to kill the crews.

The New Regime has already launched their surprise attack on Ziara; the Cassad home world. The comms are screaming with distress calls, all from Ziaran citizen ships. Looks like they're trying to flee the system. These running ships aren't military; they're civilian, trying to escape the assault of their home world. Now that the Empire is in its death throes the rest of the known is swooping in to pick the meat off its still breathing body. But none of the ships in distress are military. They're all commerce ships, industrial runners or passenger craft. The only armed ships are the long dead Cassad fighter craft which must have been trying to escort these civilian ships out of the system. With them gone the raiders are taking their time with the rest. There's no mercy being shown to the Ziaran civilians.

No mercy at all.

G-Det pings on a big ship, a passenger ship, riddled with hull breeches along its length. All about the ship, caught by its minute gravity, float the bodies of its former passengers. Whoever attacked this fleet made sure to kill them in this fashion…

…the so called Blood Tide.

Still the pirates are not a real threat until they get a bead on me and only then if they decide I'm prey and not predator.

Or if I decide to intervene.

This is how it might have been on Arcadia at the end, at least for a while before…

I check the G-det and make sure I'm clear of incoming debris, then I begin checking ship I.D.s and one stands out.

Njaro Station; not a ship at all, but a massive space facility that orbits or rather WAS in orbit around Ziara. But right now it's sitting in the middle of a field of dead ships, on the outskirts of the gravity well of the Cassad home world's system star, Orun. What on styx is it doing here?

Just as with the rest of the ships in this debris field I can see that *Njaro* is wrecked and derelict. Obliviously it was part of this battle but this could blow my whole plan. Buck! It's supposed to be orbiting the All damned Cassad home world!

The only reason I figured I had a chance to pull off this bounty in the first place is because I knew Cassad would head home after the invasion…knew that he would need to use the *Njaro* to stage his retaking of the planet. Without it he'll just abandon the planet until he can come back later with a large enough force. One too large for me to grab his ass from.

I used *WarChild's* docking thrusters to maneuver into position to try a light sensor sweep of the station. The cete-armor plates covering the front of the engine housings part to reveal *WarChild's* broussard collectors and sensor screens. The G-Det hologram is immediately augmented with new information. *Njaro's* sub-light engines show evidence of having been running at high output. Could they have been trying to escape the system?

The Coalitions invasion should be in full swing by now. It must be a more horrible battle than I anticipated. Again, the "Blood Tide"… most invading forces would have taken the *Njaro* by negotiation. Obviously the near guaranteed slaughter of every Ziaran citizen found must have made the commanders of the *Njaro* desperate. They ran, with some help it looks like, but they couldn't make a jump…or "slip" as the station used the old Cassad slipstream tech.

The bodies of the inhabitants of the station begin to come into view. *Njaro* had been home to nearly thirty million souls. Whoever attacked the station didn't let up until they breached every compartment. All damn it… even the Giaks backed off of survivors when Arcadia was burned… but with the Cassads...

Never the less, I've got a job to do there may still be a chance. The wreckage of the *Njaro* may give me an opportunity I hadn't counted on.

G-det pings again; more pirates. They're crawling all over the massive Cassad station like ants. But these ships are not carrying or at least they're not broadcasting their transponders. Now that usually means illegals…unsanctioned by the Coalition, probably running salvage. But with the nature of the revolution in the inner realm it could be renegade rebels or even Cassad regulars turning on their own people. Privateers would broadcast their transponders to warn off challengers.

Quickly I check to make sure my transponder is offline and after adjusting *WarChild's* course, I cut the engines. Likely most of them noticed my jumping in but maybe they haven't pinpointed me yet and probably care even less. Now that I'm seeing them work there seems to be an air of cooperation; there are plenty of unarmed ships to go around.

Another set of pings and a small group of the ships specification flags pop up. Three of them; one's big, a cargo hauler maybe and it probably has the facilities to breakdown salvage. The other two are shuttle…no…fighter sized. They looked to be the ones doing the stripping…one is anyway…the other is his cover. But no scans come my way, none of them seem to have noticed me.

And that lets me know they saw me. No way they missed a ship jumping right into the debris field but with all the wrecks pitching back and forth and the other raiders breaking down ships they don't know whether I'm Ziaran or more raider competition. So they're playing at being unaware.

The stripper continues breaking down the wreckage from what looks like one of *Njaro's* communications wheels while his cover continues making his security sweep as casually as he can. It's the cargo hauler that's really giving them away now. The captain of that ship thinks he can prep his engines without anyone noticing. He's either panicking or inexperienced. *WarChild* must look like trouble to somebody in this group.

They've got a pretty old comm system 'cause I'm picking up quite a bit of their coded transmissions. I subvocalize to the C.O.P. to run a decryption program but it'll take time.

I lean back heavily into the cushions of the Primary control seat. What's the play here? The station is drifting away from Orun. But it's sitting perfectly along the route Cassad should be coming in along when he gets here. I figured he would go to free *Njaro* first; it WAS in a good position to coordinate any attempt to retake his home world, has the facilities and resources needed but more importantly my recon indicated that it was his rendezvous point with some Ziaran agent. Now though… he might just pass it up and head in system if he arrives with more fleet left than he's supposed to have left after his tour on the perimeter.

What's the play, Pack?

I look at the huge station. It's mostly still functional for the time being, at least until the scavengers pull out its vital systems. But if I were coming in to stage a rescue of MY world from a bunch of rag tag rebels…

WarChild's docking thrusters fire as we near the station. Better to pick one of big rings, a habitat ring, where the scavengers are scarce; they're not here to pick personal belongings. There's another nasty rupture right in the hydrogel shield and it's large enough for me to squeeze *WarChild* in. We slide in easily enough, bumping a few odd bits of debris; small station cars…a few bodies that didn't get pulled all the way out of the station when the dome was breached.

These habitat rings were capable of sealing themselves even after sustaining multiple breaches. All known…how many times did they fire into it before those redundant systems failed?

I set *WarChild* down on a park plaza near to what I hope is an access port to one of transport bridges. There's a lot of work to do here before his royal highness arrives; I need to get moving.

CHAPTER EIGHT:

THE *NJARO*

Standard camouflage is too easily recognized by most ships sensors but a manual rig works just fine. It takes a bit to set it up but it's worth it. I finish hanging to last bit of camo netting just as a small flight of scavengers comes drifting by the breaches along this side of the *Njaro*.

They move smoothly, trying not to look as if they're looking for anyone in particular but sure as worlds turn they saw *WarChild* approach. They can't be too worried about Ziaran authorities; I figure they probably just want to be sure they aren't losing too much to the competition. They run really aggressive high level rad scans. If there are any survivors in this part of the habitat ring that rad sweep just finished them off.

Buckin' vultures.

My rad alarms barely register the levels though as the camo rig reflects just the right amount back and sucks up the rest. It's fairly new so I'll get a few more uses out of it before I'll have to drop coin to get another set. The pirates glide on by and move on to scan the rest of the habitat ring. Time to get moving.

Now's not the time to take chances. Not sure how many have boarded the *Njaro* but it's possible though not likely that I could end up running into a few looters in the habitat ring looking for small coin or what not. And I'm not sure I'll have time to set up a good ambush sight before Cassad gets here so I pull up the plating above my pirates hold and lift out my Raptor armor.

Raptor armor; it's what made the 46th so damn famous. During the "*Wars of the Blade*" it gave mere mortal men a toe to toe chance against veritable titans. It isn't the best fighting armor by far. It lacks the firepower, strength and shielding of heavy armor units and the tech sophistication of the light armor units. It's modifiable like the special ops pieces but not upgradable like the newer units coming out of the major clusters. Never the less during the *Wars of the Blade* it was absolutely perfect,

Because when the big EMFs went up and all the lights went out the Raptor armor, with its primary power cell offline, kept going.

The weave beneath the fullerene plates is all "bio-mechanical" and gives the wearer augmented strength and speed that won't disappear when an EMP pops or even an All damned Dark Field. That makes it strong enough for an ordinary Arcadian to go up against a three and a half meter tall Giak and hold his own and even, if he's been trained, win more than half the time.

My set has hunter green paint on plates trimmed with gold that are locked onto a black bio mechanical weave. There's a chipped, faded "wing" insignia painted on the right shoulder guard for my old Fire Squad. Probably should have burned it off a long time ago to protect my identity but I always manage to not bother. Anyone who would recognize that logo is far, far away.

Without specific training the armor is too complex for someone to get into, even with help. I've logged thousands of hours in the armor however, so I can don the weave and lock on the plates almost subconsciously.

The bio-mechanical microfilaments, weaved into a thick membrane, comes to life around my skin, pressurizing and making the biometric connections like it was brand new. I slide the thinking cap up over my head and run through a quick diagnostic. I don't need the cap on to know that the armor is running at optimum. It's the one thing in my life that always does.

Again I reach down into the pirate hold and this time I grab the helmet. The mandibles lay open and the winged visor is up waiting for my head. Instead I lock the helmet onto the back shoulder plate while I get the rest of the Mission Package ready.

The wing housing, which is no larger than a field pack and looks like a natural part of the armor when on, takes a pulse beat to connect to the back plate. It's essential that all the command ports make their connections or the unit won't respond in real time to the thinking cap. Though the unit was designed to work manually and I'm more than used to it in that mode, I'm going to need my hands free for this op.

My twin carbide butterfly blades lock into place beneath my thigh plates, they're good micro-edged blades. Not as amazing as the kendo blade, but since I don't have a scabbard for that I can't risk carrying it.

The Sever 3030 hand gun and holster slide on easily enough around my waist. It's a good Ops weapon; fires "smart" rounds, specialty rounds or just plain old slugs that aren't affected by counter measures. Like my armor there's a strictly mechanical aspect to the firing mechanism that allows it to stay effective even under an EMF.

Next I grab my M-11 rifle with the XR under barrel launcher. I'm not really that much of a full auto shooter but if you're alone against multiple targets you need a heavy auto weapon. It locks in at the small of my back just below the wing housing.

A few hand sized explosives including two EMP grenades. Don't like using them in sealed environments but since much of the *Njaro* is open to space anyway it won't matter.

Most importantly I set up the remote. Sweet little device I picked up during the *Wars of the Blade*. So complex…but so simple. I set the first function for the holo-imager. The second I rig to a dilapidated, obsolete plasma shield generator. It emits a small personal shield of magnetic plasma that acts like a personal heat shield for atmospheric entry. Also it can stop small arms fire…from small arms made about five centuries ago. There was a brief window of time during the *Wars of the Blade* where armies tried using old mechanical projectile weapons. Our C/O was ready for this and issued us the shield generators. It burns pel crystals in an organic acid bath, works in numerous atmos and vacuum... smells like rotting eggs.

The generator snaps securely to my hip. I check the pel tank on the way to the hatch… I'm using qualt rocks instead because the shield shows up in the visual range a little better. They're processing just fine.

Without gravity the habitat ring is filled with floating debris that didn't make it out when the shield was first breached. The magnetic cells in my armor lock on easily enough to the stations walkways but I have to float across the park plaza where I landed *WarChild* first. Microbursts from ports in my boots and gauntlets push me along where I can't get any tread. The debris knocks about, forcing me to identify every bit of it lest I let some scavenger get the drop on me.

There should be several ways to get to the stations core control levels from the Habitat ring. I find a couple of accessible railways but discount them. If someone is already in charge of the stations command center they'll know the instant I fire up the tram that I'm here. Instead I look for one that's already active…

…got one.

Just outside the industrial district there's a bit of activity. The district sits on several giant platforms that extend from the main habitat structure. The hydrogel shield that encircles the whole habitat ring shines with a bright amber glaze a few hundred meters away from the edge of the platform. Along the edge of the larger platform sit the industrial units, squat and wide buildings with skeletal spires rising up and through the far off shield. That's where the scavengers are.

Looks like they're breaking into a fabrications complex. Smart move; between what's already been produced and the fabrications units themselves there's bound to be high value, easily moved loot there.

They're good. I know that without even seeing them in action. The tell-all is the fact that this little gang of pirates is multi-species. There's a human tech specialist breaking into the complex vault, a pair of long legged braiders running through the complex searching for more valuables… I see an Afan; a female braider, using a group of bogeys to load loot onto a hover cart. You can tell they're bogeys, androids that can pass for living beings, 'cause they're moving freight with mass way above normal Afan limits without exoskeletons. Then there's… what in the All?

They've got a damn Giak standing guard at the tram. A two tonne…looks like four meter tall…humanoid from the Tri-star system back in Eastspace. The big girl is wearing light armor, not that a Giak needs much more, and carrying a Warhammer rifle. That marks her as a vet. I should know; seen more than enough of them during my tour with the 46th. She's pacing back and forth inside the port in front of the two bridges that connect the habitat ring to the main station hub here; dual spokes on the main *Njaro* "wheel" as it were.

You can't get this kind of cross species cooperation without being successful, but I've never heard of a crew like this. Maybe this is some kind of quick hatched agreement by the pirates looting the *Njaro*? Or is this an established gang?

I don't see any tats or emblems. Nothing to indicate they work together other than the smooth and efficient way they're getting the job done. They must have worked together before. Bet my ship that they've got control of the Command Center as well then.

There don't seem to be any lookouts. Could be they've got the Command Center handling over watch so I've got to be careful and not stray into the station's visual sensor sweeps. Shouldn't be a problem; *Njaro* wasn't a military outpost after all.

Getting close to the tram isn't too hard. I find a small low hanging catwalk and make my way towards the port while trying to decide what exactly to do. I need to get past the Stomper and steal the tram without alerting their people in the station's Command Center.

The catwalk brings me directly underneath the port. I can't see the tram or the Stomper from here but there's got to be some way to access the bridge from the underside.

Right?

Been a pulse beat since I used the air foils but I'm not exactly gonna be burning atmo at a five times terminal velocity. The zero-G and the short distance should make this a piece of cake. I use the manual lever and the Raptor's wings extend from the back plate. Individual air foils project from the three sections of each wing frame. When folded you'd barely notice them in the housing but at full extension they have over a six meter wingspan. My boots make no sound on the metal railing as I use it to launch myself into the air. The air foils work just fine in vacuum; they're low mass vanes filled with micro-counter weights that help to give an initial momentum boost at takeoff. It's not as effective as atmospheric flight but it helps get me to the bridge just fine.

The magnetic clamps in my boots and gauntlets don't work as well on the smooth duro-metal surface of the bridge. It's a slow, careful crawl I need to stay attached without drifting off. Makes it take forever to find an access.

"***Daphon b'kayng.***" The Giak's voice booms in the tube, it's so powerful that it vibrates through the duro-metal to the audio receptors in my armor. She's communicating with the Command Center I figure; reporting the status of their little raid.

"***PaQuashivence, berkerd. Monond sotond b'kayng.***"

Hmm…she just assured whoever she's talking to that everything was fine, I think. Been a little while since I was exposed to Giak without a translator but the last bit is a colloquialism; means something about the "ground" being stable. I'm not sure about the first part but pieces of it sounded familiar.

The only access I find is a good fifty yards further along the bridge. Who places a damn repair access this far out??

The only good thing about the distance is that the Stomper doesn't hear the panel pop open… or the hiss of the evacuating air!

FEK! Quickly as I can I climb into the tight passage and pull the panel closed behind me. I tune up the sensitivity on my armors audio receptors and listen. The Giak doesn't stir but I'm not worried about her having heard. It's her boss up in the Command Center that would be getting a steady little alert on their status board about a loss in pressure on the bridge.

With the *Njaro* in the state that's it's in there should be a load of warning lights flashing now but whoever's running the show would be paying attention to where their crew was.

One pulse...three…six go by before I can hear the Giak mumbling into her comms. Now there's a sound I haven't heard in over five cycles...

Boom. Boom.

The Giak stepped off the tram and her powerful magnetic boots stomped down the rail line towards my position. She'll cover the distance in a few beats. I grab the remote and hit the fat end. The holo-unit activates and I'm cloaked…hopefully well enough to hide me from her sensors through the bridge floor. Still I draw my M-11.

Boom. Boom! Boom!

There are lots of ways to kill a Giak, a good number of ways to kill a Giak warrior but very few ways to kill a Giak vet. My mind races over the dozens of times I've squared off against one of these bitches.

BOOM. BOOM. BOOM!

They never go down easy. We used to say that dealing with the Giaks was like dealing with the truth; undeniable and painful.

The boots stop pounding on the bridge floor a few yards away. She can't have gotten my position…

Small explosions go off all around me. Weapons fire sound from every quarter. The whole bridge shakes so violently I'm thrown headlong into the tunnel wall. That's when I hear the old familiar drone of a Giak war hammer being fired.

What in the known?

The bridge shifts violently. Feels like the structure's stability has been compromised. In zero G it won't fall but it will swing in the direction the station is spinning.

More war hammer fire. It certainly isn't directed at me. Seems like someone else tried to get the drop on this crew. Someone who's never battled Giaks before because they got the first shot and didn't put her down. Now they've got a pissed off forty decimeter giant coming after them in the tight confines of the bridge.

Another explosion and the tunnel ahead of me opens in a blaze of fire and then collapses in on itself. I crawl forward to the damage and peer through ruined ceiling out onto the bridge. Smoke and floating debris obscure so much…

…but I can still make out the huge shadow of the Giak.

She's alternately firing and swinging that war hammer, banging out her attackers as cruelly as I remember back in the *Blade*.

I can see the shadows of her attackers. They move and fight as well as any I've seen but they've never encountered a Giak vet. She'll clear the bridge of them pretty soon.

And I can see him, standing tall in his royal armor, trying to regroup his men and direct a counter attack against the goliath;

Cassad.

CHAPTER NINE:

THE LAST CASSAD

He doesn't stand a chance.

Maybe if they had critically wounded the giak on their first strike. Maybe if they had more men. Maybe if they knew what they were dealing with. Maybe if they had something they could hit her with big enough to get through that armor but like me they don't want to risk damage to the bridge.

As it is the Stomper is running riot through his men. They're Royal Guard… though they're not swathed in the Cassad family colors or displaying the Cassad family crest like I'm used to seeing. They're the best personal bodyguards in the history of the known. They've protected the Cassads for thousands of years and this Cassad for the entire bloody duration of the revolution. They're history is the stuff of legend. Their accomplishments so impossible to believe that most chalk it up to propaganda.

This is not their finest moment.

They've obviously never fought a Giak before.

You can't take them down with small arms fire. Even if you've got high caliber… or even armor piercing ammo, even after the rounds get through the mahbount plates they wouldn't have enough energy to penetrate the Giak's incredibly dense muscle. Tear up their skin all you want but the rounds never get to the squishy inside.

Even though high caliber weaponry might crack the armor unless you crack it and kill it in the same shot she'll just go even harder. And the wide area of the bridge is gonna get small real quick with a Giak swinging a five meter long war hammer. Close combat with a Giak is something you want to avoid.

Energy weapons take too much time to burn through the armor to try and use this close. The Stomper would just run you down and smash you into a nasty red paste that squirts out of your ruined gear.

Fragging it works. But again the Royal Guard doesn't want to destroy the bridge. They may have to change their minds on that if they want to survive this. There are other ways to get to core control.

I'm almost mesmerized by the fight. Between watching the Guard operate, which despite not working is still elegant…still precise on an appalling level and watching the Giak battle, which brings back all too harsh memories. I almost forget I've got a stake in this fight.

"Fall back!" his voice booms through the tunnel. Good man, realize you're outmanned…well, kind of… and get the hell out of there before that Stomper brings that hammer down on your head.

If he runs now he can get…

But Cassad doesn't run. Even as the Royal Guard retreat back around him he charges the Giak.

Insane fool.

His guardsmen can't believe it either. So graceful before, even while getting clobbered, they twist and spin about awkwardly now, taken by surprise by his ridiculous move.

But he's not awkward. Cassad moves swiftly despite wearing magnetic boots. He sprints right at her, dropping the rifle he's been holding and drawing his side arm with one hand and a long blade with the other.

Down comes the war hammer. Cassad turns off his magnetic boots…

…scratch that, he and his guard have got to be using an artificial gravity system in their uniforms, still magnetic but more sensitive to the users' needs. You can tell by the way he just launches himself over the half ton block of metal and past the stunted armored head of the Giak.

He's not the first that I've seen do this to a Giak and I don't think it's the first time it's been done to this particular Stomper. Ready for it, she spins around…DAMN!... much too fast for something that big, bringing that war hammer with her. Cassad fires his sidearm right into her helmeted face, his aim true despite that hammer passing just over his head.

He'd turned those boots back on while aiming, firing and…the blade he had is no longer in his hands.

It's lodged in the back of the Giak's rear armor plate… right in the seam!

Cassad sprints again, around the Giak now still firing at her faceplate. His Royal Guard finally recovers and runs to join their…king or whatever, but a harsh barked order from him brings them up short. He intends to finish the Giak by himself.

Fool actually thinks he's winning.

I can see the nasty toothed fighting grin on her face through the guard in her helmet just before she spins abruptly the other way, bringing that hammer around in the opposite direction. Her turn is so sharp that her boots scrap along the ground despite the powerful magnets holding her to the deck. Cassad leaps to avoid the blow but the Giak's not trying to smash him. Instead she's firing the war hammer.

And she's a smart one. She's not aiming for Cassad.

His Royal Guard, caught flatfooted and out of place by his prideful order, are cut in half when the baleful weapon opens up. All damn… half of them dead just like that.

It's very easy to forget that hammer can shoot. After you've seen it hit a fellow soldier... smash a person into wrong, unbelievably unrecognizable mush… it can make you fear being hit by it more than being shot by it. Giaks know this… and they use it to their advantage.

I pop the safety off my M-11. Can't let the stomper kill Cassad. Don't know why they're already here; I should have had more than a work rotation to set up before they reached the *Njaro*…I think. Kept falling behind my schedule but thought I still had plenty of leeway. And where the buck is his fleet? No matter, Cassad is here with only a small force so this as good a chance to grab him as I'm gonna get. My original plan is blown to vacuum now but I've invested way too much just getting to this point. Loren, don't misfire now.

Before I can even begin to sight the stomper from beneath the deck I see Cassad make his move. He takes the advantage of the death of his men to charge the Giak again. This time he grabs the hilt of the blade he'd lodged in the Stompers armor. There's a small explosion; the blade must have introduced some kind of charge. Then, with a herculean effort, he pops a wide plate of armor off of the Giak's back, exposing the dark tattooed Giak warrior flesh beneath.

The maneuver cost him position though; she turns on him and swats him aside with bone crunching force. But the opening's enough for the surviving Royal Guard to take advantage of. They open fire with smart weapons, every single round finding their way into the breach.

"ARROOO!" the Giak cries out and drops the war hammer to the ground.

Smart weapons…they blew it.

The Stomper turns on the Royal Guard and I see the fire in her eyes. Fek… I've only got a few beats.

It's easier to push through the torn bridge deck than I thought it would be, gives me maybe the extra nano-pulse that I need. Without gravity it's gonna be hard to target her and my shot window will only be open for an instant. I jam the M-11 stock hard into my shoulder as I float in between the charging Stomper and the Guard.

Smart rounds fly around me as Cassad's body guards fire uselessly. They're not hitting the breech in the armor anymore and it wouldn't matter if it did. The Stomper's lost it from the pain and gone berserker; a state of hyper elevated violent rage. She'll attack and kill everything around her until the fury passes.

And the rage can only pass when there's nothing left to kill.

But there is one thing you can count on when a stomper goes berserker; the howl. She'll howl just once as she falls into the rage. Just once…for a few beats…

"HAAAAR…."

Her huge head slides across my sights and in the instant our eyes meet I plant one magnetized foot down and pull the trigger. I get two rounds out of six in her mouth. The big girl shudders and her body goes slack. Her momentum is arrested jarringly by the auto activation of her boots bringing her to a stop not two meters in front me.

Wow… last time I pulled that off I got smashed and ground into the plasticrete of a Crodun airstrip, but I still managed to take out two of them. At least that's what they told me when I came to.

The echo of the gun fire dies down and the bridge goes quiet for a pulse beat then I hear them behind me, the Royal Guard. My armors tact-net pops with warnings as I'm targeted several times over. Cassad is laying, twitching slowly to consciousness, down on the deck on the other side of the mound of dead Giak.

"Stand down, mercenary!"

Hmm? I expected them to fire on me immediately. Looks like cutting down that Giak for them is buying me a few moments. I'm actually gonna get a chance to see if my buckin' back up tactic will work.

I lower my rifle slowly and turn as peaceably as I can. There are six…no seven of them left. Big buckers too; they've been breeding these bastards for over a millennium and the smallest is at least quarter meter taller than me. Not many in the known that can look down on a native of Arcadia.

These guys get the best training, best equipment but today they look like they've been put through the ringer and it's from more than just the Giak beating.

Their equipment is mismatched and a few even look a bit piecemeal like they've had to supplement their gear on the fly. There are some pretty nasty burn marks on their armor from energy weapon fire. But they're still standing tall…and ready to fire on me with those very deadly Royal Elite rifles.

Good.

"Mercenary?" one of them says as she strides forward. Two others move to secure their fallen Minister.

Can't have that.

I reach down and pull the cord on the plasma generator. In a beat, a thin transparent pinkish bubble envelopes me. The Guard fire before the bubble completes itself but it doesn't matter; I'm moving and the rounds never reach me. The one who advanced on me catches two from my M-11 to his midsection then I send some more fire towards the two trying to get to Cassad.

They open fire on me in mass. The plasma shield bubbles and flashes with the multiple hits but I stay unscathed as the ammo veers off just enough to miss me. There's a pregnant pause in their attack and I can't help but smile at their confusion. Doubt they've encountered countermeasures so resistant to their weapons fire before.

And it gives me more than enough time to get to Cassad. His highness is still stunned and floundering from the Giak. I give him a quick tap and zap from the crowd control unit in my gauntlets to keep him sedate. More fire opens up on me from the Royal Guard. They're not too worried about hitting their king; little known fact: Cassad and his Royal Guard carry ancient counter measures in their armor to prevent them from hitting each other in case of tight skirmishes.

Damn it…I'm still smiling as their rounds bounce neatly off my plasma shield. I return fire and scatter them, not really trying to take them down but I need them off of my back.

Can't take Cassad back to my ship until I have time to strip him of whatever tracking devices he might have on him and I can't take him back into the industrial district because the raider gang has to be alerted to the fight now. That means using the tram and heading to the station core.

I haul the last king up and toss him over my shoulder. More of their useless weapons fire explodes around me as I get Cassad up onto the tram. The Giak had the transport on standby so it's nice and warmed up for me. Simple, standard Cassad engineered controls…I activate the running program and give the Royal Guard the courtesy of a warning shout before levering the tram up to full speed and bursting through their position and across the bridge.

A few more rounds of weapons fire chase us up the tunnel but it doesn't even harm the tram at this point. We're free and clear for a pulse beat.

I take a moment and look at the view of the central core of the *Njaro* through the transparent shield as we rocket closer. It's a shame; this was one of the greatest space facilities in the Empire…

…vultures.

Ah well…the sooner I disable Cassad's equipment the sooner I can head back to my ship. One EMP grenade, slightly modified, should do the trick. I send a few blasts of highly charged electron waves over Cassad and read the results through my tactical display. A few at a time his electrical systems go off line, even the pheromone particle emitter stashed in his boots shuts down. Using the slowly dying grid of disabled macro lines as a blue print I disable the rest of his counter measures and slowly strip him free of his gear. Oddly there are no subcutaneous or deep tissue implants… guess the Cassads are above such things.

I throw a standard tech jumpsuit on him and then bind his hands to his waist, one on each hip. Whew! That didn't take too…what?

The tram is speeding up. I look at the controls and see the ominous flash on the board indicating a remote set of commands. In almost no time at all I can see the dock we're racing toward at fatal speed.

FEK!

I try the EMP on the controls but there isn't enough juice left to fry the remote connection. There's no time to jury rig another grenade…

I grab Cassad and extend my Raptor armor's air foils. They catch the wind with a neck jarring jolt and we rise out of the tram.

Too much buckin' momentum! The tram crashes into the dock ahead of us by only seconds turning into a rolling ball of scrap. Metal shards fly through the air like shrapnel and I twist in midair trying to cover Cassad with my body.

We soar past the dock at breakneck speeds but the wings finally begin to slow us considerably after we clear the still tumbling tram. Can't maneuver for position…can't maneuver for anything other than a survivable landing as the Central Cores first partitions race at us.

We're still moving too fast! I curl around Cassad protectively and shield us as best I can with the wing foils as we slam through a guard rail first then into aircar dividing wall.

UNG! The crash knocks the wind out of my lungs and in the pulse beat it takes me to recover I see that all I'm holding of Cassad is a bit of torn jumpsuit.

All damned… where?

"Lose something, Loren?"

What the buck? I look up and see a small gang of mercenaries floating in cover formation all around me. Cassad, still unconscious, is cradled loosely in the arms of a female soldier who is one of three of the mercenaries who are wearing armor… Raptor armor.

The female floats forward a bit tossing Cassad back to one of her mercs like a sack of grain. She lifts her visor and her eyes shine through with a wicked glimmer.

I take another breath, then; "Long time no see, Step-child."

"Heh," she says. "Long time no see, Picker."

CHAPTER TEN:

The FireHawks

They've repainted their armor, nasty splotches of dark red paint covering the old trim. Step-child is still wearing her "Heavy" package and is toting a MM 7&7. She's covered all the old 46th patches and insignias with the roughly drawn blazing fire emblem of the FireHawks merc gang. I supposed it's meant to look pretty dynamic but it comes off garish. Could be I'm just used to the subtle design I fought in.

The other two in armor I don't know, but I recognize the Raptor Armor easily enough.

"When the hell did you join up with the FireHawks?" Anger rises in my voice with every word.

"Join up?" she's smiling. "Picker, we STARTED the FireHawks."

"What?"

"Right after you bailed."

"You started a mercenary gang? Filled with Afans and All dammed Stompers? Using THAT emblem?" the fire bird logo was used by a pretty big merc army that operated back in Eastspace during the *Wars of the Blade*. They were a pretty impressive bunch… started by vets from some of the stronger Imperial worlds. But we pretty much ended them during the *Blade* so there's no way…

"…you started the FireHawks, Step-child."

"Oh yea…it's Phoenix now. And I never said I was the Duke."

"Phoenix…?" As casually as I can I take a look around trying to get a sit-rep. We're at the dock landing. It's separate from the main body of the Central Core. Cargo and people transferred here onto shuttles and made their way across what looks like a good hundred meters to the city proper. Below us there's a web of crossing gantries spanning down into the amber haze caused by the hydrogel dome. Armor's picking up the faintest bit of gravity here. If any of us float too far from the dock we'll start to drop.

They're clustered pretty close together… I don't see any back up…no overwatch that I can see. I glance at the other two mercs wearing Raptor armor and suddenly my gut tightens. I kick off from the wall and let the counter weights in the air foils straighten me up to face them. "These two are wearing the armor of dead men!"

She hesitates for a pulse beat and then shakes her head with a lot more venom than I'm expecting. "They've proven themselves worthy of wearing…"

"Proven what??" I point a gauntleted finger at the bigger of the two. "That's Yogger's armor, Step-child! Who is HE to be wearing that?"

The merc in question bristles a bit. But Step-child makes a dismissive gesture. "They are proven, Loren! Now what are you doing here? Who is this?"

Cassad lolls about in the arms of the smaller merc. If they recognize him…

"That armor needs to be interred with Yogger, Seph…how could you…"

"DON'T YOU DARE!" she screams and jets forward a bit. "You know…" her voices breaks only a little. "No…you wouldn't know; you left us so damn fast… what they did to the bodies of the 'traitors' we were bringing home before Arcadia fell.

"This way Baro gets honored…by those who know." She floats down toward me from her group and I lift my visor so that our eyes can meet. This close I can see the she still hasn't gotten rid of the old scars; one in the cleft of her chin and the nasty flash burn from a Junn plasma rifle still paints a dark brown "butterfly" across the copper skin of her nose and cheeks. I see the pain there and the same resentment I hold in my own heart. But it isn't enough.

"Boo-fek. Nobody should be wearing that armor, Seph. And who's armor is…" I stop myself as I recognize the battle damage pattern embedded across the wide chest plate and then the faint and poorly painted over "lightning" emblem on the shoulder guard.

"Recognize it, Picker?" Her eyes switched from pain to a dangerous anger in the space of a nanosecond.

"I do." I do…

"So it's true?" she asks.

The memory came back easily enough. It's one of the top worst in the rotation of my lucid dreams. My throat goes tight. Showboat was…it had to happen.

Step-child floats ever closer. A few thick strands of her dark brown hair escape her flight cap and poke out of her visor. "We lost a lot of our people to the *Blade*…more at Dalius, but even more after. How many are yours?" Her eyes narrow to slits. I see it now; She isn't looking to avenge Showboat, she wants to take her still seething anger over Yoggers death out on me. This is just an excuse.

"I'm not here for this." I say. It comes out as a warning.

"I don't give a hot pile of fek what you're here for." Now we're so close our helmets are almost touching. "You're gonna pay for what you did."

"You don't mean Showboat." I say with challenge in my voice. "Or Half Head, or Bingo…"

I narrow my own eyes as I peer into hers. "or even Quick…"

"Quick?" That startles her. Good; I need her to know how much trouble she's in.

"No," I press on. "Who you want me to pay for is Yogger."

She starts to shake her head but I cut her off from answering. "But you really do need to think about the others first." I say. "Yogger died with honor. Sacrificing himself for his people…fighting with his squad at his side…saving our lives…but those others? They died in situations…very much like this."

I see a moist gleam in her eyes. Not sure if she's going to back off or come at me. I don't want to hurt her. Don't even want to fight her. She's saved my life more than once.

"You buckin piece of…"

"You need to be thinking about this little squad of yours… Phoenix." I snap. "Only thing you're going get here is a handful of dead mercs."

"Maybe you recalculate the odds here, dipper" spits the merc wearing Yogger's armor. "Dipper" is an Arenn term, sister planet to Arcadia. At least there's somebody in her crew whose people I didn't used to kill.

I make sure to keep my eyes locked with Step-child's. "You think you're little gang here has what it takes? I know you were monitoring the bridge. You saw me take down your Giak. I'm still in fighting form. This is going to end badly for one of us but this does nothing for Yogger."

Step-child backs away from me. I let her go; if this goes bad I don't want more 46th blood on my hands. But she seems to be composing herself.

"I…I want to know who this is." She jabs a finger at Cassad. "And I want to know what kind of tech that is you used against that other merc crew on the bridge."

She's trying to save face for both of us, I think. I'll give her one but not the other.

"He's my business" I say. "But I'll give you the plasma shield."

"We're not letting this piece of fek go?" her squad starts to balk.

"We blew the tram to get him!"

"He killed Sieda." That objection spews from the vocal simulator perched on the shoulder of a particularly small merc. He stands just over a meter tall and covered from head to toe in EXO-combat gear. From his bow legged stance I realized he's Pan, a feral humanoid species from the Cerebus star system. Very secretive; they've managed to keep almost everything about themselves hidden from most of the known. Except for the Cassads, who had their foot on every world, no one gets cooperation from them. More points for the FireHawks.

"Not my intent to attack you." I say. Looks like Step-child doesn't run her squad with the kind of discipline we were taught in the ADF. One of her crew might decide to take it upon themselves to open fire prematurely. Can't tell which of them might pop first…they all look so damn jittery. Got to calm things down.

"Think we all should just let go what's past and move on from here." I say.

"You don't give the orders here." And the little Pan raises his weapon.

"No, I do." Step-child finally steps back up. I can tell from the way the whole crew is bracing themselves now that this challenge has been some time in coming. Not sure I want to get in the middle of this especially if the side I'm leaning to has Step-child on it. But then she says something that draws my gut tight.

"He's 46^{th,}" as if she were telling them I was part of their merc crew.

They all go silent. I don't. "What's this now?"

Step-child looks hard at me. "WE don't turn on our own."

I can't help but be curious. "Who's we?"

"Don't tell him fek!"

"Find your cover!" Step-child snaps. She stares down the merc in Yogger's armor again then looks back to me. "You only get that if you stand down and join up, Picker."

"Join up? Eat dirt with longnecks and Stompers? Not gonna happen."

"Then give me that shield tech." She floats forward and extends a hand. Her crew bristles a bit but remain in ranks. They must have all seen the plasma shield perform against the smart rounds. They want it but giving it to them is a big gamble I'm not sure I can risk losing.

Could be she thinks that my shield generator will give me an advantage in a firefight with them. So if I hand it over now she might just try and go at me.

Could be she's just looking for a way out for both of us.

All depends on how much she really blames me for Yogger falling.

I reach down and disconnect the generator from my hip, watching the small FireHawks Squad for the first signs of attack. They grow even more fidgety, but still look uncertain. Hopefully they at least wait for her to decide one way or the other.

I hold out the generator. Step-child looks it over without reaching out. I see doubt in her eyes.

"Looks a little like the bubble gennies we had during the *Blade*" she frowns. Of course it looks like that because that's exactly what it is.

"It's not. Works a little better."

"Obviously. How?" she reaches out and takes the generator. Her whole body shifts forward a bit as the mass of it surprises her; the qualt rocks I'm using weigh three times as much.

"Figure it out" I tell her. "Hand over my mark."

"He cost us, Phoenix" the Pan murmurs. "We should keep the man…take his armor…and his ship…and…"

"He's a point, Loren." Step-child says with an arrogant confidence. "Why shouldn't I just…"

"Cause you're not stupid, Step-child." I say as I give her a look I reserve for Junn pretty boys. But she's tough, 46th trained and tested in the

Wars of the Blade, she won't fold now. This is going to go ugly. I've lost Cassad.

Before we hear the shot the merc wearing Showboats armor and holding the unconscious Cassad is spun about from a long range rifle hit. The next instant we hear the rapport and suddenly several more of the FireHawks take long range blasts.

The Royal Guard have made their way across the bridge.

Step-child ducks down and to her credit she's barking regroup orders even as she's hit herself. Her heavy armor handles the hits just fine but I see she's already struggling to plug in the plasma generator.

I really should warn her but I'm too busy trying to scoop up Cassad.

The last of the House of Cassad is tumbling head over heels down…down into a chasm of crisscrossing walkways, hitting a few but still falling none the less. I go full burst from my M-11, toward the top of the docks, to get me moving in the opposite direction. Just a beat passes and as gravity takes over, I sweep the wings and shoot down after him. The lowest walkways should lead to the inner core. If I can get Cassad there…

Hot white tracers cut across my flight path to Cassad. A few of his highness' guardsmen must have come in ahead of their brothers. We're all in fast dives zigzagging past the thin walk bridges. They're coming in at an angle but in that Royal guard armor they've no real flight speed or directional control. I'll get to Cassad first so they're trying to cut me off with sporadic fire.

It costs one of them; not paying enough attention to his own flight path the guard slams into a cross bridge dead center.

Our speed picks up as the gravity in this section is almost at one full G. We're falling faster and so is Cassad.

Fek! More cross fire from the Royal Guard. I raise my M-11 and send back rounds, hitting one nicely center mass and sending him, careening, into a cross bridge rail hard enough to lose his weapon.

Ahead of me I see Cassad hit a relay antennae, spin and then head directly for a particularly wide bridge. Just moments after he slams into it, my boots come down on the same walkway harder than I anticipate, forcing me to catch myself. My rifle hits the ground, pops out of my grip and spins away down the bridge. I sprint after it and toward Cassad but more tracer fire tears up the plasteel plates around me. The bridge shudders as another of the Royal Guard lands hard in right in my path. His foot stomps on my errant rifle and with a grin; he levels his own weapon at me and pulls the trigger.

Can't help but to enjoy the look on his face as every shot veers wide of hitting me. I pull my Sever and return fire with much better results putting him down with torso shots until he falls away from the walkway.

I take a look around. The rest of the Guard seems to be engaged with Step-child and her little squad of looters. She's not doing so well herself, having taking more hits than she should have trying to depend on that useless plasma shield.

Time to go.

I recover my weapon and then walk over to Cassad who looks… well at least he's still breathing. I rack the M-11, keep the Sever in my gun hand and toss Cassad over my shoulder with the other. Without looking back I haul ass across the walkway and into the corridors of the central core of *Njaro* where I can lose anyone trailing us.

Almost done.

EPILOGUE:

I fasten the holo-emitter to the binding bar behind Cassad's neck. He's still unconscious but now only due to a sedative that won't last too long. I checked him out in my small med-bay and despite all he'd been through Cassad is going to be just fine. Well until his trial anyway.

So I position him, upright, in the cargo bay, locked into a prisoner binder. Then with the remote reconfigured, I depress the button on the wide end and the crystal clear and life like image of a large cargo container shimmers into focus hiding Cassad completely. He'll wake in a hazy darkness, unable to see where he is.

That done I return to the workshop. This time I have my own Raptor Armor up on the rack. Hardly any damage to speak of, a few plates could be reset but that's all. I check to see that the inner emlin alloy I pulled from the old guard's armor is still in place. It's doubtful that the Royal Guard will catch up to me before I turn Cassad over to the New Regime but "just in case" is what wins the argument.

Long ago the Cassads used the emlin as a safe measure to make sure that their own personnel would never be hit by friendly fire. Over the years that alloy got forgotten by most and was only used in the old ceremonial armor and perhaps in the Royal armament of Cassad himself for purely traditional reasons.

But the weak point in the weaponry was still there, hidden in their secret history, just begging to be taken advantage of. The smoke screen of the plasma generator was a fail since one of the Guard clearly saw his rounds veer off target after he fired on me when I didn't have it but at least it bought me enough time to get Cassad.

His fleet never made an appearance in system. Could he have lost it out on the edge of the known? His men looked beat up enough. Guess the money I spent getting Ziaran transponders was wasted. Maybe Sticky can get a good price for them.

The FireHawks sent out encrypted messages with 46th code keys attached but I ignore them for now. With any luck I won't be in the merc game anymore so I won't be running into them again.

C.O.P. pings and I head for control. *WarChild* has made it out of Orun's gravity well and can make the jump now. Time to get paid.

PACK LOREN:

KING'S RANSOM

by

Howard Night

A DARK UNIVERSE NOVELLETTE

THE FALL

About twenty-three cycles ago the most powerful worlds under the control of the empire got together in secret to figure out how to beat the top dog; the Cassads. Most people will tell you that was the beginning of their fall but really…it was the *Blade*. The *Blade* did to the Cassads what it did to most; cut them up and bled them numb.

The New Regime got bolder after that. The known began falling faster and the Cassads couldn't feel the reigns slipping through their cold fingers… couldn't hear the scores of worlds crying for liberation for the buzzing in their ears.

Now the Known is in chaos and the Cassads last worlds are under siege.

It's a good time to be a merc…

CHAPTER ONE:

The Graveyard

The field is particularly violent this cycle. I can see collisions flaring in the distance as an unscheduled meteorite shower races through. Of course I can't see the streaking meteors themselves through the bright plumes of burning waste fuel filling the star field, but their impacts flash bright enough.

The Targothian Graveyard; a band of space junk orbiting the star Targo, so thick that it's never been mapped and so old that it's rumored there are ships in here from before the Dark Age. The graveyard is one of the most volatile places in the known. It's filled with debris from every corner of civilization, mostly the carcasses of ships wrecked in wars, sent here because of some long forgotten tradition. There are millennia old and corrupt engine cores still spewing radiation and burning fuel, eco-spheres filled with unregistered biohazards and warheads that go off intermittently all of which make salvaging the deeper parts of the field a near certain death sentence. This is where I found my ship, *WarChild*, and where I made my living in the tough years after Arcadia fell. It took me awhile but I learned how to navigate enough of the graveyard to get by. That's why I chose this place for the exchange. It'll be hard enough for the Revolutionaries to even get this deep into the field let alone stage some kind of double cross in an environment they don't know.

Still, I keep my ports open. Streaking debris and rad leaks aren't the only hazards. When I worked here junker gangs roamed the outer edges of the field raiding legit salvagers or researchers which, with the fall of the Cassads there are less and less of. So now the junker gangs either go to war with each other over salvage they'll never be able to collect themselves, or just attack anything that they happen upon.

A burning gaseous sky silhouettes clusters of floating shipwrecks and debris crisscrossing each other's paths as they pass overhead. I'm standing on the outer hull of a Shecogan capital ship in the largest and thickest cluster in the field. She's probably a thousand years old but this deep in the graveyard it's never been cannibalized. Not much left to it anyway. Whatever war this ship had last fought in had done a number on it. Only part of the hull survived; weapons ports were holed and empty, the engine housing was simply a warped and bubbled mess of metal framing an open chasm now in the center of the ship. There might be something of worth in its computer core but it's centuries out of date and I doubt I have anything compatible enough to access it.

The ship is big though, hard to get around and positioned perfectly in the graveyard. The Coalition can only approach from one specific path, which I provided them. Prevents them from ambushing me… I hope.

They're late.

Could be that's the holdup…they're trying to set something up.

The meteor shower subsides and the field calms a bit. Maybe the path I mapped for them changed…happens enough with the movement in the graveyard but I thought I checked it out thoroughly. Hate to have to set up another…here they come.

Two ships, both looking a little worse for wear, appear out of the field about where I was expecting. Small frigates…good; another advantage of using the Graveyard as the exchange point; large ships can't get through without taking enough damage to permanently inter them.

There's a static filled squeal that comes over my comm gear; another graveyard trait, so much background noise is generated by the flotsam that complicated broadcast communications can't be read. All you can do is send a strong signal and hope whoever you're trying to talk to hears the blip.

The screech is enough to let me know they're coming in as planned. So far so good. Another few clicks and I'll have my money.

Enough money.

The frigates take their time matching velocity and direction with the Shecogan hulk. Even though they must be getting my signal they look to dock a good ways down the hull. Being cautious I expect, but this feels…

The hull shakes with the landing of a small shuttle from the nearest frigate. I watch as a small party of three disembark and make their way slowly towards my position, stomping clumsily on magnetic boots.

I don't see my money.

The leader of their little group is a small female, could be the woman who served as my contact when I brokered the deal. She's wearing a standard EV-utility armor with a dark plated face guard, but her two bodyguards are in heavy powered combat armor and carrying cheap plasma rifles. Nothing too fancy and nothing that should worry me; my own Raptor armor and load out is more than I would need to handle these two if things go glitch. And from the way they're twitching I guess they know it.

The woman reaches to the comm lines I've set up and hooks in.

"I don't see my money" I say.

"Where is the Package?" her voice comes clear over my comm. It sounds like my contact.

"Ready to be transferred to you," I say. "I soon as I'm paid."

"That's going to be a problem," she says and the two heavies thumb the safeties on their weapons. I don't make a move save to softly slide my thumb over the remote in my palm. No need to trigger it yet; the first few rounds from those plasma rifles won't get through my armor…I think. Why can't any part of this buckin' mission go smoothly?

"What…problem?" I almost growl.

"Cassad forces have captured and are holding the Alpha Gates three chief stations. Regime forces cannot get through…"

She's lying, nobody can control a gate that big, so I cut her off. "Skip to the part where this is a problem for me."

"We…can't get your money here," she says, the pitch of her voice rising a little. With her faceplate dark I can't get a read on her. Not that it matters.

I turn and begin pulling the temporary comm gear apart. "Fine, I'll find another buyer."

"Wait!" she pulls out a small data chip. "We still want…!"

"I'm sure you do," I say. "So do a lot of other people, including the Royal Guard."

"If you can get the Package to New Beia, for the trial, we can still pay you in full."

"New Beia?" She's talking about Esara, in the old Sumatran Republic, "liberated" from the Cassads shortly after the start of the *Wars of the Blade*, now the heart of the New Regime's Coalition. "Deal's off."

"You will be given safe passage…"

I cut the comm line and stuff the gear into the equipment pack on my hip. Still watching the two heavies I deactivate the magnets in my boots and unfold the air foils on the back of my armor. The inertial counterweights inside them begin pulling me away from the Shecogan wreck.

I'm so busy watching the two heavies that I miss seeing the woman launch herself at me.

"Wuff!" BUCK! I nearly pressed the button! Would've set off charges I'd planted on the Shecogan as well as two other shipwrecks floating nearby.

"Get off!" I yell knowing she can't hear me. What on styx is her game? She can't think she can take me… and her two buddies haven't even moved.

She fights through my arms and grabs a hold of my helmet, then slams her head into mine. Not hard enough to stun or even distract me…what's she…?

"Please! We need the package for the trial!" her voice comes through my helmet, muffled and distant. Desperate move; trying to communicate through vibration. This close I can see through the dark tint of her face plate. Her eyes are wide and pleading.

"I don't work for free. Get off!"

"Please! I swear you'll be paid…in full. Meet me on New Beia. Use code Seven Sierra for Maren! You'll be given safe…"

Finally I kick her off and send her spiraling down toward the hull of the wreck. With my air foils up I drift away from the ship a few meters before pulling the bulky handheld zero-G maneuvering jet from my equipment pack. Then slowly picking up more and more speed, I make my way through the debris field.

What the buck am I gonna do?

I zip along through the Graveyard until I find my old hiding spot; the remains of a Cassad colony ship, one of the ones they used to force colonize planets across the known that already had small indigenous populations. It's big enough to hide a large ship and perfect for hiding my ship…*WarChild.*

She's tucked up under the old cooling system, to protect her from probes or scans from salvagers. A Multi-purpose Utility troop Transport; a M.U.T.T, she's a drop ship from a war fought more than five hundred years ago. I found her deep in the field, when I was salvaging myself after the *Wars Of The Blade*. It took me some time to outfit her and get her up and running but she was worth it. Her body and hull are cete-Armor, made back when ships couldn't deflect incoming enemy fire with energy shields. The armor has a regenerative property so it grows over time; when I first saw her I almost didn't recognize that she was a ship at all she was covered in so much spikey growth. Of course she was little more than the hull and housings but I found most of what I needed to complete her in the Graveyard or was able to swap for in deals with buyers or looters. Even managed to fall into some G-Rock; which enables *WarChild* to fold space and get me back and forth across the known. That alone makes her worth more than most ships so I try and keep that detail quiet. The fact of the matter is that I can get the package to New Beia in just a few jumps.

I use *WarChild's* top hatch to gain access. It's a tight squeeze against the underside of the Cassad wreck but I have the other hatches rigged against tampering. The hatch is a little glitchy, like most of my ships systems, and takes me a moment to get her to pop open. This is this kind of thing I was gonna have refitted when I got paid. Hatch closed I slog down to *WarChild's* prep bay and begin stowing my armor.

What am I gonna do?

The New Regime ain't the Cassad Empire. The Cassads had the known on lock for the better part of the last thousand years. There was an…order…to things. But since they began to collapse the sectors where they lost control have become utter chaos. The New Regime likes to think of itself as the new authority but they lack the Cassad's finesse and central command structure. The many governments of the Coalition fight with each other nearly as much as they do with the Cassad forces that remain.

New Beia is where their Coalition Cabinet lies. I was there a while back and it wasn't too bad. From what I've seen on the Hub it's still sound, stable and pretty nice there. But the underground scuttlebutt says that's just hoofer-fek for the vid-heads. If I try my luck jumping there I've nothing guaranteeing me a way out.

I strip off the Raptor armor, first the helmet with its winged visor, then the hunter green armor plates which are begging to be repainted, and finally the bio-mechanical weave. It's not the best fighting armor in the known by far but it is one of the most unique and versatile. We thought it was a joke when my old C/O brought them in for us to wear back in the *Blade*, but the Raptor armor turned out to be the very thing that turned the tide. Kept mine after I left the service and have been using it ever since. When you get into as much trouble as I do you stick to what you know.

After a quick check for damage I stow the gear in a small "pirates hold" and ground it to inspection side. Funny that I hide the armor, which hardly anyone outside of the Quad, my home star group, would recognize but I leave the "package" sitting right out in the open.

It's parked in the middle of my prep bay; two thick gunmetal gray cargo boxes sitting beneath the missile loader. The most valuable cargo I've ever had. For every single pulse beat that I hold onto it my life is in danger. I was full of fek when I said I'd find another buyer. No one else has the coin to make up for what I spent on this venture…at least no one who couldn't just take the "package" and my ship by force. I could set up another exchange but I wouldn't even begin to know where to look for a safe place to trade the goods. Doubt I can use the Graveyard twice…no…that would be asking for glitch. Can't afford to bring anyone else back here.

I'm too tired…not gonna figure this out unless I get some sleep…unfortunately. I tell the Computer Ops Program to wake me after a shift then I trudge up ship to my bunk.

CHAPTER TWO:

NIGHT TERRORS!

I settle the floor panels back into place over the secret hold then turn to stare at the stacked cargo containers strapped down in the middle of the prep bay. After a pulse beat or two I pull up the virtual holo and set the C.O.P. to wake me in one ships shift. With one glance back at the cargo containers I start up ship for my quarters to bunk down.

I settle the floor panels back into place over the secret hold then turn to stare at the stacked cargo containers strapped down in the middle of the prep bay. After about a pulse beat I pull up the virtual holo and set the C.O.P. to wake me in one ships shift. With one glance back at the cargo containers I start up ship for my quarters to bunk down.

I settle the floor panels back into place over the secret hold then turn to stare at the stacked cargo containers strapped down in the middle of the prep bay. Then I pull up the virtual holo… wait… what's going on?

The holographic lights of the C.O.P. dance before me. I stop myself from sending the subvocal command to activate them but that doesn't seem to bother the holo; the C.O.P. still registers the command to wake me after one shift. What's happening?

Suddenly…I'm in the access stairwell headed up ship. This…oh…I get it.

I'm dreaming.

During my time in the ADF, I, along with my fellow soldiers, was indoctrinated into the *Wars Of The Blade* by means of Arcadian Combat Memory Training; a method of implanting combat memories into a fresh recruit via a means of lucid dreaming. Gave us much needed combat experience before we ever actually came under fire.

It was a boon but it did leave a few nasty side effects, one being that many of us would never dream the same way again. After memory training forced us to remain conscious during the implantation of memories some of the soldiers lost the ability to dream subconsciously. So we would remain lucid even after entering the rem stage of sleep. Also our dreams are no longer cobbled together images and experiences from our memories, no longer our subconscious imagination at work. Our dreams are memories, full and intact that play over and over again while our bodies sleep…they're usually the worst memories.

But this is different. I usually dream an old memory but here I sit, back in the prep bay locking down my gear. What's the mal? Maybe the stress I've been under has finally made something in my brain pop?

As I slide the panels back into place again I try and look around. Like in most of my dreams I can get at least a blurry image of what I did not directly look at. This memory I just lived. This is me stowing my gear and then heading for some rack time.

Sometimes I can control what I dream. If I go to sleep thinking about my ship, I might dream a memory of when I first found her or of repairing her. If I'm thinking about food then I'll dream about a time I was eating that food.

For the most part though, no matter what I'm thinking, I dream about being in the *Blade*. I dream the skirmishes over and over again. I see my friends die in exacting detail on a nightly basis. I see Arcadia fall…

But never have I dreamt about something as simple as stowing my gear and checking my cargo. What is this?

I settle the floor panels back into place over the secret hold then turn to stare at the stacked cargo containers strapped down in the middle of the prep bay…again! This is going to get monotonous real fast. Because I dream lucidly, I can't wake myself. So I'm trapped in my sleeping body until either it wakes on its own or the C.O.P. pings and jolts me awake.

Still, I've had worse dreams, so I guess I shouldn't complain that…

OH FEK! Did I just see what I thought I did? I struggle to turn around but I'm already heading up ship with no way to stop myself. Okay…don't panic…I did NOT just see that.

Finally, I'm in my bunk again and settling down to sleep.

I settle the floor panels back into place over the secret hold then turn to stare at the stacked cargo containers strapped down in the middle of the prep bay.

Where is it? I stare down the containers but everything looks fine.

Maybe I just imagined it; if that's even possible in a lucid dream.

But there's nothing there. I should be fine. The holo pops back up and I watch as the C.O.P. sets the wake up time again. Then as I reach the hatch I turn and…

FEK! There it is. I didn't notice when I was awake but there… just on the outside of the hologram of the cargo container, is a brown muscular arm feeling its way around. Somehow the "package" got his arm loose of the control bar.

Buck me; this dream has looped at least five times! By now he's free!

Cassad is loose on my ship and I'm trapped in my sleeping body!

CHAPTER THREE:

BURN!

WAKE UP!

WAKE UP, WAKE UP, WAKEUP! Boot up already, Loren! He's probably standing over you right now with your Kendo blade in his hands! Come on! Get that heart beating! WAKE UP!

I struggle but it's like there's nothing to fight against. I can't feel my own body. Can't feel if my heart is beating hard like it should be or even if Cassad's hands are around my throat!

And he will kill me; the late Emperors son, now king of the known, is bound to be a little bit past the redline after finding out his empire has finally fallen and his homeworld has been occupied. Not to mention his having to sit strapped to a restraining bar in the cargo bay of my ship ever since I snatched him at gunpoint for the bounty.

Uselessly I fight against the dream as I slide the cargo panels back into place and then turn to head up ship. Again I see that damn arm sliding out of the cargo container hologram. How many times have I dreamed this? How long has he had?

Come on, Loren! Get up! I've never woken myself up before. Always needed some external stimuli to shake my body out of this bucked up version of R.E.M. sleep. And I doubt I have the time for my body to naturally wake on its own.

GET UP!

I…can…almost…feel…my…

My eyes pop open to the dim light of my bunk. The chronometer on the wall reads 1300; a full three hours until next shift. Everything seems fine…

…except I can't move.

What the buck? The gravity well must be glitch. I can't lift a finger…gotta be more than Twenty G's in here. I try and subvocalize a command to the C.O.P. but I'm not getting through. Something's blocking my link.

Could this be Cassad? Could he have gotten free and somehow made his way to control or even down to the G-unit? He couldn't have hacked my systems so that means he must be smarter than a liquid A.I. to have sussed out my command codes.

Buckin' Cassad!

But why ramp up the gravity? Sure he's got me pinned but he won't be able to move about the ship either. Unless he's sitting in primary… and has figured out how to pilot *WarChild.* Since he doesn't know where I am he figured to just ramp up the grav all over the whole ship. He won't need to move himself until he has us rendezvous with whatever's left of his Royal Guard.

I try and sit up but I can only twitch a bit. Wait…something's off. This doesn't feel quite right.

There's a muted click and my eyes go right to the hatch. Slowly the door opens, pausing each time the metal hinges squealed. Then in a rush the door is slammed open and Cassad leaps into the room with a good length of cargo piping in his hand. Looks like he couldn't access my weapons locker.

But how the hell is he beating the G-rock?

He walks forward hesitantly, looking about the cabin as if he's weary of a trap. But he's not wearing any kind of exo gear…how is he not pinned to the floor?

"…yuuu…" I can't even talk! Grav-well wouldn't paralyze me… what is… All Damn… I'm in Rem Jam! My head woke up…but whatever it is that keeps your body from moving during your active dreams is still running in my head.

Cassad takes a step closer and our eyes meet. His eyes are narrow and suspicious; he still thinks this might be a trap.

How I wish that was true. I never had this happen to me before but I've seen it. Didn't take too long after Memory Training for soldiers to start getting caught in Rem Jam. I woke up one night in the barracks because a soldier we nicknamed Fanboy was gasping in his bunk. His eyes were open and his body twitched something fierce…I thought he was dying.

"Mercenary?" Cassad seems a little more confident now. He might not know about Rem Jam but he's getting to the realization that I'm bucked up.

And he's right. There's only one way out of Rem Jam. Somebody eventually got the Duke, Omega, up and he came into the barracks in a fit. Took one look at Fanboy and said only four words; "Go back to sleep".

Well, I guess when you think you're dying, it's a little hard to try and take a nap. Fanboy twitched and gasped for what felt like an hour but couldn't have been more than five minutes. Omega just stared him down, never saying another word. Finally Fanboy closed his eyes and his body calmed. Another minute and he woke up naturally, just as fine as ever.

"Go back to sleep"?…no buckin' way!

Cassad strides forward with a lot of confidence now, until he's standing right over me with that thick piece of cargo piping. He looks about my cabin a bit more, taking in the spartan décor. Most likely he went to the Captain's Cabin first, not thinking that I'd be using the pilot's cabin which is closer to the Command deck.

"You are alone on this ship" he says… or asks; it's hard to tell. Either way I can't say anything back. "Where is the crew you were working with on the *Njaro*?"

He thinks I'm with the FireHawks; the mercenary gang he and his Royal Guard were fighting when I swooped in and grabbed him. Of course he'd have no memory of me really as he'd taken a pretty good bashing from a particularly upset, twelve foot tall Giak warrior.

"Who is it you were working for?" He raises the cargo piping. One blow from that will be enough to wake me up. Of course one blow and I'll probably be just as helpless as I am now.

"Tell me, mercenary."

There's only one way to beat Rem Jam…

"Now."

I close my eyes and see Fanboy twitching in his bunk…completely helpless…

Then, just like that I'm back in mine.

"*WarChild* burn the rock!" I scream.

Cassad brings the piping down. But my coded command to the C.O.P. instructs *WarChild* to do the very thing I thought Cassad had already done. Instantly gravity jumps to about ten times normal. The piping drops straight down missing my head and hitting the edge of my bunk with a harsh ring.

Cassad follows it down, dropping to the deck in a flattened heap.

"Clever, mercenary… but you are as trapped as I am." He's not talking to bluster or scare me. He knows that I know we're both stuck. What he's really wants is for me to give away how long the grav is gonna stay hot. Right now he's got to keep struggling against it, staying tense waiting for me to give the order to normalize gravity. But I can relax…and count out the forty-six clicks till it drops on its own.

"I'll give you one chance, mercenary…"

32…33…34…

"You have shown your worth…ugh… as a warrior. But if you do not release me this moment you will learn what it means to cross a Cassad."

43…44…45…

The grav-well cools down and I leap out of my bunk. Cassad is moving too but I close on him fast landing on top of him awkwardly. He preps to grapple, to wrestle me as he's probably been trained by masters to do, but all I do is throw my forearm, with all my weight behind it, into his chest. Exposed, I catch a mean right from the toppled King that sends bright flashes across my field of vision.

Another one is coming when the G-rock fires back up and suddenly we both weigh ten times normal again…

…with me sitting right on his chest.

He gasps and wheezes but loses the fight to maintain consciousness, though it takes him longer than most. I give it another few pulse beats then order the Grav-well to normal output. Pressure off, I roll over onto my back.

Luck. Stupid luck. Trying to finish this venture will get me killed.

But what else can I do?

CHAPTER FOUR:

TAR CITY BLUE

"TARGO INNOCULATION SUITE UPLOADED." The C.O.P. tells me. I pop the forward hatch and watch as the cobalt blue afternoon sunlight pierces the dark interior of my ship. First time I visited Targo I thought the deep blue color of the atmosphere was beautiful. Didn't take long for me to find it depressing.

Targo in the afternoon is about as bright as twilight almost anywhere else in the known. It was once an industrial world, centuries ago, before the Dark Age. Whoever built this world then did a real number on it, mining it clean of all resources, then using it as an industrial reclamation center, likely for salvage of the ships in the Graveyard. But the multitude of processors needed to break down the old ships and their toxic elements fill the air with, reportedly safe, blue oxidized gas. So much so that on bad days it hangs the air like a fog, stains your clothes, your skin and sits on your tongue like a dead mint.

I check the area quickly with a scan from my visor which only tells me what *WarChild's* security suite already has; there're only the two mech techs on the dock.

"Standard?" the burlier of the two techs asks me as I walk down the ramp. She's already got the fuel linkages ready to go.

"No, clean and sweep," I tell her. "Top off the baselines only."

She grunts and moves to make the connections. The rear hatch closes behind me quickly but I wait a minute to make sure the feeds are being hooked up properly. It's easy to scam unwary ships with low feeds but my time spent here after the war made me savvy to most of the tricks.

Dock Administration tries to gauge me on the dock fees but I still have my old warrant from when I was here before. It has the true and current rate on it as well as my non-identifying ships marker. The marker can be used to relay third party messages and indeed there's a communication package waiting for me.

It's key coded right and from Arcadia but with no author I.D. so it could be anybody. Arcadian military maybe? Finally figured out where I am?

No… it's most likely…family. I was more lucky than most; I have family that managed to get offworld during the ELE attack on Arcadia. But being branded a traitor and a deserter means that I can't go home and contacting them would place them in danger of being arrested. Doesn't stop them from trying.

I dump the package without reading it. No need to dig up any more problems for myself right now and I don't want them connected to my current venture.

With everything settled I walk off the dock and head down to the public trams. With the deal bucked I need to get info on what's going on in the known. The kind they don't broadcast on the Hub. The kind you can only get by talking to some dangerous people.

The tram travels from the dock overland to Neolon City, more popularly known as "Tar City". The Targo Prime skyline is long and desolate. Most of the cities on Targo are built under domes that had been needed when the cities were founded, long before the Dark Age but not since. Still they haven't taken them down. Most of Targos inhabitants are contractors and prospectors; people using the planet as a brief port while they raid the graveyard. Those kind of people don't improve worlds; they leech them.

The tram slides under the dilapidated dome and into the first depot. Hundreds of people and beings crowd the small terminal, a lot of them look familiar.

Arcadians, lots of them are here, they stick out from the crowd because of their dress and their size. They don't look good; haggard and weathered, beaten and broken, my people are clearly refugees on this world. There were no Arcadians, no refugees I mean, when I was here almost five cycles ago. But Targo is on the fringe of Eastspace, the Quad, so it makes sense that eventually a few of the survivors of the ELE attack would make their way here. They're ignored by the rest of the commuters who are only looking to journey deeper into the city. The only people eyeballing them are hunting for prey.

I've taken a position at the back of the tram; easier to zero problems and also makes it obvious to anyone looking for trouble that you're ready for it. A pack of raider kids does a walk through from the front of the tram to the back. Doesn't take them too long to notice me, with all the refugee Arcadians there aren't any decent looking vics on the tram today. I see them deliberate silently, each trying to gauge me and their chances. Raider kids are smart, they like to look you in the eye to see where your head is, if you're "aware" or not. I just let them sneak peeks at the holographic "ghost eyes" of my visor.

They hang for two stops before deciding to move on. Like I said; raider kids are smart.

The tram plunges on through the heart of the city where the dangers get worse. I watch as passengers disembark and pay out "tolls" to the deep city street gangs that control civilian thruways. The Arcadians are getting the worst of it. I grit my teeth and pray to the All that one of those thugs gives me an excuse but the gangs never board the trams like the raider kids. They would take too much and then the city authorities would step in and sweep them out. Happened every few years when I was last here. As I'm moving to clear to the other side of Tar City, I won't get a chance to... Probably for the best…I mean; I've got money waiting so…

A small Arcadian family boards the tram, a mother, two small kids and what might be an uncle who's strapped into a cheap ambulator. They're carrying big storage packs…probably everything they own so they're broke and clearly unarmed.

The raider kids notice them too. Like a pack of sulu they always prefer weak prey...prey that's are cut off from its support. Most of the Arcadians got off on this stop but this family is getting on. Must not have been able to find work or safe lodging in the inner city and figure to try their luck on the city's edge.

The woman helps the uncle climb aboard, and the kids…can't be older than five cycles each…flitter under her with fear and sadness in their eyes. The mother is small for an Arcadian. She's probably from Uero; her golden hair, stained with many days' worth of Targo air, is tied into two tight buns on the right side of her head which means…something to do with her marriage I think.

She spots the Raider kids quickly, so does the uncle who tries to turn but the ambulator just jerks and shakes. It's an old model and it wasn't made for him because it's too small. Without it, though, he wouldn't be able to move or even speak.

The lead Raider kid, decked out in what must pass for tough street wear, smiles and blows kisses at the mother. His buddies begin to spread out, trying to surround the family.

Then the mother sees me.

Fek.

She herds her small family toward the back of the tram just managing to keep ahead of the raider kids who try to cut her off. And she's slick; nods to me like she knows me as she sits her kids down in the seats adjacent to mine. It's enough to get the Raider kids to hesitate and hang back.

But they don't just give up. The lead kid watches her, trying to gauge if she's playing them.

She tries to make eye contact with me but I'm still wearing the visor which makes me wonder how she picked me out as…

"Arcadian?" she whispers.

"No," I say…I lie… out of habit.

"Please," she calls my hooferfek. "You seem to know this place."

"I…am…looking…for…work…" the uncle says or rather the vocal box, spot welded onto the ambulator just under his jaw, squawks in barely intelligible electronic tones.

I don't answer him, instead noting how the Raider kids are just waiting for an excuse to rip into this family but their leader is eyeing me and clearly picks up on my size which matches what he's seen of Arcadian males although I'm actually a little taller than average. We're a bit bigger than most humans in the known. Makes staying inconspicuous damn hard.

"You seem…" the mother says, looking me up and down and finally noticing the Sever on my hip. "…to be working."

The lead Raider scopes the distrustful way her children are looking at me. He knows we're strangers.

"I'm…a…machinist…" the uncle says. Not likely a quick one, doubt he'll find work here on Targo.

"Hey, mama," the Raider Kid leader blows kisses across the tram at the mother. She doesn't cower or seek any more protection from me. She's Arcadian; she pulls out a blade.

I stand and place my hand on my Sever and let the "ghost eyes" on my visor stare down the leader.

He gets the message and with a subtle coded hand gesture, pulls his gang back. They move further up the tram but their leader's clearly not satisfied; the small family is still their focus.

The tram takes us all the way to the Unk pass; a large factory complex sitting under the only open section in the dome. This is where most of the reclamation facilities are…where most of the money on Targo is made. They have their own docks, a larger port than the one I used but here they monitor everything and even run ship inspections.

Can't have that which is why I berthed *WarChild* outside the city and in the commons.

Huge cargo ships make birth here, loaded down with salvage from the Graveyard which they can sell or have refurbished. But mostly they just process the ores. Few ships go deep into the graveyard where there might be something of value; it's easier to pick at the edge for more consistent albeit second-rate salvage. So there is a vast network of support businesses running here. Parts dealers to fabrication shops, union labor houses to training academies and of course, bars, game-rooms and binding houses.

The Raider kids stayed on the tram when the Arcadian family followed me off.

"I'm Vel," the mother tells me. "And you ARE Arcadian."

"No I'm not." I lie again and start to walk away.

"We…need…work…" the uncle stops me, grabbing my arm with his weak exoskeleton covered hand.

"Good luck." I mutter and pull free leaving the Arcadians behind.

The *Busted Lock*, a parts dealership on the sunset side of the complex, is where I'm headed. It's where I got my first job after the war. It's easy to find, some of the shop signs have changed but most of the buildings are the same. It was a busy place when I worked here but now it appears desolate. Styx...if I hadn't checked on the Hub first I might think the shop's closed it's so quiet and empty now.

The door slides open at my approach and immediately I'm hit with the harsh smell of gear solvent and burnt linkages. My mind goes back to my time here after the war but something's missing…sweat…the funk of a few dozen jacklegs standing ass to balls in que, desperate to get the parts they need. But that was a few cycles past. Now the inside is about as empty as the street outside.

Almost.

"What's yer need?" I don't recognize the young guy now manning the requisition station but the crew always had a quick turnover rate. He stands behind a broad counter, which has several security features built inside, none of which worked when I was here and I doubt they work now. Behind him the room opens up onto a wide expansive warehouse filled with rows and rows of categorized parts. It's a mess; ship parts lay scattered all over the floor in the aisles or are set haphazardly on the racks.

"Where's Clock?" I ask.

He bristles a bit. "I'm Parts Certified," he says, thinking I don't trust his knowledge. Fine.

"I need a phali caliber, non-conductive alloy, post-Age, with the open 30 odd bracers."

Immediately his head drops to his virtual console. "What's the ship make?"

Sigh...you don't need to know the make to find the part. Never the less, "I'm running a Bocine drive in a Four-Over Crodun housing."

"…uh…what ship is the Bocine drive from?"

"A Bocine."

"Right. Ok…a phali caliber?"

"Yup."

"What…"

"Pre-Age." I answer the redundant question before he asks.

"Oh…" and I watch him as he scrolls through his data, looking for a listing that's not there. "…uh…there's a 25th Cycle, Ramir age…"

"Where's Clock?" I ask letting the holographic "ghost eyes" on my visor narrow to slits.

"I…I'll get him." And after one final look into the data base he disappears down the row of parts right behind him, the sound of metal on tile rings out as he trips over something set on the floor.

"A WHAT?" a hoarse voice bellows out a thick Welt accent. "Who on styx is playin' games in ma shop?" Heavy footsteps and the jingle jangle of swinging mech tools ring up from the aisles. After only a few beats Clock emerges, still wearing his half frame goggle over one eye which made it appear three times as large as the other. He was also still wearing Welt mech coveralls, worn, covered in adherent stains and stretched over his massive shoulders and barrel of a belly. The jangling came from the web belt which was overrun with tools and meters. He'd let the beard grow, and it had gotten whiter so his chin was now framed in a white halo.

"Buck…Loren?" his mouth dropped open.

I can't help but smile. "Good to see you, Clock."

"Loren? Pack Loren?" the kid who had been manning the counter looks at me with wide eyes then dashes back into the aisles.

"What was that?" I ask.

"Ahh buck, Loren. You shouldn't have come back." Clock's eyes are suddenly full of regret.

"What? Why?"

"I…I got in bad…I work for Hard's Boys now."

CHAPTER FIVE:

THE HARD WAY

"How long?"

"Not too long after you was here last I guess. Salvage got real bad when the Daliuns tried to claim the Graveyard for a bit. Had to leverage the shop and Hard bought the marker."

I grimace. "Hard is dead," I should know; I killed him. "And only one of his brothers survived to make it to a Junn prison."

"Yea. It's the sister, Quan and her kids running the show now. And a cousin, I guess, who's a buckin' psycho path. They put out a watch for you after that whole thing with that ship you found." Clock raises his eyebrows and the eye behind the one goggle fills the lens. "You still got that brick?"

"And the kid?" I ask instead of answering him.

"He's Quan's youngest. Got no grey in that skull but he's got enough smarts to send a comm to his mom."

I can barely remember the sister. Only dealt with her idiot brothers and back then they had been small time but bad enough. Don't much want to risk getting caught back up in that.

"Fine. I'm gone. But I need some feed."

"I don't get much anymore, Loren. Hards ripped out most of my set up and took it back to their place."

Fek. "So if I wanted to know who's making offers on the capture of Cassad you couldn't tell me?"

"Well that's easy. No one. No one with the coin to match what the New Regime is offering."

"What about lower offers?"

"The Zande maybe. But they're about as dangerous to deal with as anybody. And any leftover Cassad allies are broke or sitting with their backs against a wall." Then Clock peers at me hard with that big eye, blinking once. "What? You hooked up with somebody thinks they can get Cassad?"

It was a longshot coming here to see if I couldn't get a line on another buyer for Cassad. Clock is compromised. What he knows Quan knows or will soon know and that could cause me problems. Without his tech gear it's a wonder he's still here at all.

"Why don't you just get out?" I ask.

"No coin, Loren. Else I'd head back home…start over." He means back home to Weltinadir, the breaking world, where the most G-rock in the known is mined. Clock always said working the graveyard was easy compared to trying to make a living on his home world.

The door chime sounds behind me. In walks…of all the…

"Hello, my name is Vel and this is my brother, Volor. We are looking for work and were told you hired out processors." Vel is followed by her kids and of course her brother who has trouble making it over the small threshold at the door.

Clock looks them up and down, especially Volor, the uncle stuck in the ambulator. "Come back tomorrow, I'll vet you then."

Vel tries not to let her face drop. "We're pretty faded. Barely made it down here from the inner city. Not looking forward to another trip back and forth."

"If ya can't hack it in Tar City ya should'na come to Targo. Now get out of my shop."

"I'm…a…Cassad…certified…machinist…" the uncle says. Clock looks at the exoskeleton he's wearing.

"Serious?" he snorts. "You've never seen a Tar City reclamation factory I'd bet… or a cutter scrapyard else ya would'na walked this hoopty in here."

"We're both capable!" she's Arcadian proud; won't beg but she has children and no way to protect them. Almost against her own will she glances at me.

"You're better off joining one of the cooperatives. You need someplace that can look after those crumb snatchers while you work." Clock tells her.

"The cooperatives?" she asks.

"That's," I start to say. The cooperatives are dangerous. She takes her family anywhere near one and she'll likely lose those kids. "…not an option." I finish.

"Not for you. But we need work." Vel argues.

"You're from Arcadia I take it?" Clock asks. "They're not all built like you huh, Loren?"

I give him a harsh glare for saying my name and indicating where I'm from but Clock is unaware why. I wasn't concealing my identity when I used to work here. It wasn't necessary with all the chaos the wars and the ELE attack caused.

"No," Vel states, again trying to catch my eye through the visor. "We're not all so lucky. Not since Arcadia fell."

"Look, Loren, Quan's gotta be on the way by now. You'd better go."

"Too late for that." I tell him while dropping my hand to the gun on my hip. My visor is picking up weapon signatures outside the shop. Quan sent some heavies; she must still be pissed about her brothers. A warning alert goes off as the shops security sweep finally picks up the weapons in the area.

"What's happening?" Vel pulls her kids to her.

"Keep your heads down. Clock, take them back into the stacks." I step to the door and peek outside. There are nine of them and they're spread out along the avenue. Only one that looks familiar is an older male with shiny dark skin. He's got that Hard head.

"You Loren?" he asks with challenge in his voice. The rest of his men look overconfident. They've been enjoying the perks of being a top gang in Tar City for a bit now. They think I'll fold or run.

I step outside, walking to the center of the street to keep the shop clear of what's coming. My visor zeros on all their gear. Hope it doesn't miss something vital.

"Yea." No point in lying.

"I'm Reg, FeReg Hard. Domo was my cousin."

He's got major countermeasures in place. Jammers, switchers and sparkers…most set to throw off smart weapons and guided slugs. Plus his clothes are lined with armor and it's a high grade plate. But, like most thugs, he's left his head unarmored.

"Domo?" I ask.

"Domo Hard! You killed him."

His crew has armor and a few counter measures, but none are as well decked out as he is…save the guy wearing ridiculously thick cover armor on his torso but none on his head or legs. Their weaknesses are easy to pick out but this is still quite the upgrade since I last dealt with these guys.

"Hard's boy?" I ask, again like I'm not sure.

"Yea!" he's barking now, a little thrown off by my indifference. He's got two side arms, both fire guided missiles. Absolutely useless with all the countermeasures he and his boys are filling the air with. The rest of them are carrying heavier weapons; full auto but again, all dependent on tracking gear. How did these guys expand the Hard gang with fekhead tactics like this?

"Actually," I shift my weight, allowing them to see the big Sever on my right hip. "His brother…I want to say…Crater?"

"Kradar."

"Kradar. Yea Kradar killed Domo. I shot Kradar and the other brother."

"I…what??"

"What was your name again?"

"Reg genetrash! You bucked…"

BOOM! His head explodes as the slug from my NOK 37 passes clear through it. It was a good shot, straight from my left hip but I don't have time to admire it.

His small gang opens fire without deactivating their countermeasures. As a result the shots are only as good as their own natural aim. This won't take…ung!

A shot from a pulsegun knocks me on my ass. The armor plate in my flight suit handles it well enough to keep my ribs from cracking. I toss out a stunner and subvocalize an order to my visor to go dark a millisecond before it explodes.

The street is filled with a bright electrical discharge designed to blind both human eyes and artificial ones. I hop up and fire at the nearest targets, who are shooting blindly into the ground. That's two down…three.

But the rest have recovered so I roll to my feet and dart back into the *Busted Lock*; the only cover I can get to on the strip. The inside of the shop is quiet until what's left of the Hard Boys begin to pepper the front with small arms fire.

"You've really got me cruked, Loren!" Clock shouts at me from deep in the stacks. I can hear Vel's kids crying back there as well.

"I told you to get them out of here, Clock!"

"And go where? Quan will have half her crew out looking to burn us all down now."

He might be right. I don't know Quan but if she's anything like her idiot brothers then she'll think nothing of killing a homeless family just for being in the wrong place at the wrong time.

"Head to the docks at Neolon south. My ship is berthed in the commons!" When I last worked here, Hard had people in seven of the major cities on Targotha. If Quan has, at least, maintained his holdings then there's no place on the planet where they can go. Off planet…it's their only chance now. Mine too.

The small arms fire stops for a moment and I can hear Clock complaining as he leads Vel and her family down into the basement and hopefully out the back. The Hard Boys will have that covered unless I keep their attention focused right here.

I fling open the door with my Sever drawn and sight the first Hard Boy I see, distracted by something when he should have been watching. I take him out with a head shot and immediately my visor flashes a warning:

WARNING: HYE ROUND INCOMING!

I see the smoke trail but not the round so I know it's too late to move!

BOOM!!

My ears are ringing from the blast. The front wall of the shop is leveled by the blast and so I'm exposed though it's hard to see for the smoke. I'm on my backside again and this time I'm sure a couple of ribs are broken. The concussion wave of the blast was absorbed by the remaining security feature the *Busted Lock* has…had; the durocrete in the walls. Despite that my head still swims a bit.

The Hard Boys're waiting for the smoke to clear. They're pretty sure the blast took me out.

It takes two tries to get my Sever back into its holster. Jamming it in at an angle trips the cylinder cartridge release and reset. At the angle I pull it out at it reloads with an explosive round cylinder. Each round is filled with oxyfernum which makes them so thick the cartridge can only hold ten of them.

Ten shots…

I subvocalize to my visor. The smoke filled hole in the front of Clock's shop is overlaid with a three dimensional map rendered from the visors sonic sensor. The street outside the shop comes in as a rough radar rendering as it and the remaining Hard Boys…and the fekhead with the launcher, are bounced back by the sonar wave. The jammers make the image hazy but they're not really designed to disrupt sonic sensors so…

BOOM!

I put the round right into his chest and the launcher drops to the ground.

BOOM!

The idiot with the thick armored jacket is gonna miss that leg.

BOOM! BOOM! BOOM!

The Hard Boys scatter for cover and now I'm seeing that there are a lot more of them than I thought. If Clock and Vel got out through the back then I can't follow; the Hard Boys would run us down because the uncle and those kids move like slugs.

I reload the Sever, toss my second and last stunner out into the street then leap out after the flash.

More gunfire follows me but it's way off the mark. Their leadership is fractured and they're sloppy now but still seem eager to finish the job. So I haul ass and cut off the strip first chance I get. The pursuit is hesitant and that's all I need to make it to a tram and head away from the Unk docks.

I can't help but slump in my seat as the tram ambles along the worn railway. My ribs aren't as bad as I first thought…I think, but they still hurt like a ride down styx. I should probably switch trams a few times but I don't want to risk Quan having the time to get the word out to all the raider gangs. The way I look now they'll definitely try me.

"Look at you now."

I snap my head up and spot a gray haired process worker sitting a few rows ahead of me. She doesn't seem to be paying me any attention, coughing out a shift's worth of burner smoke, but there's no one else close enough. Plus…the voice I heard couldn't have come out of an old clanker like her could it? Look at you now…why would she say that?

The docks are quiet when I arrive and that's just fine. I find Clock and the Arcadians waiting for me on the main walkway and they follow me to the port where I pay the docking fees. Fek; cred is gettin' low…

"All damned, Loren." Clock grumbles as we emerge from the dock administrators office above the fueling station on the landing deck.

"You've just bucked me."

Vel and her family walk out behind us and follow along down to the landing circle. She is still holding her little girl in her arms. "What have you gotten us involved in?"

"What did I get you involved in?" My words come out with a bit of a growl. "I don't remember telling you to follow me to a scrapper shop."

"We didn't follow you; we were looking for work!"

"Well I didn't follow anybody!" Clock shouts. "Now I'm on the Hard Boys fek list."

"You have an off world cache?" I ask him while I disconnect *WarChild's* supply lines from the port myself instead of waiting for the port mech techs.

"A small one…enough to book some passage but not enough to do much after. I can't…"

"Enough to reopen a repair shop though?" I ask and take a quick look about the walkway to the docks, checking for Hard Boys.

"I can't stay here, Loren! Quan will…"

"Clock! Is it enough?" My ribs are killing me.

"Just," he says. I can see a small group of raider kids running along the docks now. They're looking at everything in port. Maybe Hard's boys don't run so deep now if Quan is using them to do the scout work.

"I'll take you to the jump at the Nine-Five. You can get back to Weltinadir from there…"

"Welts not good for me, Loren. My creds won't buy a facility much less the gear I'll need."

"I can get you a hangar on Stels if you can overhaul it."

"You've got a hangar on Stels?" he asks suspiciously.

"No time, Clock. You in or out?"

"Not much choice, Loren," he grumbles and starts to walk past me to *WarChild* when I see Vel eyeing me. I grab his shoulder.

"One condition…"

Vel loses her patience. "And what about us?"

I look at her and her little girl hides her face from me. It's the visor…she's scared of the visor.

"I was getting to that," I say. "If your brother is Cassad trained then Clock can use him in on Welt."

"You expect us to go all the way to Weltinadir for work that you can't guarantee?"

"What do you care where you starve?" I am growling now. "There's no going back to Arcadia and you can't stay here."

"We…accept." Her brother speaks up.

She looks to balk a bit but notices that I'm actually watching the incoming raider kids. Seems to be more than enough to get her to decide I'm right although I'm sure I'll hear more on the way to the Nine-Five.

"So now I'm to take in orphans?" Clock asks as *WarChild* drops her rear hatch at my command.

"Better deal than you had before I showed, Clock." I tell him while checking the load on my Sever. "I can get you back to Welt space…you can go home."

The raider kids draw closer. I consider waiting and using them to send Quan a message. But that would just be waste of time and won't pan out to anything anyway; I'm never coming back here again. So I just climb the ramp to the hatch, close up and begin to prep the ship for takeoff.

This was a bust. Looks like dealing with the New Regime is my only option.

CHAPTER SIX:

STICKY SITUATION

There are more habitable worlds in the Median Belt than anywhere else in the known. It's where the Cassads first began their conquest for power and it was the most stable bit of space for the past millennia. Even when the *Wars of the Blade* broke out the Median Belt remained a sea of calm. But that was before Ziara, the Cassad home world, fell.

Almost two weeks after I dropped off Clock and the Arcadians at the Nine-Five and I'm back in Cassad space. I've got *WarChild* coasting just outside the Maren Gates Kup belt, the quickest way from the former home space of the Empire to the Median Belt. There are four…no make that… at least FIVE battle groups of major warships pinging all over my G-det between here and the Gate. Not a single group is from the same government….not one from any Cassad friendly holdouts. Looks like there are Brythons…some Denir, a Marajesh task force, a …Quaznian unit, and even an All Damned Dalian battle group. They're circling each other like packs of sulu but nobody's shooting…not yet. More than half of these forces represent the big seven worlds that started the New Regime and it looks like they aren't working too well together.

Could be this ain't gonna be as hard as I first thought. I might be able to pass right by the ruckus unnoticed. There's a ton of traffic coming in and out of the Gate itself flooding the system with ships. A lot going on beyond that Gate I guess. The G-Det is getting pings from all kinds of ships. Most of the transponders are running Coalition tags or New Beia registries. And from the flight patterns it looks like they all have to fly through the check points of each of the battle groups…and pass some kind of inspection.

Fek.

I should turn and bolt right now; take my chances jumping to New Beia on my own despite the time it would burn. Problem is showing up without being announced is even more dangerous. There are five fleets here…nope six, there's a Norlan group too…what's sitting on the other side of that Gate?

Might be other options.

The Ops station is slaved to the Primary control position. I don't have to get out of the Primary control seat to have access to ships functions like Power distribution, Tactical and Communications. It makes it possible for me to run the ship all by my lonesome. Still I hop up and step over to Ops because there is one set of protocols that I've installed that can't be accessed from Primary.

With a hard kick I pop the façade off of the Ops communication console, exposing its insides and the special modifications I'd made. Three foot sized nodes lay hidden inside the Comm station. Each is the housing for an Entangled Communications chip; a two way comm unit used to communicate instantly across the known with a twin unit.

The first node has a twin connected to the main Communications Hub at the Howard Array in the Freygent nebula. It's not that rare; there has got to be a few million twin units at the array, so just about every major city in the known has a direct connection to the HUB and so to each other. What's rare is a small ship like mine having one. Without it I'd have to connect to a local Hub and through them to one of the main ones which would mean anyone in between could tap my feeds, get my intel or even my location. I was lucky enough to grab this one off a derelict craft in the Targo Graveyard.

The second node I ripped out of the smashed Communications room of the *Eagle*, the Capital ship of the 46th Task Unit. She was listing and done for at the Battle of Saxet where we stopped the Daliuns from invading Arcadia. I haven't used that one yet; it'll read as the *Eagles* node and that might draw too much attention to me. If the main Hub back on Arcadia is even still up.

It's the third node I activate though, connecting it to my main comm lines. I put the façade back on the console and in a moment the wide Ops screen comes to life as the C.O.P. makes the connection I've dialed up. While I wait I pull up a visual on Cassad in my Prep Bay; can't be too careful.

The screen shifts and brightens as the connection solidifies on the other end. The node is connected to a pirate hub. Don't know who's running the hub or how many nodes they have out there but I got the node from a pretty reliable source so I trust it…for now.

Another moment and a plain faced woman appears on my screen. "Hello, Mr. Loren. How can I help you?"

"Sticky." I say a little too harshly but since he's the only contact I've been dealing with in their group why on styx would she ask me that?

"Of course" she says and the screen goes to a default setting displaying a basic Cassad network logo. I lean back in the Ops chair and wait, flipping the remote over in my hand. Takes a little while for the screen to light back up.

Sticky is close to my age, maybe a bit older, though Arenn years are counted a little differently. Back in the *Blade* he was what many would call a middle man, the kind of guy you go to when you want hard to get items, items that would put you in harm's way if you tried to get them on your own. He's the one who sold me the third Communications node as well as giving me a pretty good faked log to get through a few Jump Gates. So he should be able to get me what I need now to get past this one.

Unfortunately I don't exactly have the coin or even a way to get it to him right now. Means he'll have to gamble on the fact that I can pay him back later. He should be willing to take my word for it;

…he's 46th.

"Loren," his tired face pops onto the screen; must be the middle of his sleep shift. His face is drawn and filled with more lines than he earned from the *Blade* but his eyes still have that sharpness that I remember. Tall like an Arcadian but thin and lean like most from Arenn he has to stoop down some to remain on screen.

"Sticky," I say, his "call sign" that would be. Earned it back in our time with the 46th Task Unit. Even then he had a bit of a black market set up. Never used his services myself while we served;

…thought he was shady.

"What can I do for you."

"I need Intel."

He grimaces a bit and looks off screen at something and then turns back. "Your account is low, Loren. Doubt you can afford my grade of Intel."

"I'm outside the Maren Gate," I tell him. "The New Regime is six sets deep on the Median side. Need to know who's really aligned with who, who's crewing those ships and who might be a friendly." His face doesn't change.

"Like I said; Intel you can't afford. And I don't see how you can get me the creds even if you had it."

I clench my jaw. All my life I've avoided having to owe coin to anyone. Never liked having a debt hanging over my head, never liked the thought of being stalked for money. And while Sticky doesn't scare me like I'm sure I scare him, he has his own effective ways of collecting. Still, I say four words that I myself have never trusted.

"I'm good for it."

That actually gives him pause, but only a briefly. "You're 'good for it'? Are you kidding me, Loren?"

"I'll have the money."

"Loren," there's a fateful tone in his voice now. It's almost sympathetic. "You're never going to collect that bounty. No one is. The Coalition only posted that reward out of bravado… they're trying to show how strong they are."

"You're the one told me they could pay," I counter.

"Sure they've got the coin but there's no way to get Cassad and they know it."

"You're either overestimating Cassad…" I start.

"I'm not."

"…or underestimating me."

"Loren, I'll admit you're pretty good. Showed some nice skill before but there isn't any single man who can capture the son of the Alaafin… the man is, for what it's worth now, the king of the buckin' known. It'll take a fleet of ships and a damned firestorming of an entire planet just so they can declare him…"

I cut the live feed of the prep bay into our communication. Sticky's eyes go wide.

"…dead?" His mouth hangs open for a nice long and satisfying moment. Then his face twists up in doubt and he reaches off screen to tweak some control as he tries to verify that I'm not showing him some hooferfek holo. Finally his eyes widen back up and he turns and looks back at me.

"Consider the intel an investment," I tell him. "A risky one."

"How did you…All Damned, Loren… how in the known…you're…where did you GET him?"

No point in keepin that a secret now. "At Ziara."

"You went to the Ziara?" his eyes are as wide as I've ever seen them.

"No," I explain. "Just outside the kup belt. The *Njaro* was trying to escape and I'd already figured he'd make a play to use it to help take back his planet."

"So it was you who took the *Njaro*?" he looks doubtful…and a little greedy. "Where is it now?"

"I didn't take the station, Sticky, just Cassad. Left the *Njaro* to float."

"It's gone now," Sticky says. "Somebody managed to power it up and jump the damn thing."

Hmm…must have happened after I was gone. Still it doesn't concern me. "Don't know anything about that. I've got more important fek to deal with."

"Yes! They'll…" he stammers hard for a bit, takes another look a Cassad on his monitor then turns and looks far off screen. "Fek! Aldra! Put together an intel package on the New Reg forces at Maren…NOW!"

Then he turns back to me, but his eyes are on the Prep bay feed. "You're buckin' insane, Loren. They'll rip your ship apart to get Cassad before they'll pay you for him."

"This is why I need the intel."

"You want to play them against each other?" he guesses.

"Just enough get them to keep each other in check and off my back until I can get paid." It isn't the best plan but it's one that can work.

"And you think you can make that happen? You know how many people want that man dead?" His fingers are flying over the screen as he brings up data that I can't see on my end.

"More like; how many factions want to be the ones SEEN taking him down" I correct him.

"Then you'll really need to know who benefits most from actually bringing him to trial…"

"Whatever gets it done, Sticky."

"Whatever gets it done…" he says and I can almost see the wheels in his head turning. "You know what, Loren?"

"What?"

“If I’d known you had the skill to actually bring him in I’d have charged you a lot more.”

CHAPTER SEVEN:

HOT GATE

I review the intel package Sticky sends for the better part of two shifts. Got to admit, he's good; not only did he give me the battle group dossiers of the Coalition forces but he also sent me a breakdown of the major and minor "sub-alliances" inside the New Regime.

Piloting *WarChild* while wearing the Raptor armor is not something I usually do but if things gets bad…and they could go really glitch…then I may need it on as a last and very desperate measure. I stow the helmet in the holding rack above primary and don the visor for the visual communication.

All set I head in toward Maren.

Surprisingly I'm left alone for the better part of the fifteen hour trip in. Just a few directed beacons with instructions on whom to report to for inspection. I keep *WarChild* on a seemingly compliant course making sure to steer clear of the roving, circling battle groups until I find the one I'm looking for.

The Brython Flagship, the *KBS Triumph*, sits like a fat, bloated whale at the center of the formation of four battleships, two other carriers, six or seven frigates and…more than a dozen gunboats, looks like.

The Brythons give the New Regime the moral and populous legitimacy they need to challenge the Cassads. They have the worlds; the Brython home system has three completely terraformed prime worlds, two terraformed moons and dozens of habitable moons. They've "annexed" worlds in at least a dozen other systems since the end of the Dark Age…they tried to take Eastspace centuries ago. Even had a serious foothold on Arcadia until the Liberation War. So they've always represented a serious threat with both their resources and their population. Their government runs step in step with the Cathol; their major terrestrial religion. Very similar to many of the "one-god" religions, they believe that the messiah figure has already walked across the surface of all worlds. Brython Cathols zip around the known trying to spread the "word" and convert every being they encounter while searching for evidence of their messiahs passing. Though the scripture of their faith professes love and kindness in theory, the Brythons can be quite violent and misogynistic in its practice. Each Brython ship has a famed Knight of the Star onboard. It's the Knights duty to insure the purity of every mission by whatever means necessary. I've never seen one of the Knights but I've heard some pretty nasty stories.

That's the secret to the Brythons power in the known. Their complete hold over the will of their people, a hold that is dependent on strength of their Cathol faith which means their leaders must follow, or at least appear to follow, their own dogma.

The Cathols have declared that Cassad must be brought in for a trial before their lord. Means they need him alive to cement their place in the hierarchy of the New Regime…means they'll deal with me and honor the bounty.

I hope.

WarChild is halfway to their battle group formation when my Comms ping. Someone's read my new transponder and wants to chat. "Independent ship, *The Seventh Seal*, fall into formation with the Daliun ship, *Austin*, and prepare to be boarded by order of and under the authority of the Junn Empire." The holo lights up and I see the upper torso and head of the *Austins* X/O. He's got the look of a former pretty-boy so I know I'm dealing with a real fek-head.

Looking at the G-Det I see the Daliun Frigate that hailed has broken off from the battle group in an attempt to intercept me before I get to the Brythons. The rest of the battle group seems to be slowing a bit…maybe waiting to see if this comes to anything but not yet willing to be too aggressive.

G-Det tells me that the frigate will catch me before I coast close enough to the Brythons to get their interest. If I don't slow now the frigate will pursue or even open fire and if I make a break for the Brython battle group, they themselves may just open fire on me.

Instead of running I subvocalize a command to the comm station and open up a hailing channel to both the main Hub and the standard Hub.

"This is the Independent ship, *Seventh Seal*, broadcasting to all concerned parties." I say in my most officious voice. "I have important cargo that must pass through the Gate…by order of the Coalition."

"*Seventh Seal*, the Junn Empire speaks for the Coalition. You will now accept nevron control of your ships systems and prepare to be boarded." The old pretty-boy orders.

I have to be careful here. Drag this out just a bit longer. "I have clearance to pass through the Gate. Code Seven Sierra."

That gets somebody's attention because the Tact board lights up suddenly. Means that *WarChild's*'s being scanned rather aggressively right now.

There is a bit of a lull in comm traffic but Tactical fairly screams with scan warnings and the G-Det shows me that not only is the Daliun battle group turning, but several others as well. Only the Brythons are holding steady but then I was moving in their general direction anyway. They're playing it safe.

Tactical pings at a more frantic pace; the scans coming from both the Daliuns and the Marajeshi, have moved into the aggressive range. The Marajeshi have a relatively small task force, a few frigates flying vanguard for a big carrier Tactical labels; the *Mtumishi*. A ship with a good rep, noted in Sticky's dossier, but its design is so…alien it's a little unnerving. Marajeshi ships use some type of weird centrifugal force technique. The body of their ships spin about to either create gravity or locomotion, I'm not sure which, and the differing sections spin in opposing and discordant patterns. They almost look alive. The Marajeshi are not considered "alien" by the Cassads but they are one of the more segregated people. Their tech is mostly unknown but still, whatever their scanning capabilities, they'll get nothing through *WarChild's* armor.

"*Seventh Seal*, open your nevron link or be fired upon." The pretty-boy is getting angry.

"*Austin*," I keep the transmission on the open circuit. I want everyone to hear both what I'm saying as well as what the Daliuns are threatening. "Stand down. I have a high priority package to deliver to New Beia authorized by the Coalition. Code: Seven Sierra."

G-Det shows the *Austin* has increased its speed and is trying to intercept me. If I don't fire up my engines they'll catch me before I get to the Brythons. She's not that big but still a Frigate. With the condition my ship is in I'd be stupid to try and engage her in any kind of combat. But just looking at that smug Pretty-boys face on my holo makes me want to open up with my busted pulse cannon. I quell the urge and check on the

Brythons again. Other than the one scan they haven't shown any interest in me. What's their glitch? The code must be good…two other battle groups are now moving toward my position. What are they waiting for? Well…still have my trump card…

"Stand down, *Austin*. You are interfering with a High Priority mission sanctioned by the Coalition."

"We speak for the Coalition, greasy! Now open your nevron link, else we're fittin' ta open your ship ta cold black!"

Yea, he's pissed now and they're getting too close. The Brythons still haven't budged so looks like I'll have to see if anyone else is interested. I keep the comms open and connect the live feed of Cassad in the prep bay of my ship along with a biometric transmitter.

"*Austin*, New Beia is waiting for my High Priority cargo; Khalid Cassad, Alaafin of the Cassad Dynasty!"

Well, that gets everyone going. G-Det pings as several battle groups break formation and send their fastest to intercept and the Comm station lights up with overlapping holographic hails.

"*Seventh Seal*, move to position three-one-five, sheer nighty degrees of Maren. Wè will protect you." That comes from the Quaznian group. 3-1-5 is a rather nice angle for them to blow me and Cassad to atomic ash, which is what Sticky's Intel says they want very much to do.

"*Seventh Seal*, this is the Marajesh ship, the *Mtumishi*, bring your ship into our fleet formation and we will escort you safely to the Gate." Doubt it, they more likely just want to keep Cassad away from the Brythons.

"Coalition forces stand down!" The pretty-boy is flustered and spitting. "Our scans indicated that the transmission from that ship is a fake. The ships transponder is false, this is not the *Seventh Seal*, seven weeks out of Euphrates. It is in fact, *WarChild*, a mercenary ship known in Daliun space ta pirate Junn ships and assassinate Junn officials." His jarring Daliun accent is starting to come out.

The comm traffic heats up even more and my holo projector can't keep up. So I focus on the G-Det and watch as the battle groups begin to jockey for attack positions on each other. Still the All Damned Brythons are just sittin' on their asses.

"Captain of the *WarChild*, you are under arrest for crimes against the Daliun Republic. Open your nevron link!" He's even more agitated now. Could be the incoming Marajeshi or maybe it's the all the failed attempts to break into and remote access my ships systems. Buckin' pretty-boys always expect to get their way.

Fek! He just might at that; the Daliun Frigate is getting close. G-Det shows only one possible course, unless I head for the Brython Battle Group which, if they don't believe I have Cassad, would be suicide. Buck that.

I gun the engines and send *Warchild* diving for my escape corridor. G-Det pings as two score ships change course to intercept. Damn, they're fast as fek! Come on, *WarChild*, open it up!

The vibration from the engines pushing at the redline is noticeable even through the stabilizers of the Primary control seat. The spare engine I swapped in back at the Dark Gate is showing how out of sequence it is with the other. It forces the first engine to slow intermittently as *WarChild* tries to maintain the course I laid in.

Damn it…I could have tuned the engines before I even made my approach to the gate but I was too damn chambered up. Now my ship is shaking so hard she'll fly apart before she ever outruns any of these ships.

The Daliun frigate is closing. G-det pings as she enters Effective Weapons Range then, just as Tactical confirms, it pings again as the Denir get a gunboat into range. The blurry merging holos are warning each other off even as they both target us.

I'm so tempted to fire first. The pulse canon may not be as big a gun as the gunboat is armed with but it'll match anything that Daliun frigate has to offer. If the swivel mount wasn't busted…I'll have to wait until they drift into its narrow field of vision.

Another ping; the Quaznians are looking to cut me off. They might have the angle too if *WarChild* loses anymore acceleration.

"Attention Coalition forces!" the comm fairly squawks with the new incoming transmission with a voice that sounds really familiar. "The…ship claiming to be the *Seventh Seal* has been given clear passage to the Maren Gate. Please breakoff your pursuit."

My contact with the New Regime! Seems like she's genuinely trying to live up to her end of the bargain.

"That ship has committed crimes against the Daliun people and the Junn Empire! Anyone attempting to capture that ship will be…"

"The Quaznian Empires claim to the Cassad heir predates and preempts all other considerations!"

"The ship is an imposter!" not sure WHO that is. "They are a Cassad ship attempting to deliver weapons and materials to hidden Cassad forces on New Beia!"

WARNING! Tactical pings hard and the G-Det zooms in and focuses on the lead Quaznian ship. She's fired a full spread of missiles.

Even as I'm launching countermeasures Tactical pings again. The Daliuns are firing as well. Countermeasures will never get them all!

I curse and push *WarChild's* engines two clicks past the redline and pray to the All that they don't pop a coil.

"In the name of the Junns I…" the pretty-boy transmission is cut off as Tactical screams at me.

WARNING: HIGH ENERGY WEAPONS FIRE DETECTED!

There's a flash of light and a cacophony of pinging from the G-Det and Tactical as the incoming missiles are detonated. Who?

The G-det settles down and zooms out to reveal the Brython battle group has shifted position and the big girl, the *Triumph*, is moving in between *WarChild* and the Daliuns.

"Attention Coalition Forces…" a crisp clear Brython accented woman's voice joins the comm traffic. I narrow the channel and her image emerges from the bunch. She's wearing the beret and service jacket of a Brython naval officer and from the gold swords pinned on her collar I'm guessing she's one of the ships top brass.

"…the ship…this ship that you are pursuing has been granted unrestricted access to the Maren Gate." She says it with such a finality that I think she may in fact be a ship's captain.

"That ship is an imposter attempting ta gain access ta the Gate. We have analyzed the transmission from the mercenary and it is a fabrication!" If the holo didn't project the Junn forces in neon blue I'm sure I'd be seeing a red faced Daliun.

The Brython captain answers him unaffected by the Pretty-boy outburst. "We have confirmed the capture of the last blooded Cassad through a second and most reliable source. He IS on that ship."

"Then that ship belongs to the Quaznian Empire! Our claim dates back to…"

But the Brython captain insists with authority. "It has been agreed to by the Coalition that Cassad stands trial for the crimes of the Cassad

Empire. The Arch Minister and Magistrate of the King of Brython have decreed that Cassad must face justice and face God for his crimes. The Brython Naval Fleet intends to see him to New Beia."

Despite the apparent protection of the Brython battle group I only ease the engines back down to one click under the red line. Now though I can alter course and head straight for the gate.

There's a lot of cross traffic communication that's encrypted. No doubt the Quaznians, the Marajeshi or Daliuns are trying to broker side deals to take on the Brythons together. It'll never happen though; the Brythons ships are at least the equal of any of the forces here and none of the members of the Coalition would risk having the Brython Empire as an enemy with only a hastily arranged alliance to insure their security.

And I'm right. *WarChild* begins pulling away from the converging fleets now that the Brython battleships are flying in viking positions. The Quaznians give a bit of a chase but Tactical tells me they not daring enough to target the Brython ships and soon enough they back off.

The Daliuns are still screaming. "We are lodging a formal protest with the Coalition council. I demand that you bar that ship until we receive their answer!"

I'm so tempted to open my comms and raze the Daliun officer a bit. Now that the Brythons have made their move they're not going to change their minds, that's part of their virtue…and one of the things that has kept them from dominating the Coalition.

We close on the Maren Gate. One of the artificial, man-made gates, it consists of three massive space stations. Each a wonder of gyroscopic engineering; three concentric rotating rings spin up an incredibly vast amount of negative energy and fire it onto a single point in space. Enough negative energy to open a temporary wormhole to the Median Belt.

Not sure who built it…I want to say; the Cassads…? But that doesn't sound right…

"*Seventh Seal*, you are cleared for gate entry. Please open your primary nevron control circuit for…" the request is coming from the Maren Gate Custodial Authority. Might be a bit rude but I cut them off, raising the power level of my comm so that it screeches harshly.

"Just send me the timing sequence, MCA, I'll make the trip on my own." There's a moment of silence where I'm sure people are arguing about my breech in protocol. They'll let me through though, I got through before and I wasn't even delivering the buckin' king of the known.

"…understood, *Seventh Seal*, transmitting…timing sequence now."

Right.

I drop the sequence into the Nav unit and *WarChild* slows a bit. The gate stations fire off the negative energy in a brilliant display of color. Fiery spirals of blue and red fly outward from the gate as interstellar dust reacts to the overspill of negative energy waves. The center of the event starts as a dark blue hue, concave like a sunset on Targotha, then grows into a light so blinding that *WarChild* automatically drops the forward shield over the canopy.

You'd think that an event initiated by something called "negative" energy would be a little more circumspect.

Just a little further…

PACK LOREN:

KING'S COURT

by

Howard Night

A DARK UNIVERSE NOVELLA

INTERREGNUM

The Alaafin is dead, Ziara is occupied and the last king of the known is in chains. The big seven powers are set to carve up the map to their liking if they can manage to agree on who gets what. The smaller powers are going for broke now that the Cassads are off their back; settling old grievances, occupying the weaker worlds and violating every agreement they were ever forced into.

The known just got a whole lot darker.

CHAPTER ONE:

NEW BEIA

New Beia, formerly known as Esara, the one-time capital of the Sumatran Republic, is now the official home world of the New Regime. Coalition forces forged their agreement here after the start of the *Wars of the Blade*.

It's a standard terran class world, terraformed long ago to meet human requirements.

The Median Belt became their first an easiest won battleground during the revolution; there was hardly a shot fired. Most of the worlds here were long tired of Cassad rule and when the outer territories made their first push the New Regime took full advantage and "liberated" the sector.

It's a blue and white world…lots of cloud cover…heavily settled so there's very little natural vegetation. I expected that I'd be directed to one of the orbiting stations but as I approach my contact sends me a comm.

"You're directed to the Nezerian Tower, Abatan city. Landing protocols are being sent to you now." Her holo comes through clear and it's the first time I get a look at her face. She's a lot younger than I thought or at least appears to be, pretty too.

"Nezerian Tower," I subvocalize to the C.O.P., the Computer Ops Program, and the G-Det holographic display zeroes in on the landing site. The tower is…quite a site. Built on the foundation of the Nezerian Mountains, which are some of the biggest mountains in the known, the Nezerian Tower is one of the tallest planet bound structures ever built. The upper levels extend past New Beia's troposphere and into the mesosphere where they connect to transorbital elevator lines of several low orbit space facilities.

And it's big; the tower has the mass and size to host ten different cities within its walls each with a population of a few million citizens. It's so big that it has three different space ports, the biggest at its base but the other two were actually built on the upper levels.

"Abatan City Space Port," my contact confirms. The highest level city, the highest level space port… ok. I begin my approach and drop my ship, *WarChild,* into the atmo.

Damn…the tower is big! I could probably make my way there without instruments.

I lost my Brython escorts not too long after passing through the gate but soon picked up some fancy, fresh built, New Regime gunships to watch over me. They're probably crewed by a mix of officers from the member groups of the Coalition. This close to their capital though I doubt there'll be any trouble.

Still…I keep my ports open.

"*Seventh Seal*, this is Abatan Port Control, you are marked on approach. We understand you have the stick?"

"Roger that, Abatan. I have the stick."

The Nezerian Tower grows and grows as *WarChild* gets closer. Buck me it's big! Each city of the tower lies in a cup shaped ring, each one smaller than the one beneath it, though I can only see the top two for the clouds. All of them are connected by massive tower pillars that maintain the shape and stability of the structure. I can see the port; it hangs insanely over one side of the Abatan City ring. Who on styx had the engineering ability to design that?

Abatan City lies just under the "cap"; the upper most levels where the Towers control is located. It's the smallest city but it's also the New Regimes Coalition councils headquarters. I can see the fanfare from three clicks out; looks like they know Cassad is on his way.

I follow the landing protocols and circle one time around the tower. Flags from the different members of the New Regime pepper the tiers and spires of Abatan City. There are swarms of air cars racing about, a few following my progress as *WarChild* closes on the port.

Even the port itself is bigger than I'd thought. It's got three levels, any one of which is large enough to land my ship in. As it is I'm directed to the center level. Makes sense; it's protected a bit from an orbital strike or even just prying eyes.

There's a massive welcoming committee waiting for me at the landing circle. Soldiers, armored units and of course the dignitaries all jammed into the small service corridor surrounding the port. I extend the landing legs and, just for show, cut the hovering jets a good ninety decimeters off the ground. With a crash, *WarChild* comes down hard; scattering the deck techs like mice. She's a brick of a ship, the hull and most of her structure is cete-armor which makes her tough as anything in the worlds but not too pretty. She's an old drop ship so she's got impressive looking, albeit mostly empty, gun ports. A nightmare from wars centuries ago, I found her drifting in a graveyard and rebuilt her to her former glory. Well…maybe not her former glory…fek…anyway I got her running.

"Nice landing, *Seventh Seal*." I forgot my contact was still on the open comm. I throw her a smirk and a wink, which, translates as one of my "ghost" eyes winking out on my visor.

"So…" I challenge. "I still don't see my money."

"You'll get paid, mercenary. All of the known is watching now."

"Yea," Wouldn't do to see the new lords of the known reneging on their agreements. Never the less… "I'm sure. Meet me at the forward hatch…alone."

She balks but I cut the comms. It's getting tight now…that small crack of light that's my way out is getting thinner and thinner.

I strip off the armor first. Coming through the Median Gate to get here was a dangerous mission and I threw on my Raptor armor in case *WarChild* suffered catastrophic damage. But now that I'm planet-side I figure if this goes bad now it won't help me.

One last check on the "package". In *WarChild's* prep bay there sits a rather innocuous looking stack of cargo containers. I retrieve the small cylindrical remote from my equipment pack and tap the button on one end. The camouflage holographic containers shimmer and fade revealing a man bound to a restraining bar and locked in a control collar. A bit overkill maybe but he managed to free himself before and nearly killed me so now I'm not taking any chances.

He is the king of the known after all.

Catching Cassad was more fortuitous opportunity than bounty hunting prowess but regardless I got it done. It took most of my resources, all of my skill and tore up my ship in the process. All of that for a massive amount of QED that would put an end to my mercenary days. Better be worth it.

Cassad can only stare back me now, which is good, don't want him causing trouble this close to the deal getting done. I tap the remote again and the holo shimmers back up.

My contact should be at the port by now so I throw on my flight suit and field jacket then check my visor and head to the forward hatch.

CHAPTER TWO:

THE ADVOCATE

"STANDARD INOCCULATION SUITE UPLOADED," the C.O.P. tells me as my prep for the New Beia ecosystem completes itself. "VIRTUAL INTERFACE UPLOADED."

There's a roar when I pop the forward hatch followed almost immediately by a sigh of disappointment when they see it's only me coming down the ramp. Just stepping over the safety rail at the edge of the landing circle, my New Regime contact makes her way over to meet me followed by two smaller females in Coalition colors. Her dress is…formal; long, wide sleeves that cover her hands, gold flecked tunic and some kind of headdress. Whoever she is she must work in an official capacity with the Coalition itself and not merely one of the member worlds. She has a confident walk. Can't tell if she's flaring for her superiors, the crowd or maybe even just for me.

"We've got Coalition Special Guard on their way to take custody…"

I ignore her as she goes on about the transfer procedures and take a moment to take in the port. The air is almost sweet. We're too high for them not to rely on some kind of atmo generators but the port is an open deck. Must take a bit of power to continually pump in O2 and heat. It should be freezing but it feels like a mild day.

…like fall on Arcadia…

I've been to New Beia before but nowhere near the Tower. Too many procedures and official gauntlets to run through. Planet hopping among the more developed worlds is a headache that just isn't worth it if there's no cred bump. But now I'm a special visitor with all the privileges extended to a diplomat.

The view out of the hangar is amazing.

The mob awaiting Cassad is huge. For the most part they're New Beia citizens but there are plenty of off-worlders too. The virtual posts floating through the crowd are from literally hundreds of different worlds.

My visor is picking up all kinds of sensor sweeps and recording waves. No doubt a lot of them are trying to get an I.D. off of my image and bio-signature. Good luck; my flight suit masks my bio-sig and my visor actually projects a low level holo over the exposed portion of my face just outside the visible spectrum…makes a computer I.D. impossible.

I turn and look over my contact. She's got no virtual post but her two friends are sporting glowing Coalition ID tags. I don't see any bags, I don't see any crates… "I don't see my money."

"Now is not the time to…"

My ghost eyes narrow as I peer at her. "Now isn't the time? Lady, this is the buckin' transaction!"

She falters a little bit and then composes herself quickly. "You will be paid" she insists. "You do understand that very few thought it could actually be done. That anyone would be able to..."

"Is this where you try and tell me you don't have the money?"

Her face drops a bit. Oh fek… "The money is being gathered as we speak."

From her body language I thought for a pulse beat that she was about to tell me they didn't have it. But Sticky assured me they did in fact have that money…had so much coin now that the bounty shouldn't have been a problem.

"Good. I want it in…"

"It's being gathered…" she cuts me off.

"When will it get here?"

"There is still the matter of the trial," she says.

"Which has nothing to do with me."

"Mercenary," her voice rises in frustration. "…the bounty is being held by the only faction that the Coalition trusts to hold the money; the Nth Consortium."

N^{th} Consortium? The name is familiar. "And it's being brought here now?"

"No," she says. "You will receive your payment once there has been a conviction."

My eyes flare. "You expect me to sit here and wait for you to stage a trial? It took y'all twenty-three years to knock this family off the throne, I'm not waiting while half the known queues up to spit in the eye of the Cassads."

"It will not be a lengthy trial!" she argues, once again glancing to the crowds. The activity around the pad and in the corridor beyond is increasing. I can see banners, virtual, holographic and real, approaching… could be dignitaries. And there's a group of security officers, armored, headed our way.

"You've got to be kidding me." I mutter.

"You WILL be paid. I swear…" she hisses. The security group looks to be another Coalition force; some of the member groups are represented.

"Your word is no good. You're not getting Cassad till I get the coin," I tell her.

"And what will you do, mercenary?" She's talking harshly but in hushed tones. For some reason she doesn't want them to hear us. "Try and take off? They'll blow you out of the sky. You've no choice."

"Wanna bet?" I'm bluffing. I'm bucked.

The Coalition Security group slows to a stop not ten paces off. Their commanding officer, ID'ed by her floating virtual badge, looks to be a Denir, decorated in war if that braid on her shoulder means anything. She's wearing light battle armor, all spruced up in its ceremonial configuration for this little show. Quickly she looks me up and down, lingering only a little on the NOK 37 resting on my hip.

"Prim Locasta of the Coalition of Free Worlds, Nezerian Security Command," she announces herself. "Ready to take Minister Cassad into custody."

Out of the corner of my eye I see my New Regime Contact signal to one of her assistants. Then she quickly turns and addresses the Security officer. "Prim Locasta, it seems there's been a bit of a miscommunication."

The Prim narrows her eyes at that. Behind her the banners begin to emerge from the crowd. First to enter is a Daliun delegation, riding in open air cars and waving to a mesmerized crowd.

"Adila Eboro…you're the Advocate?" The Prim addresses my contact. "Fine. I was told Cassad's presence on this ship was confirmed."

Advocate?

"He has Minister Cassad," my contact, Eboro, assures her. "The miscommunication is about how we proceed with the exchange of custody."

"Then I will clear that up." The Prim steps forward. "This port, for all the commotion, is secured. You may bring Cassad down here. Now."

Horns sound. Behind the Daliuns another delegation walks in, or rather, floats in on personal hoverpads; the Brythons. The Ambassadorial royal family comes in with plenty pageantry and plenty of 'bots. Unlike many in the known the Brythons prefer their droids look like machines rather than mimic beings. They walk stiffly besides the royal carriage while carrying the royal crest and royal pendant. They're all such royal…

"I said 'now', mercenary." The Prim takes another step forward.

The "Advocate" is watching me intently. She doesn't want me arguing with them about the money. Why?

"The… Minister… remains aboard my ship until we square things up." I say. The Prim studies me with enhanced eyes. She'll get nothing through my visor.

"Square things up?"

"There are…security concerns." Advocate Eboro, interrupts. "Despite the Coalitions protocols there is worry about Cassad arriving fit for trial."

"Really, Advocate?" the Prim glowers at her.

"I want Minister Cassad," The Advocate starts with just enough hesitation that I can tell she's making it up as she goes. "…the Minister will be sequestered here for the duration of the trial."

Uh oh…

"Here?" the Prim looks over my ship like she's looking at a pile of bicafek. *WarChild* isn't a "sleek" ship by any means, she's bulky and shaped like a brick with two huge engine housings on either side. The hull is all cete-armor, a rough crystal that grows like crab plate. I added the tritansteel wings which don't quite match the hunter green pallor of the armor. "That is not acceptable."

"As Advocate for the Accused I…"

"This is NOT acceptable." The Prim steps forward boldly and points at me. "Bring Khalid Cassad down at once or you will be taken into custody as well."

Looks like I'm not the only one bluffing. Without a nevron lock on my ship they can't access it without force. Any attempt to tear into the ship, they've got to know, will end up killing Cassad.

I growl. "Not until I'm...

"I have been given custodial powers!" The 'Advocate' cuts in, stepping in between me and the Prim. "And I am not satisfied that the safety of my charge can be guaranteed if he is moved from this ship."

"Your custodial powers extend to the trial itself, under the watch of Security Command, in our own facility. Bring him down." The Prim takes a look over her shoulder. Seems she just as aware of how many eyes are on us.

"We will," The Advocate states very loudly. "For his arraignment first thing next sunside." Then without another word to the Prim she sets off across the landing circle to meet the nearing delegations.

The Prim looks to me, opens her mouth the speak, then stops to look over her shoulder again. She watches as the Advocate addresses first the Daliuns, then the Brythons.

I eyeball her too. Whatever she is telling the Daliuns they're taking it stone faced but accepting it. She moves on to the Brythons where the Ambassador begins nodding as if he expected whatever it is she's telling him.

Amazingly, the Daliuns begin gathering up their little parade and head out of the terminal. Prim Locasta mutters a curse and heads after the Advocate, trying to chase her down before she gets to the Quaznians who are just entering the landing pad.

Another wave of scans washes over me. Vid drones float just beyond the landing pad taking in every bit of data they can and transmitting it to every corner of the known. At least they're trying; the New Regime has a fek-load of counter measures passing through the air so I doubt the drones are getting more than grainy 3-d vid. Still, I double check the visor to make sure my own personal countermeasures are up. Don't want my specs on anybody's Most Wanted list.

The Quaznians get loud, their voices carrying across the landing pad as they express their objection. But the Advocate doesn't back down and from the body language of the Prim it seems she may have even gained an ally.

This goes on for a while with each delegation, as they arrive, all taking their turns at being directed away. The last few all look to have been given the heads up but even so one or two put on a show for the masses.

Finally it's done and the Advocate and the Prim head back over to me.

"It's been agreed that Minister Cassad will remain aboard this ship for the duration of the trial." Advocate Eboro is again looking at me intensely. She doesn't want me to balk in front of the Prim.

"I must first verify that Cassad is actually on this ship." The Prim is giving me the dark eye now.

"Of course." I say then pointedly give her a look over. "But you're not coming aboard my ship with all the hardware."

The Prim twists her lips up knowingly. Then, to my amazement, she begins taking off her armor right there.

"Uh..." The Advocate is as startled as I am.

The armor seemed to me to be ceremonial and of a light class but she does not so much take it off as step out of it, leaving it standing on its own behind her. The Prim steps out of her armor, nude save for a thin pair of black bottoms.

My visor takes in her body, trying to sift through the counter measures in the air to see what security tech she has left without her armor. But all I can see is how lean and muscled she is, the soft sheen of her light brown skin and the tell tail scars of a soldier. She's seen battle and she's proud of it. I'm glad the ghost eyes of my visor don't have holographic pupils; elsewise she'd see how hard I'm staring at her dark nipples.

"I've no hidden weapons, mercenary." She says.

"We'll see." What my visor can't pick up here *WarChild* will be able to detect in the airlock. "And you?"

The Advocate looks a little aghast. "I most certainly will not, mercenary! I..."

"Then you can wait right here until I come back with a portable scanner." I tell her. Her eyes move quickly from me to the Prim fast enough that I almost miss it. She doesn't want her alone with me...or with Cassad.

"Wait..." she grimaces then begins to remove her ceremonial garb. Fek...this isn't what I had intended; escorting two naked women into my ship...with the whole buckin' known watchin'. There's a collective uproar from the crowd around the dock.

But Advocate Eboro has more modest undergarments on. Her hair beneath that headdress is set in long locked braids, each set in uniform rows over her head. There aren't any battle scars but she does have some skin art over her arms and legs...probably more beneath her thin top and bottoms.

Somewhat relieved I nod and lead them into the forward hatch where *WarChild's* security sensor suite launches its check to ferret out any serious threats.

And just in case...

"What's that?" The Prim asks as I pull out a modified EMP grenade.

"Exactly what it looks like." I tell her.

"You're going to fire off an EMP right here in your ship?" she asks incredulously.

"Raise your hands."

After a pulse beat she complies and I fire off the modified EMP in short, directed bursts and watch as the last of her subcutaneous hardware is taken offline.

"Clever, mercenary" she admits, but there's a low level of anger behind her eyes; tells me I just ruined something for her.

After running the EMP over Advocate Eboro, who was carrying no hidden electronics I let *WarChild* check them over again.

No bioweapons either. Or at least none that register with *WarChild's* latest update. So…hopefully there won't be any surprises.

"Just follow the yellow guide." I tell them indicating the running lights that line the walls of the service ways through *WarChild.* Set that up before I landed; don't want to lead them through my ship, don't want either of them behind me.

Of course this is proving just as distracting. The Prim is in outstanding shape and her skin, despite the crisscrossing scars, shines like cocoa milk. Can't help but watch the muscles in her back work as she walks. It's cold in the ship…I bet her nipples are rock hard.

The Advocate isn't a fighter. That much is clear; she's more ample than I would have thought after seeing her jump me in the graveyard. It plays nicely as she tries to keep up with the much taller Prim.

"Here?" The Prim asks. We've made it all the way to the hatch sealing the Prep Bay. I take another moment, trying to act as though there was something else distracting me.

Been too damn long…

"Pull the latch." I tell her.

Clearly she's not worked aboard a ship designed to beat Dark

Fields because she pushes every indicator light like they're buttons. Then she figures it, turns the large latch and pushes open the hatch.

The Advocate slips past her to get into the room first but as she gets halfway across the bay she realizes that the yellow indicators ended back in the corridor. She looks quizzically about the room, the cargo containers, my eight-leg-walker and then turns to me as the Prim joins her.

"Where is the Minister?"

"Where is the PRISONER?" the Prim corrects her.

I pull the remote from my jacket pocket and press the small end. The cargo containers shimmer then fade revealing Khalid Cassad, son of the now dead emperor Ose Cassad, strapped to a restraining bar.

The Advocate actually bows. "Minister Cassad."

The Prim spits at his feet, onto my deck plating. "Cassad. At least it looks like him."

Cassad simply stares back at the two.

"You're using a control collar on him?" The Advocate sounds almost aghast.

"He was…disagreeable." I tell her.

"I'll need a genetic sample to confirm his I.D." The Prim says but she already seems convinced. From the way she's staring daggers into Cassad's eyes she's clearly got something personal against the man. Not sure what that could be. The Denir are the leaders of the Kujiunga Na; one of the founding members of the New Regime. But word on the Hub was that their own defection from the Cassad empire was simply a matter of business and, save for the purging of their Royal Guard, not terribly bloody at all. The Cassad embassies in Denir space had been allowed to pack up and leave. They even took in defectors themselves.

"Not a problem." I walk over to my work table, retrieve a sub-dermal surveyor then toss it to her. The Prim inspects the tool but since they're fairly simple she's quickly satisfied that it's not rigged to give her a false sample.

"Thank you, mercenary," she says then grabs Cassad by his jaw, raising the surveyor with the other hand. "Well, Cassad…"

"You will not!" the Advocate moves faster than I do and grabs for the Prim. But she's not a fighter and the Prim tosses her across the room easily.

It's enough of a delay that I have my gun out and jammed into the

Prims temple before she can drive the surveyor into Cassad's head.

"I was not going to kill him," she claims. "Just take a little flesh and cruk his perfect face."

"Liar!" The Advocate scrambles to her feet. "She wants vengeance!"

"I'll have my…" the Prim starts when I cut them both off.

"I don't care!" I take the surveyor from her clenched hand. "But nobody's damaging the merchandise until I get paid."

Eboro freezes at this, her eyes darting from me to the Prim. But the Nezerian Security commander just snorts at me, then returns to glaring at Cassad.

So I toss the surveyor to Eboro and she steps in between the Prim and Cassad.

"Apologies, Minister, but it is necessary" and as gently as she can manage she applies the subdermal surveyor to his shoulder. Cassad doesn't flinch, mostly because the control collar is set so high he can only move his eyeballs.

He's not getting loose on my ship again.

Done, Adlia turns and slaps the surveyor into the Prims hands. "Satisfied?"

"No," the Prim tells her. "Not until he pays for his crimes."

"Then we're done here" I tell them and lead them both back to the hatch. The Prim is fairly bouncing with excitement while the Advocate seems greatly subdued. At the hatch she takes my arm.

"I need to speak with Cassad privately."

"When I'm…"

"I'm his Advocate," she insists. "I need to prepare him for his trial."

The Prim laughs but doesn't seem to care one way or the other. "We will verify Cassad's I.D. but I'm sure it's him. Prepare that murderer all you wish, Advocate, he will die as surely as worlds turn." She walks down my ramp and steps back into her armor, the distinct look of anticipation on her face.

"I must have time to prep him and I'll need to council with him during the trial." Eboro says.

"But you can't get me my money until it's over?" she takes a step back and I realize I'm practically snarling.

"When he's convicted you will be paid."

"Seems to me, as his 'Advocate', you'll be working against that" I confront her.

"His conviction is assured, as the Prim was so delighted to point out. The trial is…a show for the Coalition." Eboro's eyes shade over as she speaks.

"Then what's the point of making me wait?"

"What is not known to everyone in the coalition is that there are two different factions that will pay the bounty depending on the outcome of the trial. This is something you would do well to keep to yourself. First, there are those that want him dead, they will foot the bounty if he is sentenced to be executed."

"And?"

"And there are those that want him imprisoned…sentenced to unspeakable punishments and indignities for as long as he can be kept alive. It is they that will pay the bounty for that conclusion."

I can't tell from her demeanor which fate she preferred or which would be better for me. Not that it mattered; I was going to have to sit through a trial either way. But maybe…

"Then a show of good faith."

"How do you mean?" She looks almost affronted.

"A down payment. Twenty-five percent." No way she'll go for that, but I need to try.

"I don't have access to that kind of money."

"Then I'm sure I can find one of the members of the New Regime who would like to take him off my hands for about that much."

"Doubtful."

"Guess I'll have to see for myself." I watch as she grapples with a choice.

"I can…I can see your ship refueled…and four hundred thousand New reg…" she stammers a bit.

"Not good enough. Ten million…Old reg." I say.

"Ten?? No, I couldn't…and in Old reg? Maybe five hundred thousand…"

I hit the door controls and grab her arm, moving her outside the hatch.

"Ok! I can get you one million. But not for a few rotations," she says without much certainty. One million…won't even cover all the repair work *WarChild* needs.

"Next sunside. Or I start making inquiries." A weak threat but she looks to be buying it. Still, I can't help but to be curious.

"And how did you become his Advocate? You don't seem to be Ziaran born, one of the First One Million."

"I am Akanman," she says quietly. Never heard of them. "May I council with Cassad?

It's not like I have a choice. "Get your clothes first. It gets cold in the Prep Bay."

CHAPTER THREE:

BACKDOOR

I monitor the Advocate's meeting with Cassad from Primary. Even with the Control Collar settings at minimal he doesn't say much. Eboro seems to be pretty candid with him about his chances, which doesn't seem to affect him one way or the other. Unless she's talking to him in code she's actually prepping him for his trial.

So with one eye on the monitor I do a little recon research. First I check the Nezerian atlas for the layout. They're going to hold the trial in the Hall of Kain, a converted reconstruction of an ancient sports arena. It's big but not nearly large enough to fit all the representative caucuses from the New Regime. They'll likely be broadcasting the trial on the Hub and thus to every corner of the known.

And since I'm not gonna let Cassad out of my reach until I'm paid that means my image will be broadcast across the known as well.

Fek, should have counted on that. Of course the merc that caught Cassad is gonna find himself the object of much interest. A quick check of my visor shows me it's working just fine. It ought to keep my face from registering on any vid or sensor scans. My flight suit will do fine for keeping my bio-signature private as well.

I hope.

Movement on the Prep bay monitor catches my attention. The Advocate is trying to get my attention. "What is it?" I say over the comm.

"You ship's systems are woefully archaic," she complains. "We are done here. I need to return to make preparations for the trial."

She fills me in on some of the details of what is going to happen, balking when I tell her Cassad will never leave my side and that I'll be using a control collar. Eventually she relents as we get to the forward hatch.

"The Reading of the Charges is tomorrow. They will come for him first thing sunside."

"First thing, after I get the down payment," I confirm and watch her go.

Almost home…only the hard part left.

Not halfway through last watch *WarChild's* proximity alarms ring a half a beat before the Port Admin sends me a transmission. Looks like someone wants to parlay. I check the ground feeds and see a small delegation approaching the fore of my ship. Blue, white and silver colors… Daliuns.

Hmm…

I don my flight jacket and visor and head down to the foreword hatch, along the way gathering my Sever and the remote. My comms are pinging with their hail but I take my time, don't answer and just pop the hatch when I'm ready.

There are six of them; three men, three women. Two of the males are "Pretty Boys"; the genetically altered soldiers the Junns sent against the rest of my home star sector, the Quad, during the *Wars of the Blade*. They're not in armor but I've seen and killed enough of them in combat that I can pick 'em out of a crowd.

The other male and one of the other females look like auxiliary staff, probably just there to assist. One of them is carrying a Junn banner, emblazoned with the "House" crest of the Junn family they work for. I don't recognize it but I'm only familiar with a few. The last two women are decked out in more impressive house regalia, so they must hold some higher status. Like most of the Junn reps these two have gold hair and blue eyes, all added, I'm sure after reaching their representative ranking.

I walk across the landing pad toward their group who have stopped at the pad rail. Dock security is keeping other onlookers back by the port entrance but they let these guys through with no escort; the Junns have pull. Before I'm halfway across the pad I turn and point the remote back at *WarChild*. One press on the small ended side and there's a notable flash along the sensor lenses on the front of the engine housings and an audible chirp.

In case anyone decides to try something funny.

"Greetings," The two females say in unison when I get to the rail. "We represent the House of Derai. We are House Speakers, Cherlander"

They pause for a moment where I'm sure they are expecting me to introduce myself. I cross my arms and wait.

The two of them continue on in unison, not fazed by my silence. "Our patron, Lord Lan Derai, seeks an audience with Minister Cassad."

I expect there's some kind of offer coming so I don't bother saying anything just yet. Instead I spend the time running passive scans over their group, trying to see what everyone, especially the two Pretty Boys, are carrying. But the counter measures in the air are blocking everything.

"You would of course be rewarded for your assistance in this manner," the two House reps say together.

"Fifty million," I say. "Old Reg." There's no chance that any one Junn House has that kind of money to spare or that they would even part with it if they did.

The two Reps smile those pretty white smiles at me despite what must be a very disappointing response.

They don't know me…can't know that there's no deal they could ever offer that would make me work with them… with the Junns.

"The same amount as the bounty for Minister Cassad?" Again they speak in unison. Even their facial expressions are in synch. Never seen this before…I wonder how they're connected.

"We seek only a very limited audience with him before the trial."

"Fifty million, QED certified and I don't care what you do with him." They don't have the coin.

"There must be something else that we can…"

"You can't pay fifty?" I ask.

"It's just that fifty million is certainly not commensurate with a brief audience with your prisoner."

"Then walk away."

"If you could just see…"

"Now" I growl. "Don't come back." And I turn and walk back to *WarChild.* To their credit they don't try and argue anymore.

I watch their delegation make their way off the landing deck on my ground feeds. Wonder what the Junns want with Cassad? Sticky had no intel on them one way or the other when it came to whether they needed or wanted him to make it to trial. The Cassad Empire has a few worlds left but nothing that would make them a more attractive ally than the rest of the New Regime. Unless they believe the minister has some family secrets hidden away.

Which he probably does.

I cut to the Prep Bay feed and check on his highness. Cassad is still bound. Good.

CHAPTER FOUR:

THE FIRST GRAND COUNCIL

First thing sunside they come; Coalition Security Command lead by Prim Locasta. Vid hover bots fill the golden air just beyond the dock terminal, hovering above a throng of onlookers and beyond that, in the air just outside of the city proper, New Coalition gunships patrol throngs of ships trying for a good sensor peek at Cassad. No Coalition delegations outside today; they're probably already at the Hall.

I head down to the Prep bay where the Advocate, who came aboard earlier with the good faith money, and Cassad wait. She took off the tech coveralls I had him in and now has him decked out in his…royal attire. Wonder how that went with the control collar on?

"They're here."

"Fine," she says and steps aside to allow me to release Cassad. And I do, but not before manually turning his control collar up to the top levels. Can't risk slaving the unit to my remote cause I've already used up the two slots.

"He can't have that on during the trial," she warns me.

"Not while he's testifying," I correct her.

She looks like she wants to balk but with everything she's going up against today she's probably deciding to let this battle go without a fight. I walk Cassad through the ship to the foreword hatch just to make sure the collar is working. With it on and leveled up Cassad can only manage a slow, even walk. He's had the best Cassad training and led Cassad forces out on the perimeter of the known, I'm not going to risk moving him while he's free to use that experience and training against me.

There's a deafening roar when we exit the ship. The crowd is finally getting their look at the captured leader of the Empire that ruled them for almost a thousand years. The roar is a mix of cheers, boos, and various chants that fight over each other to be heard.

My visor alerts me to all the attempted sensor sweeps as they wash over us. So many but they're probably canceling each other out as much as the ports security measures are. These things are trying to send vid feeds to the entire known. Gonna be famous… fek.

The Prim and her security detail meet us at the bottom of the ramp.

"Remove the collar, mercenary. We have our own."

Before I can tell her to take a swim down styx the Advocate speaks up.

"We will be using our own personal security tech during the trial. We wouldn't want anyone to worry that his testimony was compromised?"

The Prim twists her lips into doubt then nods. "Fine. But he will wear no collar during his actual testimony."

"Of course. Today, however, we are only hearing the charges," Eboro points out. "Please lead the way."

Nezerian Security surrounds us and I try not to look uneasy, try not to look like I'm worried at all about the hundreds of things that can go glitch right now.

We're taken to a hover platform, I climb on after Cassad and the Advocate follows. It's wide enough only for two more and the Prim and one Nez SeC officer join us. The rest of the Prims security walk beside the platform as we float out of the port and onto the main concourse.

The crowds of New Beia citizens and of course Coalition visitors from across the known have been cordoned off, providing the platform with a wide path. The barriers don't hinder the roar as we pass by. The collective power of the rage in their voices vibrates my skin under my flight jacket. Styx…I could've charged a qed a look and made the fifty million on my own.

The Tower feels even bigger now that I'm in it than it did on approach. I can't even see the other side of this city level for the huge towers that fill Ataban proper. But I can see the Hall of Kain, looming ahead of us. Over the two huge front doors stands a colossal statue of the legendary Kain, god of the Esari long ago. Or something like that. The bowl shape of the Hall is only broken by the four towers at each corner. The towers look down onto the main arena floor where the trial will take place.

Fool's gold for a sniper.

"Do not worry, mercenary." The Prim notices that I'm eyeing the towers. "My security measures have taken everything into account, including the Four Fathers. But only an amateur would attempt to attack from there"

The Four Fathers; the towers. Most assassins would avoid using them as their perch because they're way too obvious. But from my time in the 46th I learned to always look out for a way to do the very thing that everyone else thinks is impossible. There's a sniper, I once knew, that would have found a way to get up there, take the shot and then get out without getting caught.

But since she's dead…

"So how did you catch him, mercenary?" The Prim asks. She's been watching me, evaluating me most likely, the entire way here. I don't think she expected me to be around for this long after delivering Cassad.

She and I probably think more alike than not.

Still I don't answer her, instead I turn to give her a ghost eye glare.

She just smiles at that. "The whole known is going to want to know about you mercenary. Better get used to the questions."

No. The whole known might want to know about the merc that brought in Cassad, but Pack Loren and he don't have to be the same person. Soon as I'm paid I'm fading into the black.

Horns blare when we arrive at the steps to the Hall, just at the feet of Kain. I thought it might be time to move but the platform simply slides up the steps, maintaining its level angle all the way to the top. That's where we disembark. There's a contingent of Coalition security at the entrance to the Hall, along with a few officials. The Prim greets them with a bit of ceremonial flare. She announces to the arrest of Cassad and asks for permission to present him to the court. The Coalition has only been around for a little more than two decades and a lot of these ritual practices are just a mix of the differing cultural practices. So they come off a bit labored and awkward.

The huge doors to the Hall of Kain open and we stride in, making sure not to move faster than Cassad can step with the collar on. The lobby of the Hall is filled with the lesser dignitaries of the New Regime all standing behind a literal line of Coalition security personnel.

These low level ambassadors and adjuncts aren't prudish about letting Cassad know what they think. They shout curses and threats. They cajole and ridicule him as he passes by. There are insults and gestures I've never heard or seen. The Cassad's presence on Arcadia was minimal to say the least. No one even noticed when their embassy in Markett city evacuated before the Giaks launched their last attack. They'd never been much of a political factor. So we never harbored the kind of anger for the Cassads that I'm seeing here. There are more than a few dignitaries with tears in their eyes they're so angry.

"Security point," the Prim announces. We arrive at the entrance to the main part of the Hall. A red cloaked guardsman carrying what looks more like a pike than a rifle steps forward and looks us over.

"No weapons or military grade tech beyond this point. No recording or transmission devices allowed in the Hall." His voice is electronic so he might not be human beneath the garb.

"Prim Locasta, head of Nezerian Security Command," the Prim announces herself. "Special dispensation has been granted to my detail for the purposes of the trial."

"Noted, Prim Locasta. However, HE, is not a member of Nez SeC." The guard points the long pike in my direction.

"Advocate for the Accused, Adila Eboro." Eboro announces herself. "This man is a part of MY security detail. He will accompany Cassad at all times."

She looks back at me standing next to Cassad. "And he will be armed."

"That is not acceptable, Advocate Eboro. This man is not a registered citizen of any Coalition world. His identity is unknown and," the Guardsman looks me up and down then settles on my visor. "his tech is of unknown registry as well."

The visor isn't anything unusual, it's just old. "Special measures," Eboro tells him. "to insure the success of this trial."

There's a moment where it's obvious that the Guardsman is receiving instructions from someone. Then, "The mercenary must register his identity with Nez SeC," he or it says finally. The Prim looks over her shoulder at me and smirks.

"Well, mercenary?"

Eboro speaks up again. "His identity will remain secret. The mercenary…" I can tell she's thinking on the fly again. "…and his team are still engaged in locating Cassad targets."

Good one. It may even help to insure I'm paid properly. The Guardsman again waits for instructions. Then, "You are cleared to enter the Hall. You will keep your weapons holstered for the duration of the trial. You will engage in no scans of the delegates or their guests. Please proceed forth."

And they step aside as the big doors open. The cries that erupt out of the Hall overcome those of the crowd outside. I would have thought that the real royalty and dignitaries would have comported themselves with a little more reserve but this is out of control. As we enter the Hall the audience members in the stands surrounding the entrance are not only screaming worse threats than those outside, but they're throwing debris as well.

Security Command did a good job of relieving them of anything more dangerous than rolled up programs and paper service trays though, so it's mostly garbage that's hurled at us. That and… spit, but the stands seem to be beyond that reach at least.

"You die today, Cassad!"

"…of my ancestors, Cassad, finally!"

"Murderer!"

"For one thousand years of oppression!"

Once beyond the stands we make our way to the center of the Hall. The old arena floor is set apart from the stands by a wide and deep trench. From what I can see the walls down in that trench are lined with ancient barred prison cells. There are some haggard and beaten faces staring out of those cells; Ziaran citizens and officials all waiting for their inevitable fate.

I can smell blood.

Above us the Hall is open to the star filled sky. It's an illusion; the bottom of the top level of the entire tower hangs above us. The walls of the arena are so high that the Abatan city skyline is hidden, so we can only see the Four Fathers, the holo field and the sky cars floating high above trying to get live vid. They had better be careful; there's a pretty strong null field stretched across the top of the arena. At least that's what I read.

We step across the trench by way of an ornate ivory bridge and into the soft black sand of the arena floor. No…not sand really, small glossy beads so smooth they slide easily under foot.

It'll be hard to run on.

They've set up two small bunkers; one for the accused and one for the prosecution. Each has a raised platform on the top. That's where Cassad, and I, will be standing during the trial. It's only now that I'm starting to rethink whether it's really necessary to for me to escort him everywhere.

Ugh…I'm absolutely sure that if something happens to him before he's convicted I'm not gettin' paid. Just a little while longer, Pack…

The Prim and her detail stop at the bunker entrance. "We are not allowed inside. Only Cassad and his Advocate…and her team I suppose." I can barely hear her for the crowd but I get the point easy enough as she and her people leave.

We step inside. The bunker has three rooms; the main room with a platform that must raise the accused to the dais on top, there's a small alcove with a table and chairs then in the back, there's a lavatory. Along the wall of the larger main room is a one way window. From here we can see pretty much the entire Hall, the Prosecutors stand and Grand Council of the Coalition balcony. There are two rows for the council; one, the largest, for the representatives of the member worlds of the New Regime, spans the entire circumference of the stands. They sit above the main stands that are filled with citizens of those member worlds. Above them all, in smaller but shielded suites, the seven members of the Grand Council watch. The top powers of the Coalition who were the most responsible for the fall of the Cassads.

I can see the Kujiunga Na suite. The largest of the luxurious viewing boxes, it was given to them not only because it was the ex-Cassad ambassadors who were key to the start of the rebellion against Ose but because there were so damn many of them. Sitting prominently in the center of the group is the Denir representative, bare chested and adorned with a single white jewel of some kind nestled snuggly between her breasts. I can't remember her name and my visor can't get a read on her ID because of the security waves running through the hall...good thing that works both ways.

The din of the crowd is abruptly cut as the bunker door closes behind us.

"How long?" I ask. Eboro turns and fixes me with a dark stare.

"Ah! Mercenary! *He who knows and sees…*"

"Until the charges are read?" I clarify.

"Oh…well, there will be a long procession as the member world representatives are brought in one at a time."

"All the member worlds?" I mutter the question, not really needing it to be answered. This could take all sunside.

"There is no corner of the empire…the Coalition I mean, that would dare miss this." The Advocate removes her ceremonial shoal and walks Cassad to the table and chairs in the small conference room. Stiffly, he sits; the control collar limiting his movement adjusts slowly to new commands, as it is designed to do. She then tends to him, seeing to his comfort while at the same time informing him on what was to come.

I take the time to run passive scans over the inside of the bunker. The research I found on the Hall of Kain seemed to indicate that the bunkers were designed to deflect active scans and keep out snooping hardware. All in order to keep the games here played honestly. It made for the perfect Advocate chambers during trials.

There's no spy tech in the bunker, at least none my visor can detect. Eboro does not seem to be concerned with potential listeners but that could just be due to the inevitability of a conviction. She goes on to Cassad about the trial.

"I have had been given a list of witnesses who will speak on your behalf…"

"That will not be necessary. No one need risk themselves testifying for the Empire in front of the rebels." That's the most he's said since he escaped the load bar.

"Minister," Eboro says softly. "Those not willing to testify have already been…executed."

Cassad thinks for only a moment then points out, "They would have been executed immediately after regardless."

"Not necessarily, Minister. I can guide their testimony, gain them leniency." Eboro produces a small personal Hub connect and lays it on the table. The disc is small enough to fit in the palm of her hand but projects a wide holo-field that becomes her workspace complete with three wide visual fields and a small conventional key field on the table. From where I'm standing I can see the dossier holos of the first two witnesses.

"The Subjucarious of Special Operations will be one of the first to testify on your behalf, Minister." Eboro expands the holo of the man and raises it above her workspace. The Subjucarious, or S.S.O., was an older Ziaran citizen, his thick mane of braided hair was more white than grey. The holo of him was recent as his face was swollen and bleeding from the beating he had already taken

Cassad shows no reaction to hearing this. The S.S.O. was more the day to day administrator of the home world so most Ziaran citizens saw him far more frequently than Cassad himself. But from everything I've seen Cassad must have known the man very well.

The Advocate goes on about the witnesses but my attention is drawn away to the arena stands. They're clearing a path through the dignitaries…the member representatives are being brought in.

Drums sound and are followed by a low and driving horn. The arena goes dark as all lights move to one corner of the room. Fanfare sounds and out come the banners of the first rep.

"Xioung, Heavenly Sovereign of the world Appogoi!" The small man is dressed in a red and gold armor of an ancient style, his face covered in a grisly mask and his head crowned by a wide helmet. Xioung wore a ceremonial sword on his hip inside a long and curved scabbard. I've never encountered anyone from Appogoi before but I don't have to have in order to know that this is not the actual man himself.

The real Xioung would not be alone, without a court or security so it's a bogey, probably hard cased and not holographic. Likely it has its very own entangled comm node so that the real "Heavenly Sovereign" could see and even feel the experience in real time. Xioung takes his time finding his seat along the representative balcony, stopping to acknowledge the rabid crowd of the arena.

More horns and drums sound. A second set of banners, this time neon holographic projections of the flag of the people of Tennace, one of the more technologically advanced civilizations, floats into the room. Behind it walks out another bogey, no…this one's definitely a holo as she's transparent and has wings. She's likely the head representative of their Corporate Council.

"Director Suri 'a Velne, of the world Tennace!" is announced. She takes her time as well, using her fake wings to pretend to hover above the crowd. How long is this gonna take?

"Last time I checked there were more than one hundred worlds in the Coalition" the Advocate says. I had not meant to ask the question out loud. "And as the Cassads fall new worlds are added to that."

So we wait as world after world is represented. The Norlans, The Nth Consortium, the Jemsa Overmind and more and more. The Brythons actually sent a real person to represent King Brython, but then I missed seeing his courts entrance as the major Council members were seated before we came into the Hall. The Brython viewing suite is to the immediate left of the Denir suite. Almost as big but filled with more bots than actual people…damn; now that I really look the Brython rep and his wife might be the only people in the suite.

The lights flare again; the Quaznians sent actual people as well and…so did the Daliuns.

Junn Lord Lan Derai, strolls in with security and with his wife whose name is drowned out by the crowd noise. They stand a good two heads taller and a hands width thinner than everyone else. They're almost as pale as my own "ghost eyes" so they stand out a bit even from the other outlandish representatives. They're dressed in Daliun royal blue, white and silver robes and both wear silver crowns that frame their faces down to their chins in an intricate lattice. The Junns are bold for a small world; allowing an ambassador to hold their council seat instead of Lord Junn himself. I stare at them for the remainder of the introductions, wondering how hard it would be to get a shot off that would actually make it across the room.

The representatives have been seated and tucked in good when the petitioning governments are announced; worlds that want in or are being asked to join the New Regime. First up…All damn.

The ground shakes. The tunnel entrance from where the reps entered goes dark as something big blocks the running lights. In they come, three of them, big ones…Giaks.

Swathed in battle dress, that nasty dark blue Giak armor, they stomp into the arena. Each is at least forty decimeters in height, twice as big as me and as wide at the shoulder as they are tall. Their footsteps can be heard across the arena and must be shakin' up the bodies in the seats on that side of the hall 'cause the Giaks are an easy two thousand kilos a pop. These bitches aren't wearing their helmets so those mangled brutish faces are glaring out at everyone from behind thick locks of hair for all the known to see. Their rough reddish skin is covered in dark grey tattoos which marks them as being from one of the most prestigious of all the Giak "mounds".

No way they petitioned the New Regime to join. The Giaks are too prideful and they're still at war with…well everyone. Maybe it was the Coalition that did the asking. I look back across the stands to the Junns but

I can't quite tell if their faces are so pinched because that's just their usual look, or if they're upset at seeing the one group that's been keeping them from taking over Eastspace being treated as guests here. And they wouldn't be alone; most of the known have only seen Giaks on vid or holo. Seeing them live and in person can be…overwhelming. There are gasps of shock and terror at the sight of them and more than a few in the stands actually make to bolt from their seats.

The last Giak to enter the room is an officer. You can tell because though just as tall, their body proportions are a lot closer to human and a lot more feminine. Officers wear war helms that completely cover their faces and I was always told no one's seen what they look like.

But looking at those massive thighs…who would want to?

Wow. The New Regime must want the Giak shipyards pretty bad. If they're allowing them into the Coalition what's going to happen with the Junns? Will they have to give up the Cannius Gate which they're barely holding now?

Not sure if that's good or bad for Arcadia.

Of course…there is no Arcadia.

CHAPTER FIVE:

ARRAIGNMENT

"BRING FORTH THE ACCUSED!"

The Advocate, Cassad and I step up onto the platform. To my surprise it does not lift us to the top of the bunker. Instead, the entire bunker lowers itself around us. The ceiling above us shimmers and melts away. Far above, in the false New Beia night sky, New Coalition security ships have joined the party of sky car vid hounds.

Once again the crowd erupts as the bunker slides down into the black sand, disappearing from sight as we are revealed. The chants begin again, this time they seem to have come to a consensus on what to scream, outshouting Cassad's introduction.

"SHAO, SHAO, RAHN!"

"SHAO, SHAO, RAHN!"

"SHAO, SHAO, RAHN!"

"It means, 'Die tyranny'." Eboro explains though I can barely hear her.

The other bunker has receded into the sand as well. Standing across the arena from us now stands the prosecution. Three New Regime reps, two men and a woman.

"The Woman," Eboro says to Cassad. "is the Valian Conin, Advocate General. She represents the Median worlds, a coalition within the Coalition.

Conin displays Coalition colors, all in a long dress that trailed along the ground. Her head was adorned with a tall, wrapped headdress about which small colored lights orbited. The skin of her face was drawn tight giving her the appearance of having been chiseled from a solid bar of onyx. Her eyes were alight and on fire as they peered across the arena floor at us…at Cassad.

"The fair skinned man is Lord Jon Edins, Brython. Speaks for the Coalition worlds in the vast empty between the smaller clusters."

Between the small clusters included the Eastspace…the Quad.

Why would the Bythons claim to be representing those worlds? The Brython haven't made any move on the Quad or tried to implement control. At least not yet.

Lord Edins is a small but hard looking Brython. His dress is a sharp contrast to the Conins, as it's far less ceremonial; a simple black suit over white underdress. His eyes are covered with dark, archaic glass lenses set in frames perched on his nose. There is a small gold crest on the fold of his jacket. My visor zooms in and shows me the shield, spilt into two sections each bearing an animal. A ram on one side and a winged serpent on the other.

"The last man is the most dangerous" Eboro warns. I turn my attention to the darker man who stands to the fore of the others. His dress is…odd. It's…oh I get it; he's dressed like a Cassad Official except the colors of his trim are like that of the New Regime.

"Onted Galvin, First Equal of the Grand Revolutionary Council," Eboro says. "He's been executing the Cassads in trials all over the known."

Galvin's eyes are on our bunker. If they were filled with the anger and fury that's pretty much standard in the room then I wouldn't be worried. Instead there's a cold clarity in his eyes and a solid unwavering readiness in his stance. He's not just standing in front of the others, he's standing…apart, as if he's not bothering to follow the protocol of the New Regime trial process… as if his own agenda takes priority.

The "First Equal" is also carrying a blade. It's ceremonial, long, curved and clearly lethal. The way his hand rests on the hilt makes it clear as open sky to me; he intends to kill Cassad himself.

"Executing Cassads?" I ask.

"Yes. Anyone who's had any position in the Cassad administration" Eboro tells me. "Very public and very brutal executions."

"What's the position of the First Equal?"

"Consider him…the 'Hand' of the Coalition. Broad power and responsibility, he executes their will" she says with a hint of fear in her voice.

Fek. The more I look at Galvin the more sure I am that he'll bring that swords edge to Cassad as soon as he get a chance. What's he got to lose? The crowd here would go wild and the Coalition Council would be satisfied collectively. I can't let him near Cassad.

"What's his responsibility during the trial?"

Eboro looks at me then and follows my ghost eyes to Galvin. "He will question the witnesses and of course he will attempt to question Minister Cassad."

Galvin doesn't have another weapon that I can see. If he's only carrying the scimitar then maybe all I need to do is keep him at a distance. "He'll make a play at Cassad if you let him get near."

"He wouldn't dare. There are too many council members who want this trial played out," she argues.

"If you let him near Cassad…he will kill him."

"Then…" Eboro turns away from me and says over her shoulder, "Protect your bounty, mercenary."

The chants of 'Die tyranny' die down as the light in the Hall rises just a bit. The Coalition Council is illuminated softly in golden light. Then three beams of light swirl through the arena, passing over the crowd, the three Coalition prosecutors and us before settling on an even patch of black sand.

The patch slowly shifts as something beneath the sand rises. Another bunker…no wait, a tower, as black as the sand, pushes its way up to stand a good ten meters high. The top splits like an egg, the walls falling away and down to the arena floor where they sink into the beads and disappear. Standing on the top of the tower now is a woman wearing a bizarre spiral shaped outfit that was more sculpture than dress. She holds her hands out to her sides with her palms facing up and stands on one leg with the other bent so that her foot is resting just behind the knee of the first. Her face is decorated with a very convincing holo-set giving her leonine features.

"The pall of oppression has been lifted!" the lion lady speaks. "The reign of the tyrant family has ended!"

The crowd roars its agreement and applauds. I can still hear threats against Cassad being called out.

"For one thousand cycles Cassad has plagued the galactic proper with their self-proclaimed right of sovereignty. Their thousand cycle dominion has been one of torture, theft, slavery and genocide."

The arena rumbles. I notice a small icon flashing on the HUD of my visor and subvocalize a command to check the virtual audience. This trial is being broadcast across the known but more than that, just as most of the New Regime council is only here in virtual form, so are many other spectators throughout the known. Virtually, there are billions of citizens in the stands, their holographic representations overlapping each other so much that they're just one nasty multicolored moving blob with flashes of pumping fists and angry faces. I could set the visor to only show certain holos…I could see those holos from the quad only if I wanted…or even…

"Here now stands the Cassad. The LAST of his line! The LAST CASSAD!" the lioness waits as the crowd loses it again. "Come forth any who accuse the Cassad of crimes against their worlds. Come forth any who lay claim to his wretched life!"

From the other side of the arena, out of a tunnel much like the one the Council entered from, emerges a small group. They step onto the sand, four of them, Virogens; one of many peoples that had been conquered by the Cassads. Their world was once called Viro, and it was supposed to be a pretty nice agricultural planet. Still is, though now it's called Zuna and the Virogen people are down to their last few hundred living in orbiting reserve stations above the planet itself. These four men are all lean and sallow, like most Virogen I've seen. Their worn, outdated utility flight suits are ill fitting and have been patched with sealant tape.

The Virogen stand in the spotlight now for all the known to hear their story.

The First Equal steps away from the other prosecutors and marches across the arena toward the Virogen. I notice that the light that follows him is a slightly more reddish gold than the light that remains on the Brython and the Advocate General.

"Identify yourselves" he commands the Virogen.

Of the four, all men, the tallest speaks up. "I am Petrov Musinovic, Chief of the Watch, *Solar Enterprise*, Zuna…"

"You mean, 'Viro', do you not?" Galvin corrects him.

"I…yes…Yes, *Solar Enterprise* in orbit of our homeworld Viro," the man corrects himself hesitantly. I wonder if the New Regime has actually allowed the Virogen back onto their homeworld now that it's been liberated.

"And what," Galvin asks. "charges do you lay against Cassad?"

The Virogen all look directly at Cassad. Musinovic points a long boney finger at us. "The Cassad took our world. They invaded and imposed their sick law upon us. Their Empress denied our ancestors the very right to have their own children! They forced us to breed with them; a privilege they called it, but we soon realized that we were being slowly exterminated. Those who defied them were 'quarantined' to the orbiting Colony stations. Our numbers have slowly dropped for the past four centuries…"

"First Equal," Eboro interrupts the Virogen. "If we could please simply hear the charges."

Onted Galvin turns around like he's been assaulted, his hand on the hilt of his sword tense and tight. He steps sharply in our direction a few meters and if he'd been reasonably closer I swear he would have walked right up to us. As it is he stops almost midway.

"How dare you, Advocate?" he says, his eyes wide with anger. "The Virogen may be a small member of the Coalition but they deserve to face the accused. They, as well as any who have suffered at the hands of the Cassad, deserve to let the worlds of the universe know their story!"

The crowd goes wild and the very air shakes. The First Equal speaks with a genuine passion that I've rarely seen in a politician. He believes in this.

Eboro, to her credit, does not cower to the thunder of New Regime storm. "I agree, First Equal. We will no doubt hear the story of the Virogen when you present them to testify. Today, however, they must simply present their charges against the accused."

The First Equal, Galvin, stares at the Advocate for a long tense moment. Then he draws his sword and points it at her. "You speak with Cassad bravura, Advocate. How long have you been in their employ?"

Eboro shudders slightly at this but answers quickly and confidently. "I am of the Akan, First Equal, and I was set to this task by the Coalition of Free Worlds Council itself."

"You are the Advocate of the Cassad…" he's shouting now but Eboro raises her voice as well.

"Have them present their charges or remove them from the court, Prosecutor!"

Wow… I'm impressed.

The crowd boos. The chants of 'die tyranny' start up again. Some are screaming, accusing her of being a Cassad. Even more flaming debris falls onto the black sand. Unnoticed to most, the First Equal dips his head slightly; he's talking to someone on a subvocal channel.

"Virogen!" he shouts, and the crowd dies down. "Cassad's snake is correct."

Boos arise again but the First Equal shouts it down. "You will be given the chance to testify. The worlds will know your struggle, your pain and the triumph of your return to your home world. I swear it."

The crowd is somewhat mollified by this though I sense they're anticipating a long and satisfying trial.

"Please, my Coalition colleagues, present your charges." Galvin almost bows.

The Virogen hesitate and look to each other. Then the tall leader, Musinovic, speaks up.

"The Virogen charge the Cassad with…Murder…"

"MURDER!" The crowd repeats each charge as he lists them.

"…theft…"

"THEFT!"

"…and geno…ATTEMPTED genocide!"

"GENOCIDE!!"

And so it goes. World after world is brought in to list their charges against the Cassad Empire. Most of the charges are similar of course but there are a few special charges. The Tennace charged the Cassad with technological oppression; stifling the growth of their knowledge base. The Jorean accused the Cassad of exploiting their planets natural resources to the point of rendering it uninhabitable. There were charges of "crimes against humanity" and "crimes against nature".

The Brython accused the Cassad of crimes against the cathol god and of hiding evidence of his existence. The multi-cultural crowd does not respond as heartily at that.

After almost half a solar day of this, a small but unusual group takes to the arena floor to bear witness against Cassad; children.

Small, very meek looking and dressed practically in rags. they enter the bright light for all the known to see. Gasps and cries come from the arena stands at the sight. These kids could be from practically any world in the known…they could be Arcadian.

The First Equal addresses them without the overbearing tenor which he's been using all day. "You are the Nerum of the moon Gaspara?"

The children all nod.

"First Equal, with all due respect, we have already heard from the Gaspara representatives," Eboro points out. Did we? I can't remember.

"With no respect, Advocate Eboro, I tell you that we have not heard from the Nerum people. They are a separate group, self-governing on the moon of Gaspara before the Cassad imposed their wicked law. They deserve to be heard now."

"Are we going to subject children to the stress of a trial, First Equal?"

Galvin turns, fixes Eboro with that "I'm going to cut your head off" gaze and says; "Unfortunately, due to the Cassad, these children are all that's left of the Nerum."

Hmm…yea…Cassad is dead.

The First Equal addresses the kids again. "Children of the Nerum, please state your charges against the Cassad."

The children huddle together, their eyes wide with fear. The First Equal finally puts that sword away.

"Please, children, don't be afraid to speak for your people. You are safe here from the Cassad, safe under the protection of the Coalition of Free Worlds."

The first child to speak is a small brown skinned girl, her hair tied with bright red barrettes in twin braids one on each side of her small head. Her eyes are big, wide and crescent, like dawn on a new world but sad. She can't be more than four Arcadian cycles old. So small is her voice that the amplifier doesn't pick it up. Another child, a taller boy, whispers to her and she tries again.

"My mommy is dead," she says. The crowd cries their sympathy. The First Equal bows his head. Even Eboro has her hands clasped over her heart.

"Your name, child?" Galvin asks her.

Her tiny lips barely part as she speaks. "Ceri."

Another kid, an even smaller, lumpy haired boy, steps forward and speaks up in soft voice. "We…we don't have any food."

Ok…even I want to kill Cassad now. The arena cries again, this time there are several pledges to take the kids in.

"Children…" the First Equal is looking back at Cassad. "Even children were not to be spared under your rule. How many? On how many worlds?"

He turns back to the kids. "It is my understanding that your parents, the last Nerum tribe, sacrificed themselves so that you could live."

They all nod. The girl in braids speaks again. "My mommy said she had to go away. For us to be ok."

"Your mother," Galvin says, "must have loved you very much."

"She said the Ca-shah…" she mispronounces Cassad and looks back to the other children. "they made our food bad."

I sneak a sidelong look at Cassad, but with the collar on it's hard to tell if he's affected by this.

"And made the our rain bad…" tears fall from her wide eyes.

There is open sobbing in the stands now. Eboro drops her hands and addresses Onted.

"First Equal, surely this is not…"

"Have you no sense of compassion woman? Let these children speak!"

After a pause the big eyed girl goes on. "She said they had to go away to make us better…so that we…would be better…" the other kids are wiping tears now.

"Yes, child, they sacrificed themselves for you. And it was not in vain, I promise you." The First Equal looks truly moved.

"And the Ca-shahs have to go away now" her little lips curl in a horribly sad pout.

"This," The First Equal points to Cassad. "is the last of the Cassads, child. And he will go away…forever."

The kids heads all snap in our direction so suddenly that it's a little unnerving. "He's got to go away now," the girl says and the others all nod and all of them… all of them stop crying.

"I've got to stop this." Eboro mutters, marches off the pad and heads across the arena floor in the direction of the Council. She won't have any luck; this is the show they all wanted.

The Advocates movement is noticed by the First Equal but he continues with the kids none the less. No one seems to notice how dark their gazes have gotten. "He will child. Cassad will pay for what was done to your parents. I will see to it… personally."

"Now," she insists.

"Yea," says another of the kids. "now!"

There's actually a soft kindness in the First Equals eyes now. "He is not going anywhere, children. The Cassads have taken away many mothers just like yours across all the worlds known. We all have a right to…"

"Now!" the little big eyed girl finds her boldness and the others back her up.

"They must go away now!"

"Now!"

A little caught off guard the First Equal tries to quell them. "Children, please, do not…"

But the girl begins marching across the sand toward Cassad. "He must go away!"

The First Equal, arms outstretched to stop her, moves to block her path. "No child, this is not the way…"

"NOW!!" whoa…her voice gets suddenly deep. Her mouth opens wide…too wide; her jaw descends far enough to fit a gourd in!

There's the disgusting sound of flesh ripping and suddenly the girl expands. It looks at first like she's exploding on the inside but she's still moving…and changing! Her chest pops right out of the ragged shirt she has on, a nasty bulge of muscle and a riot of ribcage that grow impossibly fast. And her legs swell with even more muscle and her feet elongate until she is standing on her toes.

The kids arms balloon as well, with ugly bone protrusions bursting up out of her skin at her elbows and shoulders. One immense arm swings and catches the First Equal, surprised and off guard, under his chin. He's sent flying across the arena floor and lands in a splash of black sand.

The other kids're transforming as well. Each changing from a small timid little innocent into a hulking three meter tall beast.

And they all have eyes on Cassad.

"NARRRGH!" they bellow… and charge.

CHAPTER SIX:

THE CHILDREN OF NERUM

They gallop at us on all fours with such ferocity that the black sand kicks up several meters in their wake. Their roars echo across the arena and the crowd responds with a collective gasp. Some kind of meta-morphs but transforming faster than any I've ever heard of.

Three…four…five...with at least one more behind them that I can't see… "Run Cassad!" I scream. The bunker will never rise in time and security in the arena itself is nonexistent due to the various treaties.

But I'm still armed.

I whip the NOK 37 off of my hip, sight down the lead beast and try not to think about how it had been a toddler just a pulse beat ago. The gun bangs against my palm after each squeeze of the trigger.

The first round hits it square in the chest in a spray of blood that the thing hardly notices. The second tags it a little father up where its clavicle should be and still the transformed girl rumbles across the sand at us. What the buck are they made of?

The next shot I put into her forehead. The NOK 37 hits with good enough stopping power that her head is thrown back forcing her to stumble and fall. But no penetration; skulls're too damned thick! Should've brought the Sever!

I reset and target the next the beast, sending every round to its cranium. The first misses but the next two catch it in the jaw and temple causing him to swerve and stumble to the sand as well.

The third leaps over his fallen playmates. Training takes over for a pulse beat and makes me target him center mass. Two shots wasted; he just ignores them.

Fek! One of the first two is getting back up even as I reset and pop another three rounds at his head. He drops but they're all getting closer…this ain't working!

But it's too late to change tactics. I sight the big girls head and force her to stop again, switch targets once more and bring down the fourth.

I can see three more behind the first group bounding on the sand. Too many and too close now, I'm gonna have to make a break for it. But I turn and see something I'm didn't expect.

Cassad…walking.

The All Damned control collar! He can't move any faster!

"NAHHRGH!" the roar is right behind me and I spin hard, drawing my kendo blade at the same time and leading with gunfire. One shot, right into the eye of the beast almost on top of me. The furenium bullet doesn't explode out the back of the dense skull, instead, after rattling around inside, it pops out the other eye . Almost at my feet the thing drops into the sand.

I reset and target the next, not daring to hope for another shot that good. Still I manage head shots and get it turned a bit. It's enough that it won't maul me and as it passes by, I rip the kendo blade through its leg, severing it completely.

It drops and I'm targeting the next of them, trying the same strategy; head shots, get it turned, then use the Kendo blade. This time the head shots fail to push the thing it off its course and I have to sidestep to avoid the blind swipe of a clawed hand. Though off balance I'm still able to take its head off with one swing of the kendo.

Another howl, and I turn and sight the next Nerum.

WARNING: SABERNOK 37 FURY ROUND COUNT: 05

The warning chime distracts me enough to allow the mutated kid to dodge me and go for Cassad. I'm forced to turn my back on its buddies while I track it and pull a spare round cap from my belt. I sight the big thing but it's back is filled with rolls of muscle and sheaths of bone. There's no shooting through that, damn it!

I throw the kendo blade. It spins end over end, singing a shrill song and leaving a trail of vapor behind as it's single molecule lined edge, now glowing, rends the air. It sinks deep into the monsters back, right into its spine. Already turning back to rest of them I hear it hit the sand rather than see it.

Fek! I duck to avoid another clawed swipe and fire rounds into the bone covered knees that are right in my face. Something gets through because the beast drops nearly on top on me. With a grunt I shove the thing away and before it can get its bearings I jam the muzzle of my NOK against its neck and pull the trigger. Blood splashes over my visor and blocks my vision.

So I fire blind where I think the next one is coming from. Drawing my gloved hand across the holo-glass of my visor I sweep off the blood in time to see a wall of muscle and bone before it barrels into me.

"Wuff!" I don't resist, letting the thing knock me back across the arena. My still tender ribs howl at me but don't break, yet. The sand is surprisingly soft to land in but hard to get a footing on. So I can't spring back up. I settle for firing from off my back. Now I target knees and ankles, the narrowest parts of these things, hoping I can hoopty the rest of them.

One down…and another before the others retreat and sprint around…trying to outflank me. But now that I've got them off of me I should be able to hold them long enough for the Nez SeC to finally respond.

Just as I'm lining up another shot along the sights of my NOK, the Nerum I'm targeting leaps up, twists in midair and dives into the black sand as if it was so much dark water.

What in the known?

It disappears completely. And his buddies follow suit; all of them diving into the glossy black sand, their clawed hands digging faster than my eye can follow and they're gone…just like that.

WARNING: CHEMICAL EXPLOSIVE DETECTED!

The bomb warning flashes across my visor. How on styx did someone get a chem bomb in the arena? A primitive one too for my old visor to detect it when the New Regime did not. I follow the flashing warning icons to the source. The beast, the first one I managed to stop by cutting its leg off, it's still crawling after Cassad, it's the source of the warning. Ah buck; A bio-bomb!

I sprint after Cassad, who's walking with as much speed as he can muster with the control collar on. The All damned sand shifts under every footfall…kept the Nerum from charging me faster than I could respond but now it's slowing me down.

There's no point in killing the Nerum anymore, the bomb is likely to go off no matter what at this point. Never the less I snap off a shot at her head as I pass by, might be enough to slow her.

Might be the pulse beat I need to get Cassad to safety.

POOSH! One of the Nerum beasts explodes up out of the sand right next to me as I run. It rakes a clawed hand across my shoulder as it flies up over me and then back down, claws digging insanely fast to slip it beneath the sand again. The other Nerum beasts begin bursting from the arena floor like gulfish bounding from the sea. I'm firing left and right now, catch one in mid-leap and send him sprawling away. But the others are hot on my heels at this point and my visor flashes two more bomb warnings. Fek! I thought they dove beneath the sand to escape the bomb but…

WARNING: CHEMICAL BOMB READS AT CRITICAL MASS!

Where on styx is Nez SeC?

POOSH! Hot fire rips across my leg as I'm tagged by another slash of those claws.

Cassad has nearly reached the bridge at the edge of the arena. The crowd on that end of the floor hasn't even moved. They're watching everything as if it were another All Damned sporting event here in the Hall of Kain.

POOSH! I shoot the next leaper down and have to jump over it when it tumbles to the ground in front of me.

WARNING: CHEMICAL BOMB DETONATION IMMINENT!

Finally I reach Cassad and grab his arm. Instead of pulling him up onto the bridge I spin him hard and hurl him into the trench.

POOSH! Another Nerum beast bursts out of the sand behind me, clawed hands extended. It's got too much momentum for my NOK to stop it…

WARNING: SABERNOK 37 FURY ROUND COUNT: 05

…04…

03…

02…

BOOM!!!

I'm hit by a wall of black sand, lifted up and hurled across the trench. The ledge of the cell wall catches me in the small of my back and I drop down to the prison level in a limp heap.

A pulse beat passes and I'm not sure where I am or what I'm doing…the trial…Cassad…the Nerum! One of the beasts must have blown itself up but was still beneath the sand …only reason I'm still alive.

Ugh! Lost my visor…fek…lost my NOK…can't hear a thing over that ringing…

"CRA-SHAH!!" Heard that! There's another Nerum perched above me on the edge of the arena floor. Its eyes are on Cassad who lay still against a prison cell gate.

Down to my last weapons, I pull the twin ferron carbide butterfly blades from the hidden scabbards in the back of my jacket. They're micro edged, not as sharp or as durable as the kendo but the first couple of strikes will be just as effective, if I can get any hits in.

The Nerum leaps down a little shakily; looks like the blast did a number on it as well. Can't let it recover!

But a wave of dizziness washes over me as I rush at it. Can't stop… got to get at it before it can kill Cassad.

"HA!" I drive the first of the blades right into its neck just where it meets the boney shoulder. The Nerum tries to shrug me off but I don't let go of the blade so it rips its way free and blood sprays in gushes.

I spin and drive the other into the monsters gut but get the angle wrong. The blade only cuts the skin, stopping dead when it hits the dense muscle.

"NARGH!" it cries. One clawed hand reaches out and shoves me away. My ribs…feels like two of them actually, wail again but it doesn't feel like they broke. I stumble across the trench and slam into the bars of a cell. Another Nerum, this one burned and missing an arm, lands next to the first. They both ignore me, look to Cassad and move toward him.

I climb to my feet and rush them from behind. So intent on getting to Cassad the Nerum closest to him doesn't even notice when I shove a blade straight down through the top of his lagging buddy's head.

The blade gets stuck in the tough bone and I'm so glitch that I don't let go. I get dragged down to the cell block floor with the dead Nerum.

The last of them, at least I hope it's the last, closes on Cassad. I can't get there in time…I can't…my NOK!

Just a meter away, I dive for the gun and roll to a kneeling stance. But the bucka's got its back to me. All I can see are the thick shoulder plates and bulbous knots of muscles.

"Nerum!" I shout. But the creature ignores me and raises its nasty clawed paw to rip Cassad open.

Then I see the bright red beret in the tufts of scraggly, wire hair jutting out of its cranium.

"C-Ceri!"

The misshapen head turns at once and our eyes meet over my gun sights. It's…hers are so big…like dawn on a new world…

The NOK 37 bangs in my hand twice. The first shot was the killer; right in her left eye. The second smashes into her forehead a sends her falling backward over Cassad.

There's a crash behind me and I twist, gun first, to find Prim Locasta and her Nez SeC officers landing in the trench. From somewhere on the floor behind me I can hear the tiny warning chime of my visor sounding.

WARNING: SABERNOK 37 FURY ROUND COUNT: 00

It takes me a moment to lower my gun.

The Prim walks up and looks past me to Cassad, who's pinned beneath the Nerum but clearly alive. She then looks me up and down, nodding appreciatively but when our eyes meet she hesitates a bit.

"There's a common saying, mercenary; 'better late than never'."

"Bitch, the fight is over. What the buck do you think 'never' means?"

CHAPTER SEVEN:

THE HERALD

"…genetic array that isn't on any profile anywhere. Never caused so much as an inquiry from the Security checks" a smaller but more haggard looking Nez SeC officer explains to the Prim. He's dressed in security combat fatigues and wears an armored band around his head.

We're aboard an Esari emergency medical boat that's circling the Nezerian Tower at about a kilometer out, having been shuttled here right after the Nerum attack.

"So have we identified who they really were, Walsh?" the Prim asks him.

"All the security checks we used to I.D. them are coming back good," the Nez SeC officer told her. "It seems like they actually were the children of the last Nerum tribe."

"How many?"

Walsh activates a small holo emitter on his head band. The dossiers of the children digitally coalesce into being in the air in front him.

"There were twelve here in the Hall, eight down in the court. All of them transmuted into a class of weapon we have not yet identified."

The Prim glances in my direction. I'm leaning against a bio-bed next to an unconscious Cassad. For a short time he had been revived but the med techs put him back under while they checked him for injuries.

Meanwhile I'm using a cell stimulator to treat some of my own wounds. The bone claws of the Nerum beasts didn't get past my body armor to anything vital but they did tear me up at the edges… and my legs. My ribs managed to hold but there are micro-fractures that will take a while to heal.

"The mercenary took care of… what? Five of them?"

"He eliminated six, seven if you count the one that exploded beneath the sand, and he hobbled the other one. The remaining Nerum ran riot outside the court until Nez SeC officers were able to kill them, as you know."

I twist and turn trying to get the stimulator to all my ripped up parts while I listen but there's a particularly hard to get to wound on my back where a Nerum claw slid under the armor plate in my jacket.

"How bad was it…overall?" the Prim asks.

"There were…several casualties."

"How many?" she insists.

"The Nerum killed or wounded at least fifty members of various delegations, their security personnel included, before Nez SeC arrived. Nez SeC lost ten officers before the Nerum were either put down or activated their biological explosives. So…looks like sixty-two," Walsh says gravely.

Guess they're not counting the Nerum kids as casualties. I look at Cassad. He and his family probably weren't counting the Nerum either. They weren't thinking of them at all while those children's planet dried up and their people began to starve. While the Cassads enjoyed all the amenities of being the most powerful family in the history of humankind the regents on Gaspara did unspeakable things to the Nerum people, things so horrible that the parents sacrificed themselves not in a bid to save their children, but in an attempt to turn them into the instruments of their revenge.

The room has gotten quiet. I can feel the Prims eyes on me so I turn to find she has her hand extended. For a moment I think she's looking to shake mine but then she reaches for the stimulator instead. I let her take it and turn around while she radiates my back.

"You managed to keep Cassad alive…took out seven of them…and you are still breathing," she says.

The hatch alert chimes and her officer, Walsh, opens it to reveal a thick necked Med Tech carrying what looks like a portable internal imager.

"I'm to check the Cassad for secondary internal injuries."

Walsh checks his ID. "Checks out," he reports.

The Prim looks like she's about to let him through so I shake my head. "Not gonna happen."

"I've been ordered to…" he actually seems to have an attitude.

"YO!" I bark placing my hand on my holstered NOK. "Walk… away." A harsher threat than I should be giving to a med tech maybe, but I just got blown up.

The Prim turns back to me and continues tending to the wound on my back to hide her smile as the tech flees.

Done, she clicks off the stimulator and I turn to face her again. Her eyes are appraising me from my boots to my visor.

"Who ARE you, Mercenary?"

"Cassad is done for the day," I tell her. She looks hard into my visor trying to see past the ghost eyes. I know she got a good look at me down on the prison level. Figure she recorded my face and has already begun running it through her files. Hopefully she's the only one who got my image on vid. No doubt she'll look among the big boys for my dossier, never thinking for a moment that I might come from a world outside of the clusters, from so insignificant a place as backwoods Arcadia.

"Indeed… Mercenary. We are returning you to your ship now. The advocate is awaiting you there," she agrees. She then regards Cassad, still unconscious in the bio-bed. "You risked much to keep him alive, but you were the one who captured him, who brought him in for his execution."

I'm not sure what her question is so I wait. Another Med Tech tries to get access to Cassad and I shoo them away as well. After a pulse beat where she goes back to trying to see past the holographic ghost eyes of my visor she asks, "Why, Mercenary? Why not just let him die? He deserves it."

"Thought the New Regime was intent on a trial?" I ask her.

"Yes. The Council Members and representatives can solidify their reigns if the peoples of the worlds see them convict and execute the last Cassad. His father died in the taking of Ziara. So they want the trial with all this ridiculous pomp and ceremony. Each representative can pose with the prostrate Cassad before his people to gain status and prestige. But never doubt in the end he is going to die for his families crimes. Why risk your life just to give him another earning cycle at the most?"

Cause I haven't gotten my money. She's angling for more than just who I'm working for but I'm not sure what. Her interest seems almost… personal.

Another med tech stops by the bay door. The Nez SeC officer checks her ID and turns to the Prim.

"BioOfficer."

"For?" The Prim asks.

"Cognitive check." The tech answers, holding up a small neural data recorder. At once I go edge. She's an average sized woman with a soft, almost meek voice. But her eyes are sharp and she's got a slight hint of scaring about her chin. Who is she? Really?

"Taj" the word comes from nowhere…almost my Pops voice…but it hits the mark. Immediately I look to her neck, just below her right ear for the telltale tattoo that they wear. But her skin there is clear; just a smooth unblemished patch of skin…that doesn't quite match the rest of her neck.

Yea…she's a Taj Pirate and I think I actually know her. She's changed her hair since I last saw her and added...something, I'm not sure what…some kind of facial manipulation…but…yea… it's her.

Breer.

The Taj are famous "bond breakers", especially in Eastspace where they helped smash open the Brython Welfare program. But that was a few rotations ago…a few cycles before I was born. By the time I encountered them the Taj were split into different factions, had become brutal and were dealing in human cargo themselves. Breer and the Taj she was a part of got into a tight spot when they tried to jack a shipment of kidnapped Arcadians. Her small band of Taj pirates found themselves outclassed by some heavy hitters and she was the only one of the pirates that managed to survive.

Breer…she's not as tough as she looks but she's smarter than a liquid A.I. It was her that tracked down the kidnappers and figured how to recover the Arcadians. And she was smart enough to stay out of my way when the fighting started.

Still, she's greedy and aggressive…like the Taj are… tried to double cross me at the end of that mess but I caught her. Only let her go after I made her give up the coin the Taj had made.

Gave me the excuse not to kill her.

The Prim notices my hesitation. Luckily, with my visor on, nobody can tell what I'm really looking at. I only have to raise my head slightly to give the appearance that I had been looking down instead of directly at the fake Med tech.

"You want to wake him up?" I ask her. The tension in her shoulders relaxes a bit as she realizes I'm not going to blow her cover to the Prim.

At least not yet.

"Only to check for cognitive damage that may impair his ability to testify." She says.

"Fine ," I say "but if he's going to wake up then everyone else out."

The Prim looks like she wants to argue but I stare her down and tell her, "You can't talk with him without the Advocate present"

To her credit, she only nods. "Fine, Mercenary, it is you I want to know more of now anyway. Cassad will soon be only a memory. I will speak with you later." And the hatch closes behind her.

For a long moment the fake Med Tech and I stare at each other. I can't tell what she's thinking but I'm wondering why I didn't have the Prim shove her out the airlock.

"Thank you, Lieutenant," she says, using my old rank from the 46th.

"What for?" It comes out harsh and angry. Somewhat because I just got blown up but mostly because I'm she's got that same tone of voice as she had the last time I saw her. She glossed my finish enough to get me to drop my guard and tried to turn me into Arcadian security. Even as that made me want to put a bullet in her head, I held back because I owed her.

"For maintaining my cover," she admits speaking with a humility that I haven't ever seen in one of the Taj, who are the biggest bunch of fek heads in Eastspace. I can see, just a bit in the way that she carries herself, there's some burden that weighs on her.

"How did you get aboard as a medical technician?" I ask her. Got to say; her covert ops skill set has grown since I last saw her. Another thing that's atypical for the brutal Taj.

“It wasn't difficult. But they will find me out soon enough. I need to see Cassad.”

“What do the Taj want with Cassad,” I say.

“I ain't Taj no more.”

“Since when?”

“Since your buddies killed the rest,” she almost spits. I can't tell if she's on the level. Sure, her little Taj group got a lot of their people sent down styx but I didn't figure that to be too many of them.

“So…what do YOU want with Cassad?”

“That's my business, Lieutenant,” she throws her chin up. There's the Taj Pirate. “Ain't gonna set you back in the least.”

She's right and I'm tired…and a bit blown up. "You're right. Talk to him after the trial."

"You owe me, Lieutenant," she insists and her eyes flash a sudden anger. "I never told anyone what went down with y'all at Osage."

Here it comes. She'll try and extort me…try and use that whole buckin' mess as leverage. "You can still walk out of here," I warn her.

Now she hesitates as now my anger becomes apparent to her. But her mission, her duty to the Taj maybe, if that's the weight I see pressing on her, compels her to try me once again.

"And you have a chance to make fek right. All I need is a scan of Cassad's bio sig and what happened with your…"

"Fifty million" I spit out, trying to stop her from talking out of her fekhole.

She looks lost for a pulse beat, clearly sensing that her position has lost some leverage. But she presses on, forced by that burden maybe. But her tone has an undercurrent of rage. "Maybe the FireHawks should learn about Osage then?"

There it is. Breer was there…she saw the whole thing. She watched as I put down my former squad mates…as I killed my fellow Four-Six… she thought to use that to hold me. Figured then that she could turn me into either the other rogue 46th or to what was left of the Arcadian military. She was trying to get back some of what she thought was owed after what happened to the rest of the Taj so it didn't anger me as much as it's doing right now. I'm a soldier. I've killed plenty and after she made her play… I was ready to kill then. But she was unarmed, helpless and murder is a far cry from combat.

So I just let her go…after leaving her stranded among the dead on Osage. I was mad then but now…well I just got blown up.

The NOK 37 is out of my holster and pointed in her face so fast even I'm a little shocked. She back pedals and comes up against the med bay hatch.

"A-Arcadian?"

"You don't know a damned thing about the Four-Six…" I let five cycles of unreleased grief and pain boil up out of my gut and slam against the back on my eyes. "If you did, you'd' never would've risked this."

"They're here…"

"I just killed six little kids while the richest people in the known cheered! You think I'm in the mood for your fek? Bring it up again." I place the barrel of the NOK against her forehead. "Bring. It. Up. Again."

She goes quiet. Even as I have the gun to her head her eyes move away from it to peer over my shoulder at Cassad. I see it now…her desperation…it's not for her own life.

The NOK is back in my holster and I step away from her. "Find your way off this boat quick. I'll give you a five minute head start before I alert the Prim."

Breer doesn't hesitate and is out the hatch in a flash. I secure the door and then take a moment to let the anger work its way back down into the hole I keep it in. Anger won't help me get to my payday.

Fek… this was just day two.

CHAPTER EIGHT:

THE ARC RAPTOR

"They are continuing the Reading of the Charges without us," Eboro tells me. She was waiting for us at the port, which has become a congested thoroughfare of demonstrators. Now she's tending to Cassad in my small med bay, double checking the med techs work. I'm checking too, removing the spyware they installed in his body while pretending to be healing him. It's haphazard; they were in a rush, so it's easy to find. If they'd more notice or time they would've been able to get something in him I wouldn't be able to find or remove.

"But next sunside you'll be required to appear again" she tells Cassad. He remains silent even though the control collar is set low. "They've added extra security measures but…"

"It won't be enough," I finish for her. "The next attempt won't be as… moderate."

"We can hire our own security," she suggests.

"No." Cassad and I answer at the same time. His broken silence flusters Eboro.

"But Minister, Nezerian Security Command is somewhat less than eager to protect you. The Mercenary is right…about the next attempt being worse."

Cassad once again lapses into silence, as if his answer was more than enough to end the debate. Eboro waits a moment more then turns to me.

"Perhaps your crewmates can assist us?"

"Who?"

She frowns at me. "The mercenary crew who aided your capture of Cassad."

Oh…she means the FireHawks. She thinks I'm with them.

"How do you know about that?" Must have been Cassad.

"It was your…associates who provided the evidence that you had in fact captured Cassad. Clear vid of him in your possession. As well as the fire fight with the Royal Guard"

So that's who validated my rep at the gate. But why? It wasn't exactly a pleasant reunion with my old squad. If they had known, at the time, that the man I was hauling around was Cassad the whole thing might have ended in bloodshed…

…well MORE bloodshed anyway.

Cassad seems interested now. He's not looking at me but I can tell he wants to know about my "crew".

"That's not an option," I tell her.

"But we can't trust anyone here," Eboro insists.

"No," I say, looking at her pointedly. "We can't."

"We barely survived that attack. What if there's another? With trained soldiers this time? Or even worse?" she stands away from Cassad, looking for the first time like she's a bit fed up with him as well.

"Nez SeC and the New Regime gunboats should keep anything big from getting to the trial. And anything that can get past their inspections should be enough for the Court security or myself to handle." I say.

"Look," Eboro moves a wayward lock back behind her ear. "What you did in the court…saving the Minister, was amazing. But you both…we all very nearly died. I've already argued with the council at length and they are not going to change the format of the trial. If even the same attack were to occur…"

"We'll be better prepared." I assure her.

"How?"

"I'm too close…" to getting my payday to play it conservative now. "What's next?"

Eboro looks at me quizzically but answers me. "Statements of Intent tomorrow morn. Then the prosecution begins with witness statements. Which means more witnesses will have access to the Minister."

"As will the prosecutors," I point out.

"Yes but they wouldn't dare…"

"No," I growl. "No they won't."

"Let the Prosecution declare their Statement of Intent!" the lion lady is back and booming her voice across the arena. There's a ton of added security; seems after the Nerum beasts cut a bloody path through the delegations outside the New Regime members insisted on their own personal protections. Looks like they found a compromise with Nez SeC and now the regular security personnel of over a hundred worlds has flooded the Hall. It makes for quite the confusing mess as everyone is checking everyone else's security passes and jurisdictions are being stepped on all over the place.

Nez SeC commander… the Prim, Locasta, is having one nasty ride on styx trying to keep everything under control. I counted three times that I could see where differing forces drew guns on each other with Nez SeC coming in and stopping the escalation in the nick of time.

Not that I'm helping. Locasta nearly lost her mind when I came down off the ship wearing my Raptor armor, plates freshly painted with an urban camo pattern, complete with the air foils, my MX-11 rifle slung over my shoulder and my Sever 3030 handgun on my hip. In addition I've ditched Cassad's control collar in favor of a neck binder and hand manacles both attached to a simple duranium chain I've latched to my forearm.

"You continue to surprise, Mercenary," she told me through clenched teeth. "But today I'm not so impressed. That thin armor is only going to drive Council Security into a fit. We'll have to enter the Hall through the third tier undercourse."

My armor is thin compared to most. The bio-mechanical weave that covers me head to foot is only a few millimeters thick and the biggest of the plates sitting over the bio-mechanical weave are about as wide a finger. To most it looks a lot like the armor is no more protective or useful than a simple flak jacket but it's powered. On the right body…a trained body, it's absolutely a war winner.

Never the less it seems as though I already made a big impression with my less than formalwear. The even larger number of people out to witness the trial isn't unexpected, what surprises me is the large number of "ghost eyes" I saw staring back at me on our ride back to the Hall. Terrible copies of my visor were being worn by people lining the route.

"There's a new Griotale circulating too," The Advocate told me. "You're portrayed by Zelden Lincoln."

I guess I should be honored or something, but I'm thinking with this many people walking around wearing fake visors that I might be able to sneak out into Abatan city a bit without rousing attention.

Like I'm doing right now.

The crowd inside the Hall goes into an uproar as the bunker slides down around the Advocate, Cassad and I. Immediately I search out the Giaks for their reaction to my armor and I'm not disappointed. The big girls leap to their feet and bellow war cries across the arena at me scaring the fek out of everyone in the surrounding sections.

Then I look to see the Daliuns reaction. Lord Lan Derai is stone faced but I can still see the rage behind his eyes. His wife doesn't seem too upset, must not be familiar with Raptor armor. Further up in the stands I zoom in with the helmet visor to find a couple of Daliun Pretty Boys standing from their seats as well.

Well…it won't be long before I'm I.D.'d now.

If the Prim can't find the Raptor armor in her databases I'm sure the Giaks or the Junns would only be too happy to give her the skinny on the 46th, my old unit and the only soldiers in the Arcadian military to wear it.

But I can't come out here without it. There's likely to be another attempt on Cassad and I can't let him get taken out. Not until I'm paid.

The trial proceeds slowly. Onted Galvin is absent; injured more seriously from his encounter with the Nerum than was previously reported. In his place a junior officer gives the prosecutions Statement of Intent. She looks a bit glossy in comparison to the First Equal but her speech is just as passionate. The other prosecutors also make declarations and soon the witnesses are brought out.

Things go pretty much the same as they did during the reading of the charges save for some pretty impressive presentations.

The Viro return and bring with them a holo display of their collective family tree showing how line after line died out. If the Cassads had not been stopped by the New Regime when they were, there would not have been enough Viro left to repopulate their own planet.

A Brython conservation group…I missed the name, brings in the massive rotting corpse of something they called a galu. It had been killed by poachers in a liberated system. Ironically the Cassads who once controlled that system, had been protecting the creatures.

It becomes apparent that the conservation group is only here to make their plea to the Coalition to protect those creatures they are promptly booed and rushed out of the arena. The rotting corpse of the huge indiscernible material takes a while longer to remove. A recess is called for the day.

The Prim returns to escort us out, her Nez SeC security contingent considerably larger now.

"We've been ordered to return you to your ship via the platform."

"What's wrong with the undercourse?" I ask her.

"Nothing," she grimaces. "The Council wants Cassad on display for a little while longer."

"You mean," Eboro steps in between us. "They want to deshine him! For the crowds outside to see Cassad in this chain!"

The Prim nods slowly.

"This is a mistake," I warn her, popping open the mandible on my helmet. "Any more attempts will likely come outside the Hall or at the port where my ship is…while we're in transit."

"I've called for hovercar escorts," she tries to convince us. "And this is a last minute change. Any attempt won't be ready in time to do anything."

"Unless they're already set and waiting."

The Prim looks me up and down. "Hope your new decks are up to the task then, Mercenary."

They bring the floating platform into the arena again and we all embark. Cassad, even with more freedom now that he's no longer in the control collar, looks about at the raucous crowd with an impassive face. Is he resigned to his fate? Or just…confident?

I get caught up in watching Cassad that I don't notice the Prim is subvocalizing like crazy until it's too late. The doors open onto the outer corridor and immediately I unsling my MX-11 and sight the three large Giaks standing there blocking our path.

"HOLD FIRE! HOLD FIRE!" The Prim screams. She leaps off the platform her own gun drawn.

The Giaks are already being drawn on, however, by Nez SeC security who had been patrolling the outer corridor. But now they had their backs to the Hall doors, clearly intimidated by the Stompers.

"Pajack Legeder, Hojap, remove your personnel from the Hall!" the Prim orders. She hasn't sighted the Giaks with her firearm but she's got it out.

The Giaks ignore her, all of them staring over her and right at us on the platform. Two of them are soldiers, still not wearing their helmets but now carrying those formidable Warhammer rifles of theirs.

Fek. Who gave THEM permission to carry weapons into the Hall?

"S'TA'EN ARCADIAN B'KAYNG," comes from the Giak commander, their Pajack Legeder. She wears the helm of a decorated officer in the Giaks military. A bit taller than her soldiers but with a body much more human and feminine looking. She points a muscular finger…right at me.

"Arcadian?" The Prim asks as her comm system gives her the translation. She actually glances at me for a moment before demanding that the Giaks step aside.

"ARCADIAN SPET'KAH."

"You will make a request with the Council!" The Prim says "Otherwise you will not interrupt the proceedings of this trial." More Nez SeC officers arrive then, backing her command. The Giak commander doesn't even seem to notice them and continues to stare daggers at me while I keep her sighted down the barrel of my Eleven.

The Prim steals another glance at me, no doubt wondering why the Giaks have a stick up their asses for me. I don't have an answer for her…I honestly don't know. Sure we fought them hard in the *Wars of the Blade* but our battles and skirmishes never had the nasty tones that the ones with the Daliuns or the Irlon did. I knew they'd recognize the armor but didn't think they would be so pissed they would come down here.

But if it's a fight they want I'd be much better off with it happening right here and now, with a ton a Nez SeC officers between them and Cassad. Just got to get them to commit to an attack.

Keeping my trigger hand steady on my rifle I lift two fingers of the other off of the fore-stock and beckon the big girls to come over.

The bigger of the two Giak soldiers bellows her rage and actually starts to move forward. But the Giak commander, with only a hand on the enraged girls shoulder, stops her cold.

For another few moments she simply stares at me across the sea of armed Nez SeC officers. Then she nods, to me I guess, and she and her group step aside.

The Prim gives the command for the platform to continue on. Closely we pass by the Giaks who watch through those dark, inset eyes. Their deep, earthy scents make me wish I still had the mandible of my helmet closed. I keep them sighted, turning as we pass by and find Eboro, hiding behind me, and there's Cassad…

Only now do I realize that I never felt him jerk on the chain still attached to my arm. He never moved, not a bit. And even now he wasn't watching the Giaks, he was looking right at me…like a predator…like an eight-leg that's found a buzzer stuck tight and close to the center of its web.

And he's not the only one looking at me with new eyes now. The Prim hops back up onto the platform and looks me up and down again.

"You are from Arcadia," she says triumphantly. From the way her pupils are jumping I can tell she's accessing files even as she's talking to me.

"There is no Arcadia."

CHAPTER NINE:

THE END OF ALL THINGS

My cover is glitch but it I figured that when I decided to go to the trial in the armor. Just got to hope that I'm in the pipe now; that I'm close enough to getting paid that it won't matter.

With nothing to do because of the early recess of the trial I head to primary and run systems checks to pass the time. Running the engines hard have made them a bit twitchy but they were built to withstand a lot more. I'm not going to risk trying to tune them now as I may have to take off with very little notice if this trial falls apart.

I'm halfway through the inspection when I see the little indicator flashing on my comm console. Looks like Sticky is trying to contact me. After a quick check on Eboro and Cassad as well as a security sweep of the ship itself, I open the comm station up and hook the communications node up to my system.

To my surprise it isn't Sticky's face I see when my monitor comes up. Buckin' ass! He broke our comm agreement!

"What's the skinny, Picker?" he says. He's gotten bigger; I can see that in his face. Probably has a lot more down time to work out now…and grow his hair. It was close shaven the entire time I served with him but now it's long and wild, falling about his shoulders in thick locks. There's a new scar on his face, just above his chin…looks like something actually got through his helmet and tagged him. I wonder if it happened at Rogue One?

"Tight, O. As usual," I tell him. He grins but only for a pulse beat.

"We need to meet."

He can't be serious. "Line's secure, O. Speak your peace."

"We need to meet, Loren face to face."

"O…" He can't figure I've got away to get away from my ship right now…even though I do. "I'm kind'a in the middle of a delicate op right now."

“No fek, Picker. We need to meet before you get yourself killed.”

“I’m all clear, O.”

His face hardens. “We need…to meet.”

Fek! I’m not sure what his game is but Omega is not playing. Face to face? “You’re here, I take it? On New Beia?”

Omega leans back away from the monitor and I can see he’s wearing his Raptor armor. I can also see it’s been painted with the garish red “FireHawk” insignia.

“We’re in Morgan city, Adams district.”

Omega is the leader of the FireHawks…that thought hits me like a tonne of bricks. I figured there to be a bunch 46th members in that crew but not our Duke commanding it. Fek…Step-Child told me she wasn’t the “Duke”…she wouldn’t have used that term for just anyone.

“My ship is on lock down,” I say but then, “it’ll take a bit to get to you.” There’s no point in forcing him to try and get to me…don’t want that.

“Whatever gets it done, Picker.” And the monitor goes dead.

Yea…whatever gets it done.

“No more than seventeen hundred R.A.U.s,” I instruct the deck hand. He raises the fuel connecting pipeline to *WarChild’s* rear engine housing access. “I’ll release the safety clamps.” I duck under the thick wide piping and head back to *WarChild’s* forward hatch.

Another wave of overlapping scans washes over me. With so much attention on my ship I can’t possibly walk away and expect to move through the city without a ton of vid drones on my back.

So I’ve got to slip past them somehow and that means using a nice trick I worked out when I first put this ship together.

The engine housings have to “swept” every now and then; cleaned of rads, chems and debris. Most ports do this at the same time they refuel a ship. But if you’re already topped off then the mechanism inside the fuel pipeline won’t extend, leaving a nice wide cavity inside that a person could crawl through.

No one ever thinks of this because the odezium used to clean out the housings is molten hot and irradiated. But the cete housings *WarChild* is made up of shield the cavity from the heat just fine.

Eboro approaches me as I'm making my way through the ship to the engine housings.

"I need you to release Cassad from the…"

"No."

"Only for a few minutes, Mercenary!"

"No."

"The stress of being held in that restraining bar is…"

"Causing his muscles to cramp?" I ask, stopping and turning to face her. She only backs up a little from my ghost eye glare. "Putting a strain on him physically? Is he suffering from joint atrophy?"

"Yes!"

"Good." I snap and continue on to the lockers in the Prep bay. "That way he's easier to manage."

"Is this how he must spend his last days? In pain and torment?"

"You could pay me now and take him to the buckin' Phoede`-Phoede` lounge!" I snap. "This trial and everything that's happening now is your peoples doing."

"This trial is a test," she says gravely. "One we must pass if the known is going to progress forward."

Eboro follows me to the lockers and continues her pleading. "Cassad rule, for all its failings, kept the known stable for the past millennia. They protected the weak…"

"That's not what I'm seeing at the trial," I argue. "The Cassads were a bloated empire, too big for their own good. Your Alaafin here may or may not have been a monster, but sure as styx ends he had monsters who worked for him."

"Cassad was not the Alaafin and there will be monsters in the Coalition as well," she goes on. "dangerous beings with no regard for anything save their own machinations. But there are those of us who are working toward a much brighter future for all the citizens of the known and beyond. In this interregnum between the Old Regime and the New, there is an opportunity to fix the problems of the past. The Coalition can be the guiding force that accelerates all intelligent life in the known toward much greater heights."

"Yea," I flash a grim smirk. "You guys are off to a great start. I've been to Orun, I've seen the debris belt of floating Ziarans who would have preferred their monsters to yours. Their future disappeared in the *blood tide*."

"I know," she admits quietly. "We are failing. The horrors of many of the Cassad regents were too vile, too unspeakable. We haven't been able to convince our own not to take their vengeance. But if we continue the cycle of violence…if we allow ourselves to engage in the darkest practices of the Old Regime to satiate our hunger for reprisal, we will become them in nature. All of their vices without the any of their virtues, however few you might think there were."

She's right, not that I care. "Good luck."

Eboro places her hand on my arm. "We can start right now," she says. "We can treat Cassad…we can treat this man with the respect due him as a citizen of the known. He is on trial for his alleged crimes, not serving his sentence. The restraints are a punishment."

…got to be kidding me! "Advocate, the moment Cassad escapes that bar he'll kill both you and me. Then try and take this ship out of atmo." I swap out my flight suit and jacket for more contemporary civilian gear and my old field jacket. "If he manages to get free of that bar… and he's done that once already… then I don't want him at his best."

"You're exaggerating. Cassad understands his fate." Eboro says but I can see the doubt in her body language.

"Right." I roll my eyes as I move past her into the engine access hatchway. "The king of the known is just gonna give up to the rabble of the New Regime for your 'bright future'."

Morgan city, seven city levels beneath Abatan City on the Nezerian Tower. It's the bottom level city in more ways than one. It's dirty, at least the inner districts are. A lot of the Tower workers live here as well as the land dock workers. This is where you go if you want to get into Nezerian Tower without a lot of security red tape.

The Adams section is a small port receiving district just off the river. I can smell the water as I the tram I'm on gets closer. Deep as we are in the city and late as it is on this planets sunside there's very little natural light here.

I adjust my visor, which I have configured to project a false holo of natural eyes instead of the ghost ones. Can't be too careful.

Of course that doesn't throw off the two heavies I've got tailing me.

I zeroed them easy but they clearly don't care to be inconspicuous, not scoping me the way they are. They're armed and aren't really hiding the bulges beneath their mech fatigues very well.

So I hop off the tram at the first stop in the Adams district and my two escorts follow. At no time do they make any attempt to contact me or even direct me to where I'm supposed to go. Not that they have to, even as we approached from the tram I could see there's only one place of note in the Adams district; a club called "the Pitt".

The facility used to be a water processing plant, it's suspended over the river by thick cables and connected to the city proper by wide hanging walkways. It's appropriately raucous outside the club with the party spilling out onto upper decks and the wide bridges. The party goers look like a working crowd. I don't see any exotics and my visor isn't picking up any more than the usual amount of arms so there's not a lot of violent criminal activity here.

I cross the walkway and join the crowd just outside the door when finally one of my escort walks up to me.

"This way." And he leads me around the crowd to a side door, not a VIP entrance, more like the opening to a service way. The two sandwich me in the tight corridor beyond the door and we make our way up into the building. My visor throws up an alert, goes dark and the ghost eye holos switch on automatically; there are proximity mines in the ceiling; a trick the 46th learned on an Irlon controlled outpost.

Starting to feel like home.

The corridor ends after a long walk up and opens into a lush, dimly lit VIP balcony overlooking the club. The noise and music is deadened by the thin tinted bubble screen hanging three feet beyond the railing but it also makes the air in the lounge stale. Smells like binding. The screen also keeps anyone down below from I.D.ing those in the VIP.

There are several plush sofas… enough for a pretty large party by itself but the only person in the room is standing by the balcony rail. Omega…Major Jhan Ayrs, my former Flight Commander…the guy that put the 46th together…trained me…and on more than one occasion saved my life. Last time I saw him, Omega was so shot up I swore the only thing holding him together was his bio-weave.

Looks like he got better… and yea… he's been hitting the weights. He's decked out pretty nice though; no gear, just some slick dark dress civvies. Like he actually came to this club to party.

"So you showed up." Omega says. He unfolds those big arms and walks across the balcony to meet me. I turn off the holo on my visor.

"I figured it would be better than you coming to the port." I look past him and see that one of my escorts has taken up a flanking position on the other side of the balcony, in front of a dimly lit doorway filled with more tough faces; mercs I don't know…members of the FireHawks. They're glaring at me, hands on weapons…not drawn but definitely ready to burn.

Omega extends his hand. I take it and get pulled into a quick hug.

"You never fail to impress me, Picker." Picker; my call sign when I was in the Four-Six.

"How's that, O?"

"Cassad?" he's grinning, almost prideful. "How on styx did you track him down?"

"Recon." Again I look about pointedly, taking in the mercs I don't know. They're carrying Bradshaws 12's; Welt rifles, and wearing pretty good armor under their field jackets.

"So you weren't with the other crew on the *Njaro*?" he asks.

Other crew? Doesn't matter to me. "What do you want, Omega?"

The smile on his face fades a bit. "Our cut."

If I'd had any bit of a smile going it's gone now. "Cut? Of what?"

"How do you think you got through Maren?" he asks.

"You sent them the vid feed of my capture of Cassad to get a cut in the bounty?"

"We helped get Cassad," comes from behind me in a thick Arcadian Farlands accent. Fek…didn't see him come into the room; Bounty, the short, stubby, pasty, beady eyed former leader of *Monster,* my first squad. Back in the *Blade* he would post and pay out bounties on enemy commanders. Like Omega, he's gained weight since the end of the war, just not in muscle. His baggy civvies don't hide the bulge of his big sidearm or his wide belly roll. How'd his fat ass sneak in here?

"No. You. Didn't." I tell him flat out.

"You owe us, Loren," he spits. Behind him stands a copper colored Braider with black tipped shingles. It's big… and likely an ex-con if I know Bounty.

"I didn't ask you for fek," I spit back.

"So you're gonna cut us out?" Omega asks.

"Don't play me, Omega."

"You really think you were going to get through Maren without our help?"

"I wasn't at the buckin' gate 'cause I thought I couldn't get through, O."

"You were two AUs from being blown outta the sky." Bounty again with his big ass mouth.

"I had it handled. Didn't ask for your help."

"So…" Omega says calmly, that smile creeping back up on his face. "…you gonna cut us out?"

Omega has always had me scouted. He knows I'm grateful they covered me at Maren. Still…I bet it's not just a cut he wants.

"What do you want, O"

"Cassad."

What? I look from him to Bounty and back again. Is that what they're thinking? "You don't think that's gonna happen."

"You want get paid don't you?" he says with way too much confidence. I don't answer, I just wait for him to explain 'cause I'm sure he's got something figured.

"You gotta take Cassad to Deggar after the trial," he tells me. "That's where they have the payment."

"So?" how the buck did he know that?

"So…" Bounty cuts in. "Deggar is controlled by the Nth Consortium. Run by a guy named Alt, former Median space gangster. He's not gonna turn fifty million qed over to you, Loren."

"He'll just gut your ass, take Cassad and keep the coin." That comes from one of the mercs I don't know, standing by the door.

"And?"

"Picker," Omega. "Alt would try you. He won't try us when we arrive with a small fleet of ships."

"So," He's got a point there. "What are you offering for Cassad?"

"Depends," Bounty again. "…on what we figure you already owe us for getting you through Maren and..."

"And what?"

"And for Showboat, Bingo and Half-Head," he says with dark eyes. Showboat had been his Second in *Monster*; his last squad.

This could be a problem. "You can kill that fek right now. I don't owe you anything. And any debts I had with Showboat, Bingo and Half-Head… I already settled."

"You killed your own brothers, Loren!" Bounty opens up on me, walking right up to me and pointing a stubby finger in my face. "You betrayed men who you fought side by side with and…"

"And," I look down into his small eyes. "…men I once killed ticket-boys and stompers side by side with too."

His braider buddies bristle a bit at this.

"He killed Seida," says the merc at the doorway behind me. Hard, squinting eyes…looks Welt. He's talking about the Giak I took down while capturing Cassad.

"When did the Four-Six start running with boots and longnecks?" I demand.

"This ain't the ADF, Picker." Omega says. ""We're the FireHawks and you killed one of ours."

"The stomper went berserker on my mark."

"Buck this waste, Omega! Why are we…" the merc says.

"Not now." Omega doesn't shout but his voice shuts the guy up.

"Ain't we getting' off topic?" says the other merc.

"Yea, we was talkin' about takin' Cassad off of this waste!"

Omega picks up a holo pad and a display of the prison planet Deggar rises in perfect three dimensional clarity off of its surface. "Give us Cassad. We've got the strength to actually get the coin from them."

He's right. Deggar is a whole other batch of problems for me he could solve right now. But I've already sunk coin into this venture.

"What's your offer?"

"We'll give you five million for Cassad."

"You want Forty-Five million in Old Reg just to ship him? YOU didn't catch him, O."

"We pretty much did, Loren, you just snuck past us to grab him," says Bounty.

"Forty," I say. "And I'm not haggling. It's forty or I go get the fifty myself."

"Not haggling?" Omega smiles that same old smile. The smile he had when he first interviewed me for the 46th Task Force. Almost like he was proud of me. He once said it was 'cause we were both from the Tri-

Valley in Libertine…on Arcadia.

"We'll go ten and no more," he says.

"Then you know what my answer is." I turn and head back the way I came. "We're done."

"You ain't going nowhere, Loren," Bounty spits, moves to block my path and is joined by the big merc, who escorted me in and the braider. Should've recognized them when I first saw them; Bounty's Boys. Back in the *Blade* Bounty always picked the biggest soldiers for his squad.

They try their best to intimidate me with that Bounty Boy swagger and I try my best not to laugh in their faces. I was one of the original Bounty Boys and it looks like he's lowered his standards.

"Step aside."

The braider actually speaks for them, rolling it's tongue and clicking its teeth into its approximation of human vocal tones. "Make us."

"You gotta answer for the deaths of our brothers, Loren." Bounty is red faced. Never seen him this mad before. Showboat was one of his picks and even though Bounty always favored the bigger, tougher guys, he doted on the little bastard.

"Last time I'm gonna say this; back off, Bounty," Omega orders and the Braider and the other merc stand down, retreating to the far edges of the balcony leaving Bounty alone blocking my path.

"Omega, what on styx??" Bounty is screaming.

"They were about to draw on Loren, Bounty," He says.

"So??"

A little angry, Omega locks eyes with Bounty. "He's Four-Six."

But Bounty is as fearless as they come…about as stupid too. "Yea? And what was Showboat?" he shouts. "And Bingo? Or Half-Head?"

Omega turns that glare on me. "Well, Picker?"

Even with the club raging below the room gets damn quiet.

"You don't want to know what they were." He doesn't…I wish I didn't. There's a longer moment of silence until Bounty erupts again.

"You piece of fek!"

"Get him out of here," Omega orders. For a moment Bounty's crew looks to balk but only for a moment then they grab their squad commander by the arms and drag him, cussing and fighting, off the balcony. "I'm gonna burn you down, Loren!"

"Same old Bounty," I tell Omega and again turn to leave.

"You were his favorite, Picker."

"No I wasn't."

"I got one more piece of business, Loren." There's a darkness in his tone that I can't ignore. Plus I didn't expect him to back off on trying to get Cassad so now I'm worried.

"What's that?"

"You won't deal us in? Then I need a favor." Omega subvocalizes, sending a transmission to someone outside.

"What kind of favor, O?" He held this back so it's gotta be worse than trying to buck me out of fifty million qed.

"I need access to Cassad."

"What for?"

His only answer is to look past me to the balcony entrance. In walks Gray, a tall Arcadian who used to be in the Rescue unit of the 46th. No longer is she wearing the distinctive red and white armor of a field medic, Gray is dressed in N'Rin modern half robes but I can tell she's got body armor on underneath as well. She nods to me as if it hasn't been cycles since we last saw each other.

Back in the Four-Six she was always tied at the hip to…Madigan. Wonder if he joined the FireHawks too.

Gray's dragging in a hooded woman, wrists locked behind her back with binders, who has obviously been through a gauntlet. Her clothes are torn and burned in some places and there are bruises all over her exposed skin. Gray walks the woman right over to us and Omega yanks the hood off. Even beaten, wild haired and bruised she holds her chin up defiantly.

Breer.

She blinks a few times as she takes in Omega and then, after looking about the rest of the lounge, she notices me.

"Lieutenant? …I hate to bring this up again, but…"

CHAPTER TEN:

Breer STUCK

"Get her out of here, O!"

"Hear me out, Pick." Omega already has his hands up trying to calm me.

"What? She told you about Osage so you think you can trust…?"

"Let me talk, Pick!"

"She's a Taj Pirate!"

"I know!"

"She's doesn't know fek!"

"All damn it, Loren! I KNOW!"

Breer tries to shrug free of Grays grasp only to get jerked back harshly. "I do know about Osage. I was there!"

"Shut your mouth!" Omega and I say in unison.

Omega stares her down. "We know all we need to know about Osage. Loren told us."

"He…he…killed your people…" Breer is taken aback by Omega's fierce glare.

"He did what needed to be done." he says gravely and looks to me. I can see the pain in his eyes now…he already knew about Osage.

"Omega," I take a breath and grind the memory out of my head for a moment knowing it'll be back during my next sleep shift. "If you know then why is she here?"

He clenches his jaw…in embarrassment? "There's an encrypted file in the Daliun Security Hub. The file has information on the Daliun development of synthetic cells."

"I…" Does he mean the bomb? "…the…?"

"Yup."

All damn it! I'm not getting into this! Arcadia is gone. "So? What's that got to do with her?"

"I want her to get it for me."

"What??" Breer and I say in unison.

Omega turns back to her. "I'll give you access to Cassad if you can get me that file."

"Omega, YOU don't have access to Cassad," I tell him.

"I need that file, Picker. WE need that file."

"What for? You tryin' to clear us? After how many cycles?"

He narrows his eyes at me now. "You saw them. Giaks are joining the Coalition. Soon enough they'll be in a truce with the Junns. The Four-Six needs to return before then to protect the system."

"The system doesn't need a bunch of burnt out mercs, Omega. It needs a fleet." I tell him and again it seems as though the club gets quiet.

"Is that why you went after the bounty, Picker?" Omega asks. "To buy a fleet? Fifty million in Old reg is enough to put together a pretty impressive fleet in Eastspace. A good start to protecting Arcadia."

"There is no Arcadia."

"Then why do you want the money?"

"Cause it's money," I say. "What makes you think she can get that file?"

"You can get access to the Daliun Security Hub from their embassy here on New Beia," he explains but it's not enough.

"What makes you think she can get access to that? She was the reason the Taj got fragged in the first place. She bucked up the hacking job on…fek! O, she's got Lott and his crew lookin' for her."

Omega grimaces again and looks sidelong at Breer. She smirks.

"It wasn't a bad hack," she argues. "Lott made a good guess. And your Captain knows I can do it because I got into the FireHawks."

"What?"

Breer laughs in a hard, mocking bark, "Ha! I broke into their base ship."

"You have a base ship?" I ask, a little impressed.

"An old Cassad Firebird, we snatched it from a merc gang who snatched it right out of a Giak decommissioning yard."

"Good ship," I say. If Breer infiltrated them on a Firebird then she really had stepped up her skill set. Never the less, "So she broke into your ship and you think that means she can get inside the Junns embassy?"

"I think she can give it a shot."

We both turn and look at her. Breer glares back at us defiantly. "I want to see Cassad first."

"Nope." What do I look like?

"Why would I…"

"You get what Omega wants…and you get an audience with Cassad." She'll never get it.

"Why should I trust you?"

Now, finally, I turn to leave for what had better be the last time. "Trust ME? I never played with the memories of YOUR dead friends."

CHAPTER ELEVEN:

WITNESSES FOR THE DEFENSE

The next few days of the trial go pretty much the same. Evidence is given in grandiose fashion. It reminds me a bit of Union Day on Arcadia with all the dais presentations. The trial is stopped twice because of some commotion going on outside the hall and twice more for something the Prim won't talk to us about. Whatever it was, it kept her off of my back during that time and the trial moved on to the defense stage.

It was ugly. Unlike the witnesses testifying about the horrors and crimes of the Cassad Empire, who were brought in with pageantry and splendor, the witnesses giving testimony on behalf of Cassad were brought into the court… into the arena, in chains.

Taking their cue from the chain I had on Cassad I guess, the prisoners were bound hand, foot and neck by oversized and deliberately rusted manacles.

They'd been beaten.

They'd been tortured.

The first witness is a woman, a tall ex-magistrate from a Ziara Colony that I miss hearing the name of when they announced her. The Subjucarious was set to testify first but word was he was killed in the Nerum attack.

That's hoofer-fek. He was probably assassinated. Wonder what he might have said at trial?

I'm struck by the fact that this woman was magistrate of practically an entire world and now she was being dragged to the center of the Hall by two Coalition guards, bruised about her face and wearing clothes she clearly had been in for at least a month.

Her name is Cleona Wilmana and from the outrage of the crowd at her appearance and the dark look in the First Equals eye she won't survive this testimonial.

The lights go dark in the arena save, again, for the spotlight on Cassad which has taken on red tones, the light on Wilmana which also has red in its spectrum and now the white light on the Coalition representative, Conin. She walks across the black sand in her long one piece, New Regime gown until her light almost touches the victims…I mean witness'.

"State your name," she commands. The lights orbiting her headdress pulse in rhythm with her voice.

Wilmana stares at her, trying and failing to conceal her fear. Her voice quivers a bit. "Magistrate Cleona Wilmana…"

"No prisoner," Conin cuts her off. Her tone is soft, filled with false sympathy and dripping with condescension. "You are no longer a magistrate."

Wilmana has the good sense to stay quiet and wait for Conin to ask her next question.

"You WERE the Magistrate of the Ziara colony on Phaestus, correct?"

"Yes," she admits. She's staring down Conin, but out of fear. She's afraid to look away.

"The Phaestus Colony provided the Cassad Empire with support during the liberation of the Cassad sector, is that right?"

"Yes," she stammers a bit. "…we…we were a Cassad world. We had to defend our..."

"And as Magistrate," Conin cut her off. "you ordered your Colony's militia against the 3rd Coalition Expeditionary Force?"

"…they were invading," she pleads.

"You were given the option, were you not, to have those forces turn back without reprisal?" Conin takes a step forward. The pulsing lights circling her headdress change colors from New Regime to blood red.

"We were ordered to defend our sector." Wilmana eyes grow even wider, more pleading.

"No, former magistrate, YOU gave the orders." The lights now pulse out of sequence, and increase their pace towards…

I lean forward and whisper to Eboro, "She's about to kill her."

"Representative Conin?" Eboro asks loudly and abruptly. "I thought this witness was to give testimony for Minister Cassad?"

The Valian, Conin, turns and gives Eboro a murderous look, which then shifts to that false a sympathetic look, which she holds for several pulse beats before returning to Wilmana.

"What was your standing order, Former Magistrate Wilmana, in regards to Coalition forces entering the gravitational boundary of Orun?"

"We were ordered to send ships to intercept and repel rebel forces if the Kupier sensor suite reported a breach," she says.

"Who gave the standing order?"

For the first time, the ex-magistrate looks away from Conin and looks toward our small illuminated group, to Cassad.

"The order was given by the Ziara Defense Commander in Chief, Alaafin of the Empire, Cassad himself," she says with wide sorrowful eyes. She's not talking about this Cassad, she means Ose, his father. Khalid Cassad wasn't in the system during the attack.

"And what was your response when the Expeditionary Force passed through the Kupier boundary of Orun?"

"I ordered Phaestus ships to join the Ziaran forces already there to help defend the system," Wilmana says quietly.

"Did not the Coalition liberators give you the option to call them back?" Conin asks.

"er…yes, the Coalition commander…issued us a…directive, but we were under…"

"And despite that you sent the ships anyway?" Conin presses on.

"I…yes…we were defending…"

"The forces you sent crippled two Coalition ships, killing more than one hundred fifty Liberation personnel?" She phrased it as a question.

"…I'm not sure what the results were of the battle at the boundary," Wilamana admitted.

"The results of your support of the treacherous Cassad Empire was death, Former Magistrate…" for a pulse beat, Conin looks about the arena then, "…IS death!"

Faster than my eye can follow those lights strike, extending their orbits far enough to reach Wilmana and then just as suddenly they return to Conins headdress and their New Regime colors. The only evidence of their passing…Wilmana's head drops to the sand a full five pulse beats ahead of her collapsing body.

"Council!" Eboro shouts, both angry and horrified at the same time. "This is…This… How am I supposed to cross examine the witness?"

For the moment, Conin stares down at the body and head of the former Magistrate, and appears to be holding in her extreme satisfaction. Then she looks up toward the Council. "My apologies Council, we shall strike her testimony from the record..."

She turns and looks back across the sand at us... at Cassad. "...in the name of fairness," she says in that false sympathetic tone.

Several more witnesses are brought before the council dragging this whole thing on and on. Now, however, Eboro is allowed to question them before the New Regime Reps, who rotate chances at questioning them. She attempts to lead their testimony toward their own innocence, as well as being sure to mention that her charge, Khalid Cassad was not the Emperor.

"...and has not in fact been named Alaafin by any Cassad authority," she finishes.

It doesn't help. One after another they are all questioned then executed. It's grisly; the black sand shines with blood. All the while Cassad watches impassively, showing little regard for the lives being taken. Then...

It's not much, just the slightest twitch of his eye; Cassad's only reaction this entire time... to the next witness being brought out.

My first thought is that this guy must be borged or an alien because he's brought into the arena accompanied by an attendant and locked inside some kind of full body harness. But his face is exposed; old and wrinkled, the guy is clearly an elder human no matter how many cycles he actually might have lived. Who or what could he be to warrant such over the top security measures?

There's a bit of an uproar from the Brython section of the stands. A mix of awe and... anger maybe? It doesn't give me a clue to this guy's identity. Neither does the reaction of the Brython rep, Edins. He's in a heated argument with the Denir rep while trying to gain access to the council section.

As the witness is brought closer I can see that the full body harness is actually a complex life support system. There are nutrient pods lined along the sides and a standard medical terminal mounted on his chest plate. The whole unit is streamlined and fits his body like a glove but the frame keeps him stiff as a board. I've seen this before...he's...

"Honor Lammergeier, Averator of the Cassad Empire," Eboro tells me. An Averator? Ok...yea; the Cassads' top thinkers are given the title of "Averator" once their genius or accomplishment met some big brain criteria. There was an Averator who held a position on Arenn in the Arcadian system. Pretty sure he birded home once the ELE dropped. This guy, Lammergeier…he's pretty well known I think…he's trapped in the body harness because he's suffering from some kind of radiation sickness. Not sure why it's not treatable but he's not getting out of that thing. Hmm… guy like him should be too valuable to execute.

"A strange last minute addition to the witness list," Eboro looks worried. "I'm not sure why."

Lammergeier is attended to by a bogey, an A.I. 'droid designed to look like a human male. It's an older model, looks almost too old to have still been in service to the Empire and it's been done up to look like an elder as well. There are black age dots peppering the dark brown skin of his face, giving it an almost innocent look. The bogey's got a large mane of silver white hair with two or three beaded braid lengths dangling from its temples, but the meaning is unfamiliar to me. The old 'bot is dressed simply in civilian attire, not marking it as anything special in the Cassad political machine or even as a medical attendant.

Eboro steps across the arena, careful to stop where the blood stained sand begins. She accesses a holo, displaying for all to see the name and position of the witness.

"Honor Lammergeier," she states formally. "Grand member of the Royal Society of Brython…former. Knight of the Realm of Brython…former."

The Brython section of the arena becomes raucous and Eboro has to project her voice to continue to be heard. "Appointed Oye of Mathematical Theory, Ziaran Circle of the Mind. A position you currently hold, sir?"

Lammergeier does not move; he can't but his eyes hold a strong defiance in them. The bogey reaches out and places its hand in a small cleft at the shoulder of the body brace. At once its body language changes and it stands a little taller. Then it speaks with a voice that does not match its appearance in the least.

"Yes, Advocate, I currently hold the position of Oye of Mathematical Theory given to me by the former Allafin, Ose Cassad." The android is acting as Lammergeiers voice. Why would they use a bogey as such an awkward proxy? Wait…there's a fair amount of damage done to his body brace. Could be they tore up his speech tech when they captured him.

"However," The Averator explains. "The title of 'Knight of the Realm', given to me by King Brython himself, cannot be revoked once given."

There's another outcry from the Brython section. Some are screaming "shamed" down from the stands. Eboro tries to barrel through.

"Why did the Alaafin grant you the title of Averator?"

The bogey tilts its head. "Alaafin Ose Cassad granted me the title and position of Averator after I published 'Known to Unknown'. He called me to Ziara to confer and consult on the expansion of the empire."

"That will be more than enough!" The Brython rep, Lord Edins is marching across the sand followed by his own security force. "This witness was never approved by the council!"

Even as his group makes its way toward the circle of light the Averator sits in there's a stirring in the stands behind them. More of the delegates are headed into the arena and the whole crowd seems to be anticipating a clash.

They're probably right. Gotta watch them closely…can't let one of these overzealous rebels get past me to Cassad.

There's a Marajeshi group stepping onto the sand behind a lone Green Fed rep, who looks over his shoulder… and proceeds to veer off to give them plenty of room. The Marajeshi come from an extremely isolated world and are known to carry deadly mutations of bacteria and pathogens. The leader of these Marajeshi is strong jawed woman with dark hair who's flanked by a small floating device that's throwing out scans of everyone in the area. Reads like a medical scanner…

"This witness was not requested by my office," Eboro states. "He is then free to leave as far as we are concerned."

"No," The Brython rep, Lord Edins, is glaring at the trapped Averator. "He will be returned to Brython to pay for his crimes against…"

"The Averator," the Marajesh woman steps into the circle of light and nearly everyone…save Edins and his personal security 'bots, step away. "…is a prisoner of Marajeshi."

In the light now it's apparent that she's an elder but maybe only by a few cycles depending on how long the Marajeshi live. Dressed in flowing robes she appears as any delegate but I can still see the tight containment suit poking out at her neck and wrists. There's a pretty sophisticated filter system pulling in the air around her head. How can such open system protect anyone from exposure? Or maybe that's the point. I wonder if my military grade nanobodies can handle whatever it is she's carrying.

"…Sublimator Mallon?" Edins snaps his fingers sharply and the closest of his personal security 'bots produces an embroidered white cloth square. Edins snatches it up then places it over his nose and mouth like a mask.

The tact net in my helmet picks up some low level tech in that cloth. Probably acts as filter and more, which he's gonna need. The Marajeshi Sublimators are high level operators; security, assassinations… all kinds of Special Operations I think. While the people of Marajesh are dangerous because they're plague carriers, the Sublimators are particularly dangerous because they use the pathogens they carry to kill… at least according to rumor. Edins takes a wise step back behind his service bot. I stop myself from leaning back like everyone else but I keep checking my filter sensors for alerts.

…though I doubt they'll be able to catch anything the Sublimator is throwing out. I look to the passive Averator…he seems fine at least. Makes sense though; if he's been in Marajesh custody all this time they would have given him whatever inoculations were necessary.

"The Marajeshi have no right to imprison Brython citizens," Edins argues.

"The Averator," The Sublimator, Mallon, throws a disdainful look at the Brythons cloth covered face. "…was captured by our forces during the freeing of Ziara. He was given Ziaran citizenship by Ose himself. That makes him an enemy combatant. That makes him ours." She's got a peaceful, almost humble manner but it's laced with an unstated menace. Everyone here knows her very presence is a threat.

Save for Cassad. His eyes are on her but only when most are watching him. More often he looks to the captured Brython. Can't help to wonder where the value is; in what the man knows or what he might be able to figure out? Could be some profit there if Cassad is more worried about welfare of a scientist rather than the threat of getting infected by the Marajesh woman.

"You…" Edins points a stark white finger at the Sublimator. "…will leave this area at once, lest your cursed blood foul this arena and sicken Cassad before his judgment."

Without answering Mallon turns to the small floating device that's fliting about her. It breaks off its erratic orbit and floats over toward Edins. The med scans don't get any more intense of invasive but that doesn't mean its passive scans haven't changed. After a few pulses the face of the device lights up yellow.

"Please keep your distance, Lord Edins," Mallon says simply. "While we find a solution to our disagreement."

The little med scanner floats past the Brython security 'bots without pausing and makes its way over to Eboro. A little sooner than it had flashed yellow for Edins it now flashes bright red in the Advocates face and emits a series of warning beeps.

"What does this mean?" Eboro asks nervously.

"It means," Edins hisses. "That this woman can kill you with her breath."

I can't help but notice how the rest of the Coalition Reps are willing to let this play out from a distance. Even the First equal, who watches impassively, keeps his distance. Maybe it doesn't matter to him how Cassad dies as long as it's done.

"You will be fine, Advocate Eboro. I will do you no harm." The Sublimator placed a slight emphasis on "you". Eboro never the less retreats behind Cassad and I.

The device then makes its way over to me and after a few long pulses it flashes no warning light at all, letting me know that Marajesh tech can't read through my armor. There's a quiet murmur from the arena at that but Mallon doesn't seem the least bit surprised.

Finally the device hovers before Cassad who eyes it dismissively. The face lights up bright green and it moves back to Mallon.

"Interesting," she says. "I've never seen a safe reading outside of treated Ambassadors."

"Perhaps you should all have this discussion away from the accused and the witnesses," Eboro says over my shoulder. She's stretched her oversized sleeves over her nose and mouth.

"I agree," Edins pronounces. "Security, take Lammergeier into custody." At once the small contingent of Brython security 'bots begin to move, spreading out and producing arms.

"Lord Brython," Mallon slides her hands out of view beneath her robes and my Tact net flashes a vague weapons alert. Her own security force raise arms as well. “You will become accustomed to the fact that the Averator is under the protection of the Marajeshi.”

What in styx end is Edins thinking? Buckin’ pampered Brython privilege! He figures those ‘bots are gonna handle this fight for him but his pride’s been too insulted for him realize that if any of the Marajeshi suits are breached in a firefight then we’re all dead.

I extend my wings in a snap; got to get Cassad out of here…

“HOLD!”

Finally! Galvin Onted steps in between the advancing Brython ‘bots and the Marajeshi. “Lord Edins you will recall your security force!”

“Lammergeier is a fugitive of the Brython Kingdom. He will stand before god, Lord Brython and the Prime Cathol for his crimes or…” Edins words, though heartfelt are somewhat muffled by his makeshift mask.

“The Council has decided,” the First Equal announces. At once everyone on the arena floor looks up to the ring of suites housing the seven major powers of the New Regimes Coalition. The Brython suite is full of activity while the Marajesh suite is opaque.

Without an order from Edins the Brython ‘bots, save for one lone personal attendant ‘bot, stop and retreat back to the edges of the arena. Edins shoulders drop a bit and he turns and glares daggers at Mallon.

Galvin doesn’t give them a chance to continue arguing. “Sublimator Mallon, you will remove the witness so that we may continue with the trial.”

The Sublimator nods passively, then, followed by the attendant and Averator, she exits the arena floor.

Edins snaps his fingers at his own attendant ‘bot and they walk briskly toward the far exit.

“We will continue the proceedings next sunside,” Galvin says to Eboro, then he shouts to someone far outside the witness spotlight before making his exit. “Sanitize the area!”

Beneath us the bunker rises up out of the sand as the Lion lady announces, “The witness is dismissed.” And for the first time, one of the prisoners testifying for Cassad and the Empire survives.

Get out.

CHAPTER TWELVE:

BREER TRIUMPHANT

The survival of the witness must have thrown off the Council a bit. The sunside after, the trial is recessed. Probably everyone who came within arm's length of the Sublimator wanted to get themselves checked out. I take the opportunity to inspect *WarChild's* hull. The demonstrators, media and other groups scream questions and threats at me but security keeps them all away, just beyond a thin rail. The crazies with the faux "visors" are thick in the crowd as well with one particularly raunchy and naked group whistling lurid invitations. It's like Free Day on Niera Prime.

On my visors H.U.D. I keep watch on a small virtual monitor of Eboro in the prep bay with Cassad, while I check for damage. There's some minor new growth which is easy to chip away, but no scoring or compromises. I do find a bunch of crumpled up tech-bots; infiltration units used to spy and sabotage vehicles and tech outposts. They couldn't deal with the cete-armor, looks like or more likely they couldn't survive the countless counter measures being waved through the port right now. Either way, *WarChild* is still secure.

"Arcadian."

Whoa! I turn and see the Prim standing not forty decimeters away. She smirks, showing that she knows she caught me off guard. But by more than just her sudden appearance; the Coalition armor is gone, as are her ceremonial weapons. In their place she's wearing a thin one piece day dress, which clings to her body outlining every curve of her body. Her hair is no longer pulled back and tied so that her Nez SeC head gear can fit. Now her thick locks gambol about her head in a free but not wild mane. There's fresh wound sealant on her shoulder reminding me that she got tore up in the Nerum attack as well… which just adds to how impressive she looks.

She pads over to me on soft sandals that lace all the way up her calves.

"Arcadian from the 46th Task Unit of the now defunct Arcadian Defense Force…" she says looking me up and down. I knew it was only a matter of time before she I.D.ed me.

"The 46th who are blamed for the loss of your own home world," she continues and begins to circle me, her eyes looking me up and down from visor to boot. "Though, officially, Arcadia only filed charges of Deserting During a Time of War and…"

Slowly, carefully and with a look to me as if asking permission, the Prim touches my arm at the bicep and holds it there.
"…insubordination. No charges of murder or mass geneocide?"

I look down at her hand on my arm, take a peek at the ample amount of cleavage she's showing, then back up to her eyes. "You should ask the Arcadian War Crimes Unit instead of me."

"I did," she nods. "When I sent the request for your file."

"And?" I actually can't help but to wonder.

"And while they confirmed that you were in the 46th Task Force under the command of the deceased…Tavarez, they would not even tell me your name let alone give me your file."

"If all you wanted was my name you didn't have to go to the A.D.F." Guess her contacts aren't as good as the Old Denir Royal Guard. He got my name in the time it took to order a drink.

"Oh, I want more than your name. Arcadian stock has gone up since you arrived."

"What?"

"Surely you've seen the griotales? Since it was discovered that it was an Arcadian who captured Cassad, interest in your people has risen, then…" she squeezes my arm gently but firmly, feeling the mechanics muscles just beneath the skin.

"…after your battle with the meta-morphs in the arena and the vid of you staring down the Giaks outside the Hall landed on the Hub…well who wouldn't want to see a little Arcadian D.N.A. in their gene pool now?"

Uh…huh?

"But I think that there is something special about you, Mercenary. So I'd like for you to honor me."

"Honor you?"

"My position is secure," she says while placing her other hand on my other bicep. "I am well past due to produce and you, Arcadian, are healthy, clearly intelligent and…well made."

All Damn, it's been too long. She stands on tip toe as she slides her hands up to my shoulders…and I… I'm just letting her.

"I think we would make a good match." She says

"If you've researched Arcadia," I say through clenched teeth. She's not Arcadian…but she's about as forward as an Arcadian woman. "Then you know how we are about our children."

She lowers a bit to her heels in disappointment. "Yes, I read you acata are 'Blood Bound' to your children."

Then she rises to her toes again, her eyes narrowing and her hands slide up to my visor which she begins to lift gently until she can just see my real eyes. "But perhaps we might still show each other exactly how well made we are?"

I'm can feel her breath fluttering against my lips…can just smell the gray orchid oil she's rubbed into her skin… when *WarChild* sends my visor a proximity warning on weapons. The port alert flashes just as I see the Daliuns have sent another delegation.

Whoa…this time they mean business.

The large group proceeds past the docking rail and the Nez SeC stops them briefly then lets them approach without getting clearance from me or the Prim.

Last time they were here it was a smaller party. This time Junn Lord Lan Derai has come himself… along with his wife.

All damn he's tall, at least twenty-two decimeters so he stands almost a full head taller than me and two heads taller than the rest of his delegation…except for his wife.

She's just a decimeter taller than I am. Their height is supposed to be an indication of how old they are. Like the Irlons, it's said the Junn Lords never stop growing. Daliuns are usually much shorter than Arcadians. These two may be a few hundred years old...maybe more.

And they look ancient, but not elderly. Their skin is like smooth porcelain and just as pale, as if someone drained the blood from their bodies. Like I've seen in people who've had their lives lengthened through treatment, their eyes are both washed out and gray. But they're faces are perfect; the best symmetry augmentation cred can buy.

Both of them are wearing Daliun colors, blue on white robes with the matching metal headdresses they'd had on at the trial framing their faces.

They're not walking; the Ambassador and his wife are standing on low hovering service pads. It's the rest of their delegation; the two women who had come to the port before, a small group of veiled women tending to the wife and now several Daliun Pretty boy guards, who have to walk. At least Nez SeC is relieving them of their weapons.

The ones they can find.

The Prim quickly steps away to address one of the security personel. She must have taken a bit of official leave to come down here to talk to me or else she would have been alerted that the Junns were coming to the port. She looks about as happy as I feel having to deal with the approaching Junns.

I head out to meet them, wanting to halt them before they get too close to my ship. My Sever is on my hip…good.

"Greetings again, Arcadian," the two female reps still speak in unison though now they both appear to be quite nervous It shows as they have to raise their voices a bit over the boisterous crowd of onlookers surrounding the hangar deck. "May we present to you Lord Lan Derai Ambassador of the Daliun people and Governess Lan Uwin, his wife."

"I've already spoken to your two mouth pieces." I point at the two double talking Daliun women, who look somewhat embarrassed.

"Lord Lan Derai thought it best to come himself," the two blonds say. Then their voices add just a hint of threat. "To impress upon you his most grave intent to speak with Cassad."

"He thought it best?" I look Derai up and down. "I've never accused the Junns of having the sense the All gave a rock. The price for an audience with Cassad hasn't changed."

Derai doesn't as much as blink. He and his wife look down at me with a mix of disdain and…something else…

The two women answer for him. "But the situation has."

"I don't see it that way." I keep my eyes on him and Derai just stares back into my visor undaunted.

"We recognized the armor you wear. Something we are sure you hated to have to reveal but we understand circumstances demanded it." Derai is still stone faced and silent, it's his wife that finally speaks.

"As I assured you, husband," Lan Uwin says, her voice bitter and haughty. "meeting with the Arcadian criminal is simply a waste of our time."

She watches for my reaction with a large insect-like glare but she's not gonna get one through the "ghost" eyes of my visor. Lan Derai, subtlety squeezes her hand but shows no other sign of life as he remains silent.

A small icon flashes on my heads up display;

WARNING: SUBPERCEPTION TRANSMISSION DETECTED…

…TRANSMISSION NEUTRALIZED…

Looks like the Junns are trying to influence me with some bio-waves, an old trick. Lucky my visor is just as old so it managed to catch it.

The two blonds jump in again. "We of course respect the now famed hero who captured the Alaafins son, Khalid. You are no criminal here on New Beia."

"But he is in Eastspace," she corrects them.

"We're not in the Quad now," I direct this to Lan Uwin, letting the bright whites of my holographic eyes meet her large black pupils. My hatred of the Junns hasn't abated not one bit in the years since the ELE attack. Just looking at her is giving me a headache.

"No, we are not, Arcadian." For the first time, it seems, Uwin is actually talking to me instead of about me. And there's an added bit of menace in her voice so I guess she got that I was threatening them. But the moment seems to pass as Uwin waves off her Pretty-boy guards and steps off her platform. As she approaches me, her long, bare legs slide in and out of her blue and silver gown with each step. They're shockingly white but end with flame red paint on the toe nails of her bare feet. "We are deep in Coalition space, far from this mercenary's mud pit of a world."

She looks me up and down, "That he managed to capture Khalid… I find that… inconceivable."

Now there's less than a meters distance between us. I could pull my Sever in less than a pulse beat and…

"The… proud Arcadians…" The two mouth pieces begin to stumble over their words, though still in unison. "… have always managed to be surprisingly adept at beating the odds. You are no different. And while our two peoples have often found ourselves with challenging disagreements…"

"And yet," Uwin cuts in with that sharp contempt, her voice burrowing into my buckin' skull like an arrow-toothed Digger. "…he is of the same group of Arcadians responsible for the burning of their own world."

"Governess…" The two blonds try to stem Uwins' obvious lack of tact.

"Junn," I say. "We both know who's responsible for what happened to Arcadia." It's been cycles…but their arrogance…their expectation of privilege… I'm so buckin' sick of it!

Her eyes actually open a bit with surprise, an expression she must not have made for many years. For the brief second she allows herself the lapse in composure her unbelievably smooth and marble like skin wrinkles horribly.

"Our need to speak with Cassad is great, Arcadian." The two mouth pieces try yet again. "Surely we can come to an… agreement?"

Their eyes go wide, as do the eyes of Uwin and even her husband, Lan Derai. Again their faces are horrible wrinkled masks, fixed in an expression of shock and offense, giving everyone a glimpse of their true nature. The Pretty-Boy guard detail all move hesitantly in their direction, but with their eyes on me…

"Arcadian!" The Prim shouts from behind me. Her voice echoes across the suddenly quiet hangar; the crowds surrounding the deck have gone silent.

Derai is staring hard at me, as is his wife but the blonds and the Pretty-boys are actually looking down a bit at…

Oh…when did I draw my gun?

How could I not notice pulling my own weapon? I look to Derai and my head begins to pound just a bit harder. His sneaky buckin' bio waves…they must be having an effect after all.

"You're gonna want to turn it off, Junn."

Without making a move Derai complies, the pressure on my temples drops instantly but I'm still hot. "Now get your asses away from my ship."

"Perhaps," a cool sultry voice cuts through the air. From behind the floating platform, one of Uwin's veiled handmaidens stands and walks forward. Neatly she bows before me.

"May I present myself to you, Master Arcadian?" Though veiled and robed the shape of her body is clearly defined through the sheer material.

"A gift for the Arcadian." Uwin says her contempt not so biting now that the subperception wave is off. She glances past me to regard the Prim. "We have seen what it takes to gain an invitation to board the mercenary's ship."

They're talking about my forcing the Prim and Eboro to disrobe when I first got here. They think that…

…is that what everyone has been thinking?

"Take your whore with you, Junn."

"Please, Master Arcadian," the woman says and lifts her veil. "allow me to provide service to you."

Buck me…Breer.

CHAPTER THIRTEEN:

CROSSING THE KING

"It was not easy." Breer tells me once I close the hatch. The Junns agreed to allow her to speak to Cassad on their behalf, to deliver a message and to receive his response in exchange for a small monetary bonus and of course…her services. The Prim wasn't too happy about that and stormed off herself.

And I'm not happy about that.

"Why did they agree to work with you? To trust you?" I ask Breer.

"They did not," she explains as I walk her through the ship. It's now that I notice that her speech patterns have changed. "They believe I am as you see, a lowly concubine, useful for only binding and delivering messages."

"You infiltrated the Dalian Embassy as a concubine in that little bit of time?"

"That part of it was not so difficult, Arcadian."

"The Junns are an overconfident bunch of elitists but Derai has got to be more than half a millennia old. He's no fool. New accent or not."

"No," she laughs a bit. "He's not stupid enough to just fall for proper Daliun speech patterns. But they are desperate. They are…they're in need of something Cassad has. Something of such importance…something so important… that they willing to side with the Cassads against the Coalition."

"What? That's insane. The Cassads are done. What do they need?" Anything the Junns want so desperately I want to know about.

"I do not know. I'm unable to decipher their coded message."

I grab her arm and stop her just outside the cargo bay. "Don't lie to me."

Her arm tightens and I feel her shift her weight as she instinctively prepares to strike me. Then she relaxes.

"I would tell you if I knew, Arcad…Lieutenant. During my brief time with the Junns I found them…there may not be a more vile people in the known."

Breer has indeed advanced her skill set. Infiltration…swapping dialects…new skills or old ones that she hid before? These skills probably include lying but I've seen the look that's now in her eyes before, in anyone who's seen what the Junns really are.

"Most people like the Junns." I say, releasing her arm.

"Yes," she admits. "Unlike their Daliun subclass the Junn Lords can be very alluring…seductive. And they employ…they got a vast array of methods to augment their natural likability. You just experienced a bit of that down on the port floor. How did you manage to neutralize that?"

"How did you?" I counter.

"That part wasn't easy, but I can't stop now," there's that anger again.

Again I wonder at the burden this woman must be carrying…it's starting to feel more like a desire for vengeance…but I think about only briefly. "Did you get the file?"

"Of course." She produces a small blue data orb, the size of a fingertip. "We had an agreement, right?"

"You'll get your scans." I tell her after examining the orb. It shouldn't be hard to verify her success.

"Alone, Lieutenant, and unmonitored."

"Don't push it."

Breer produces a small portable scanner…from where exactly I don't want to know. But she doesn't just scan Cassad, she questions him. More surprising is that he actually answers her.

I can't tell what's being said though. She talks in code for the entire time they meet. I record it all but doubt I'll ever find the cipher so it's probably not worth the bother. One thing they can't hide, though, is the clear fact that Cassad is not happy with whatever it is the Junns have her telling him. And surprisingly Breer isn't happy with him either, having raised her voice once or twice. Their meeting ends when Cassad stops responding to her coded inquiries.

Breer is silent as I walk her back out of the ship. I watch as she rejoins the much smaller Daliun delegation that stayed behind during her "visit". Whatever burden she had been carrying…it had just gotten darker.

The bunker slides down around us again and the roar of the crowd is no less deafening. The black sand is still covered with blood but at least the bodies have been cleared away. Across the arena floor awaits the original three New Regime reps, the First, Onted Galvin, the Valian, Conin and the Brython rep, Lord Edins, but behind them were several others.

"More representatives from the Coalition worlds," Eboro explained. "Here to have their chance to spit in Cassad's eye. I'm afraid we are going to disappoint them."

The lioness roars to begin the proceedings. The Hall goes dark and the arena spotlights shine again.

"Now it is time for the Cassad to respond to the allegations!" the lioness proclaims and the Hall goes mad as never before. The spotlights on the New Regime reps begin shifting colors as each rep is given her or his own individual light and shading.

"How is this going down?" I ask Eboro.

"It's not," she says with determination. As the shifting lights on the reps continue pulsing, she steps off the platform, into the sand and calls out.

"Khalid Cassad exercises his right to *Kitu Yenyewe Anaongea.* There is no need for him to defend himself."

The crowd doesn't like that, not one bit. The roar that issues forth is as angry as there's been during this whole circus. Once again fiery debris rains down onto the arena floor. Oddly, the Giaks are the only ones in the crowd still in their undersized, hastily customized seats.

Predictably, it's Galvin that comes marching across the sand, one hand on his sword…the other on the on his still holstered sidearm. Ever since the Nerum attack everybody is carrying despite the previously agreed to stipulations.

"This is not the Cassad Imperial Court, snake!" The First Equal hisses at her. He's getting close…how close do I let him get to us before I have to do something?

"And yet, First Equal," Eboro stands her ground. "We are still a civilized people, even without the rule of the Cassads. Our courts will be cradles of justice, not the blood stained killing floors of vengeance."

What trial has she been at?

"Justice?" Still marching, the First Equal shouts across the arena at her. "You will not deny the worlds of the known THEIR justice, Advocate. Long have the Cassads raped our women, enslaved our children and destroyed our homes."

Galvin is getting close. "He will answer to the known…he will speak on his families crimes!"

"According to Coalition law," Eboro doesn't yell but she projects her voice over the rumble of the crowd. "…law set during the first Kujiunga Na conference here in this very tower, no accused being would ever be compelled to testify if they so choose. It was the intent of the…"

Now the arena drowns her out with their outrage. This is the moment they've been waiting for and she was trying to take it away from them. Ose, Khalid's father, died in the taking of Ziara. The "Blood Tide" could not be blocked with a simple report of his death, not after the thousand years these worlds sat under Cassad rule, not after the testimonies of near a hundred worlds. If even a tenth of it was true…Galvin is only a few meters away.

"The Cassad will answer to the known for what HE has done!" He's not slowing and his hands are still on his gun… and his sword. Too close, I should have told Eboro to…buck it!

Carefully, but deliberately I take a step forward, enough to place my right shoulder directly between the First Equal and Cassad. Nothing too threatening but Galvin notices and comes to an abrupt halt, his gun hand still resting on his holstered weapon flexes ever so much. He eyes me hard but the visor on my Raptor helmet is just as opaque as my virtual visor, save there are no holographic eyes.

My tiny subtle step doesn't go unnoticed by the crowd either. There's a sudden, collective drawn breath and then the Hall goes quiet. Galvin had stopped midstride and now was caught between taking another step forward or one backward.

Fek.

The First Equals face flashes surprise for an instant; shocked outrage next, then settles into the narrowed eyes and set jaw of suspicion. "You are the mercenary that captured Cassad, correct?"

With measure, he sets his foot down next to other, neither advancing nor retreating. I glance at Eboro who looks like she wants to run but the All is in her. She only stutters a bit as she speaks up. "He is, First Equal, but he has no testimony to offer."

"You managed what few thought could be accomplished. …Arcadian, right? You brought us Khalid Cassad when many thought he and his fleet would never be seen again. The worlds of the known owe you a debt," There's a short bit of hesitant applause that dies out as Galvin's face hardens. "But why are you still here?"

"His purpose, First Equal," Eboro cuts in. "is too insure that the trial, this trial that so many citizens have fought and died for, proceeds as it should."

Galvin doesn't like that. He eyeballs me, staring hard into the my silver visor, unable to see me looking right back at him behind his own reflection. "This trial won't proceed until Cassad answers his accusers. Justice will prevail."

"Won't proceed', First Equal?" Eboro challenges. "With all due respect it is not for you to decide how or if the trial should proceed. The Council has set Coalition law and we proceed according to those guidelines."

Galvin's eyes are on fire now. No longer listening to Eboro he addresses me with his gun hand now on the his gun handle. "Mercenary…"

"Perhaps," WHOA! Didn't see her walk up I was so focused on the First Equal. The Valian, Conin, stands not a meter behind Galvin. "We can reach a compromise?" she asks, her voice dripping with that false concern.

The blood lust on the First Equals face doesn't go away but he does take a step back. The Valian steps gingerly across the black sand to stand in front of Cassad and I, sparing me a dismissive glance.

"The Cassad need not speak if he is too cowardly to answer. But we will all have our chance to question him." She says.

The First Equal doesn't like that. "He will answer."

"*Kitu Yenyewe Anaongea* , First Equal. He will not." Eboro says as she moves in between the New Regime reps and Cassad, alongside me. "Or Coalition Law means nothing."

The Hall of Kain explodes in outcry again but now it's hard to tell the consensus. I can hear some demanding Cassad be forced to testify but there are just as many chanting for the Kujiunga Na conference referendums to be honored. More of the Coalition reps are treading across the black sand now, all voicing their demands of either forcing Cassad to answer or keeping to New Regime law. Just as the noise reaches its highest level of the trial the lion lady appears on her dais high above the arena floor.

"Coalition Law will be observed! *Kitu Yenyewe Anaongea* must be invoked for each examination."

This doesn't quiet the crowd but it helps to send the New Regime reps back to their side of the arena. The First Equal, Onted Galvin, is the last to leave and he does so after a long moment of staring me down. He's not wearing armor, so he was never serious about pulling his weapon on me despite my "thin" Raptor set. But next time he might be…

And so it went. For the better part of the next two days the Representatives of the Coalition questioned Cassad one after another. Brutal questions, really just more charges cleverly disguised but shouted at him with the rage of all the worlds. Spit flies at Cassad, a few of the members had a bit more range than I anticipate. But the accusations are far worse, even those charges targeted directly at Khalid himself and not the Cassad family dynasty. Some are so horrible that I can't help but to think they can't be true. I hope, that is, that crimes like those never happened anywhere…to anyone.

Eboro invokes his right not to testify each and every time so Cassad doesn't answer.

Not once.

CHAPTER FOURTEEN:

CLOSING ARGUMENTS

The New Regime Prosecution takes three days for their closing arguments. Eboro takes just one morning.

"They are not even listening now," she laments. She's right. The Hall was respectful and solemn during the each of the Prosecutors long speeches. But they would not stop jeering and chanting during hers. Even as we stood once again on the platform before the Coalition Council, the crowd roars profanely, spitting and throwing bits of flaming debris into the arena. It's ugly. They want blood.

And the Council deliberates for a ridiculous amount of time before finally the Lion lady is back on her pedestal.

"The time of judgment is now!" she adds a very realistic roar at the end to stir up the Hall.

"Khalid Cassad, twenty first ruling Alaafin of the Cassad Dynasty and the LAST…" and the Hall shakes from the roar. "For the a thousand cycles of inhumane control over that which you had no right; the lives of every living being in the known universe. Your cruel bloodline reigns no more."

She lets forth another roar and the crowd joins her. I feel my own anticipation rise; as soon as the verdict is read I can get on to getting paid.

But the list of crimes comes next. Like everything else in this trial it's overindulgent and drags on. I could almost drift off if the Giaks in the stands weren't staring me down like they are.

Mercifully it comes to an end. The Lion speaks again, directing her gaze to the Council. "We ask those now entrusted with the direction of our collective; what is your judgment?"

As a group the Council stands, the Seven of the inner Council, those holding the true power in the New regime. I notice that Lan Derai is not among them and can't help but smile beneath my helmet.

The Seven members look to one another, back to the Lioness then without a word they sit. As if they had actually said something the Lion roars again.

"Judgment has been made. Khalid Cassad, last Alaafin of the Cassad dynasty, son of Ose Cassad, you are sentenced to the One Year Death…"

The Hall once again erupts. So loud, at first it's hard to know whether or not they're satisfied. I look for the Junns but oddly they've left the Hall. Standing behind Eboro I see her shoulders slump. Cassad seems dispassionate and continues to study the crowd coolly.

"Sentence to be carried out on the dark, hidden, prison world of Deggar."

"My apologies, Minister." Eboro says without turning to face Cassad. "It seems our brave new society has not passed its first test."

"Did you really think it would be so different?" Cassad says to my surprise. "Rulers often find it is they who are ruled by those they subjugate. These rebels must serve the whims of their uncivilized masses."

I reach up and open the mandible on my helmet, allowing me to freely ask Eboro, "What happens now?"

She turns and I see her eyes are full of tears. "You will be given the coordinates to the Deggar prison facility. Place Cassad into their custody and you will be paid."

Finally! I yank on the chain connecting me to Cassad. "Time to go, your highness."

Claxons blare, and the lights of the arena suddenly flicker. Almost at once twenty something of the New Regime ambassadors who were holograms disappear and the rest begin to leave in a hurry. From the entrance to the arena the Prim and her Nez SeC detail come running in.

Before they can reach us the Lion Lady roars again. "Clear the Hall, the Nezerian Tower is under attack!"

Even as she's speaking there comes an explosion overhead. High above the Hall, above the Four Father Towers, past the plasma shielding… in the substructure of the top level of the Nezerian Tower, there's the flash from something detonating, and another…and another one!

"Lower the bunker!" I scream at Eboro. But before she can comply there's another explosion that rocks the entire Hall from beneath us. The black sand is thrown up from the blast and for a moment I'm blind.

WHAM! My head is thrown back hard as I get rocked from a blow to my jaw. Buckin' Cassad! I hit the sand and feel him jerk on the chain, trying to yank it around my neck. It was a good kick; I spit blood.

Really good…probably designed to break the neck of someone wearing powered armor. Where'd he learn something like that? But Raptor armor isn't like most exo-armor; it's bio-mechanically powered. So instead of killing me Cassad just pissed me off.

Rather than return the favor, however, I just send a charge from my gauntlet up the chain to the young king that shorts out his nervous system. He drops like a wet sack to the arena floor.

"What's happening?" Eboro isn't asking me. She's talking over her on comm unit to someone outside the Hall.

I call up my own Tactical display and the H.U.D. in my helmet shows me… a lot of comm traffic…and a ton of alerts. A small icon flashes warning of…All Damn…City Strikers!

BOOM!

The entire Hall shudders. Black sand spills over the edge of the arena into the cell block.

BOOM!

Another strike and I'm sure it's not just the Hall that's shaking, it's the entire Tower.

BOOM!

City Strikers usually can only be fired from big ships. How did anyone get an attack ship all the way to New Beia without an alert going up? With so many different Coalition ships in this sector it should have been impossible.

BOOM!

Buck it. Time to go.

I haul Cassad up and look to the exits. They're jammed full of scrambling dignitaries, I'll never get him out that way without killing him. I look back to the platform that sits above the bunker. Whatever exploded beneath the Hall must have wrecked the underground concourse. Couldn't have been the strikers…a coordinated attack with agents in the tower?

"The system is under attack!" Eboro shouts. My Tactical HUD hasn't pulled any reasonable data from the crisscrossing coms. I turn about, looking for another exit when a small mound of black sand explodes a meter in front of me.

Then another…someone is shooting at us! Where?

I see them, they're non-descript so I can't I.D. them but I do recognize the pulse guns they're firing. They should've knocked me on my ass but they must never have fired them without the auto targeting system live. The Hall's security measures are still engaged as well as whatever myriad number of countermeasures are waving through the air from the various delegations so computer targeting isn't going to work.

I pull the Sever from my hip and pop off five quick rounds. The little attack group falls in a mess of lost limbs and blown off heads. Any vet of the *Blade* knows how to shoot without a computer to do it for you.

More gunfire; another group…two more groups, rushing from either side of the arena are bearing down on us. I throw the Sever back into its holster, let go of Cassad and dropping to a shooters stance, I whip my rifle off my back.

Before I line up a shot the first group is fired on from my ninety…the Prim and her team open up on them. Her auto target systems have to be down too but you wouldn't know that from the head shots she's poppin' off. Tactical HUD tells me she's targeting the attackers with the long range rifles. The two groups still run at us heedless of their fallen comrades.

I recognize these guys, particularly blood thirsty witnesses from the trial; demanded they be allowed access to Cassad's DNA so they could clone him over and over enough times to kill him once for every one of the citizens they lost to the Old Regime.

I go full auto on them, rotating between both groups. Like before, they're not used to having to fire manually and not a single round of theirs reaches home and like before, my heavier rounds tear into them in very ugly ways.

Ok… they're down or scattered but I see at least one more group getting ready to make a run at Cassad. We've got to move…

"The Advocate!" the Prim screams at me from across the floor. Her team is under fire from yet another batch of fighters but she's pointing over my shoulder.

Fek. One of their shots got through…Eboro is lying on the arena floor, not moving and with a growing pool of blood spreading onto the black sand.

I move to grab her when our position comes under more fire. Berserkers are breaking through the NezSec field of fire because the number of groups attacking now are overwhelming.

I pop off controlled, two round, bursts at the first waves. Their armor is fek and they drop but it's not enough to keep them from over running me if I stay here.

The Prim sees it as I do. She sprints across the arena floor and skids to a halt over the unmoving Advocate. "Is she..."

"Still breathing," I say. "They want Cassad," And not the Advocate. He and I are drawing too much fire.

"I'll take her," she says and scoops up Eboro in one armored arm easily, then looks about desperately. "The concourse has been destroyed! There is no easy escape."

The Hall entrances are jammed with fleeing delegates and the cell block in the trench is a dead end. But none of that matters because; "They aren't after you or the Advocate. They'll track Cassad wherever he goes."

My air foils extend as I slap my helmet mandible closed and gather up the unconscious Cassad. This time they open into full wings and rotate down hard then, with the internal micro counter weights moving at full throttle, they swing upward in a lurching burst; launching Cassad and I into the air.

Above us the vid cars and the holo of the night sky is gone as is the null field. Something has compromised the Halls power network. The Nez SeC gunboats are gone as well. What on styx could be attacking the Tower that the New Regime forces couldn't keep out of the system let alone from making planet fall?

The air is getting thin fast, with the power down the atmosphere regulator must be offline as well. Banking is difficult but I manage to get us around to the third of the Four Fathers towers and land with little difficulty.

The view from the top of the tower would be breath taking on any other day. From here I can see the entire Abatan City skyline, the bottom of the Tower cap above us and the arc of the New Beia horizon beyond it. Gunboats, Coalition fighter craft...they're swooping past the city on their way to fight...what?

Doesn't matter, Cassad has been convicted. Get him to my ship...get him to Deggar...get paid.

From the top of the Hall I can see the thoroughfare that leads back to the hangar. Don't think my air foils will get us all the way back in this thin air...

There's a sudden deluge of aircraft fire raining down outside the city rim. The procession of Coalition fighters and gunboats are forced to break formation and scramble. The incoming fire is coming from multiple points.

Multiple attackers?

Then I see them, streaking past the city proper in formations of three. Tiny fighter craft, too small and too agile to be manned. And they must be autonomous, preprogrammed, because the Nezerian defenses, or any of the hundred Coalition members defense craft, would have cut off any remote signals before they got this close.

Too long, I watch them zip past the panoramic view of the New Beia horizon…they begin to fly their way under the cap and into Abatan City.

No way I make it the hangar now. Might not have to.

I pull the remote from my hip and press the wide ended side. Last chance, if the signal even got through, if I blow this then Cassad and I are done.

The small remote craft are unleashing a torrent of fire onto the city. Can't tell if they're targeting anything special but they're spread out. What kind of attack is this? Some renegade member of the Coalition making a play for power? Or even… none of the remotes are coming anywhere near the Hall. Could this be some remnant Cassad force trying to free him?

Even as the thought occurs to me a sliver of light pierces the dark rooftop of the Fourth Father Tower just across from us. Four quick moving bodies climb out of the lit hole onto the roof. Looks like they expected us to be up there so somebody got mixed up. My tactical HUD zooms in but can't identify who they are. It does identify the energy rifles they're carrying and the high density carbon in their body armor. Right now would be the best time to get the drop on them but I can't guarantee their return fire won't clip Cassad. My instinct is to make a leap and glide in on them, firing on approach to catch them off guard. But I can't do that effectively while towing Cassad. Damn it! I don't want to give up this position but we're too exposed.

Gotta bird.

I haul Cassad up again, extend my air foils and dive off the Tower; the side facing away from the ambush. His weight pulls me off angle but I've done this before. It'll just make it hard to get to another rooftop.

Too hard! Fek. We're drifting into the area the remotes are attacking. I gamble and bank hard, throwing the counter weights in my wings hard to the fore. It's not enough and we spiral down to the top of a nearby municipal building.

"WUFF!" We land hard and I'm forced to roll to keep Cassad from breaking his neck. Remote fire strafes the buildings around us but no near strikes just yet. People are scrambling for shelter on the streets below. It's mayhem; New Beia hasn't seen this kind of fighting in hundreds of years. Doubt there are even any fallout shelters.

Got to get back to higher ground if I want to get out of here so again I extend my air foils, swing them hard and launch us hire into the air.

At once my tactical sensors tell me we're being painted by small arms trying to get a lock. I pivot in mid-air, the Ataban city scape spins around me and I draw my Sever searching for the contact.

Looks like the ambush crew has tracked us but even though they got us painted they're not firing. They must want Cassad alive.

Can't help the predator's grin that slides across my face.

I fire off the Sever before one of them decides that he can get me without hitting Cassad. They scatter for cover at my return fire but we're getting high enough that it won't help them. Two of them dive off the roof so I'm sure they're wearing powered gear of some sort.

WARNING: ENEMY TACTICAL LOCK ESTABLISHED

Fek! The remotes beat the countermeasures and got a lock! How on styx did autonomous systems do that? I throw us into a dive and try a hard bank to get us around a building. Buckin' Cassad is throwing my center of gravity off too much for me to effectively shake off the lock.

So I let us drop down onto another rooftop, ditching the unconscious Cassad as soon as we hit. I sprint to the far end skidding to a stop just a few meters shy of the roofs edge. Down on one knee I let tactical show me the remote that's locked on. I unsling the M-11 and sight it just as it opens fire on my position. The Ataban countermeasures aren't compromising their systems as effectively, high temperature rounds speckle the rooftop around me way too close, but none hit home. No time for patience, I target it quickly and return fire. No hit, but somehow I manage to force it off and cause it to lose its lock on me. Never seen a 'bot back off like that before…

Might not matter; I can see four more remotes, in formation, making an attack run on me. Four of them…can't outrun that…can't outshoot that…

Something falls in behind them, a ship much bigger and mal shaped…could be a…

It doesn't fire on the remotes, it smashes into them!

It's *WarChild*!

My signal got through! She's making the run through the city I pre-programmed into nav. Not a lot of time...WHOA!...

One of the remotes exploded in a bright red plume… of blood What the buck is inside them? Humans can't maneuver that tight.

I run back to the other side of the roof and gather up Cassad. Gotta stow the gun; need one hand for the grapple unit. I'm only going to get one chance at this. If we miss it we're done; *WarChild* is only going to make one sweep through the city. After that she'll just circle the Tower at a few hundred metersuntil New Regime gunboats bring her down.

Need a running start. The pre-programmed route takes her over the Hall, specifically over the last two Towers. I need to get high enough that I can still get in range of her.

With Cassad once more in tow I sprint for the roofs edge. Bio-mechanically enhanced strength and the whipping of the air foils launch us into the air again. *WarChild* bears down on the Tower at attack speed. Remotes are trailing it, firing on her as well as the rest of the Coalition ships. But this is what she's made for; dropping off or picking up troops in heavily contested war zones.

She swoops in and I fire the grapple. *WarChild* moves too fast for me to see if I made a decent connection but almost at once Cassad and I are snatched hard and pulled along.

Fek! I could feel the lurch through my armor and the bio-mechanical weave!

She pulls us through Ataban city, the remotes still after us. The grapple begins winching us up slowly. Still can't see where the claw made contact.

Cluster fire bounces off her hull as more and more remotes fall into formation behind us. There's little room for the ship to maneuver between the tops of the buildings and the bottom of the upper city level. She won't use her G-rock powered shields until we make contact with the hull so for now the cete-armor will have to take the punishment. *WarChild* will be fine but high impact tracer fire slices through the air around Cassad and I. It'll only take one…

BOOM! *WarChild* shudders, the grapple line jerks…then pops free!

At once I extend the air foils to full. *WarChild* brought us all of the way to the edge of the city…

We're going over the side!

CHAPTER FIFTEEN:

THE MOUNTAIN FALLS

I watch as *WarChild* drops ahead of us, flying parallel to the tower. The grapple sent a connection signal telling her we were attached but the disconnection didn't tell her we broke free. She'll dive, at minimum speed until I'm aboard and give the escape command or until she has to pull up to avoid smashing into the surface.

There's a propulsion unit that I could have attached to my armor to give me breakaway speed but I never got around to finding one since the war. So I sweep my wings and dive after. The thin atmosphere slides easily around my aerodynamic armor as we fall but Cassad's drag is holding us up. *WarChild* isn't racing though, so we're catching up slowly.

The bright gold light of New Beia's setting sun washes over us and blinds me until my helmet visor can compensate.

There are more remotes out here, attacking anything and everything. The Coalition gunboats are joined by fighters of various New Regime members. And there's another ship…a big ship.

A dreadnaught…maybe, I can't tell it's make but it's big…really big. Still, there's no way they're trying to take New Beia with one ship...

…Wait…I twist and spin around so I can get a better look. It's not a dreadnaught but whatever it is it's taking an immense amount of damage from multiple New Regime ships. Not enough damage to stop it though, it's still plowing atmo toward the Nezerian Tower. A suicide mission?

My visor zooms in on the big ship until it comes in clear. How in the known…it's the buckin' *Njaro*!! The massive city station where I captured Cassad has somehow gotten here all the way from Ziara. That's…not…possible!! But it's right there and it's the ship that's been spitting out the drones. A desperate attempt to retrieve Cassad? Or something else?

A station like that can't land! It's gonna hit the Nezerian Tower and kill a few hundred million people!

The remotes chasing my ship catch up to us, close enough that Cassad and I become a bigger targeting priority. They drop in so close that I can see past the shaded plasteel dome covers to the pale, big eyed heads of whatever is piloting these remotes…or mini-fighters. Never seen anything like this before but then I doubt they've ever fought against anyone from the 46th or they wouldn't risk getting so close. Of course they have to with; so many ships spewing counter measures their auto-targeting and smart seeking weapons are mostly ineffective.

I grab the Sever in my holster, pull it out and then jam it back in at an angle; manually changing its load-out to explosive rounds. Even as we continue to drop closer to *WarChild* I spin us about and fire on the mini-fighters.

Miss!

Miss! Come on, Loren! You're a buckin' Raptor!

BOOM! Hit! The explosion knocks us a bit off course and slows our fall.

Miss!

BOOM! Another hit! This one hits the thing through the plasteel dome and blows its head off. The small fighter spins off out of control and slams into the one behind it. Two more shots take out third remote and I jam the Sever back into my holster to reload it. I can feel the snap of the round chamber being replaced against my thigh. The next mini needs three hits to take it out and then my HUD warns of another ship getting too close…my ship!

WarChild's hunter green plates come within reach and I slide my hand along its rough skin as we get closer and closer to the top hatch.

Almost there…

Explosions send shockwaves through the air. The minis and the gunboats are fighting even more heavily further down the Tower but the explosions are too big to be from those craft. The sky has grown darker from the ridiculous amount of ships in the air now. Never seen a battle like this!

Almost there…

My hand is centimeters from the safety bar at the hatch.

WHAM! UGN! Stars flash before my eyes and for a moment the

world is spinning and I'm tumbling. *WarChild* bucked, adjusting her descent for some reason and my helmet slammed right into the hatch.

My eyes clear and I see Cassad, still attached to the chain on my arm, the *Njaro*, billowing smoke and erupting with small explosions and finally, thankfully, I see my other hand holding tight to *WarChild's* top hatch bar. Thank the All!

Everything goes dark. We pass through a patch of thick hot smoke and when we clear beneath it I can see massive jet plumes shooting through the cloud. It's the Tower! But it's not breaking up under fire…it's breaking… apart?

We pass through another band of smoke and now I can see that each of the city levels of the Nezerian Tower are pulling apart…disconnecting from the group and launching themselves like gargantuan hoverpads. They're trying to get out of the way of the falling *Njaro*. The Nezerian pillars are falling away from the structure like so much scaffolding. If the city levels below are moving too then I don't have much time..

I key open the hatch and pull myself in. The wind outside fights me, pulling at Cassad but I growl and jerk him inside as well.

"*WarChild*," I open my helmets mandible and try to give the vocal command to escape but the air inside is too thin. I'm forced to wait, what feels like forever, for the hatch to close, watching the *Njaro* begin to break apart as the battleships take her down. They won't do enough damage though; the station is too big.

A lot of people are going to die.

Then at last, "*WarChild*… BIRD!"

G-forces smash Cassad down on top of me as my ship pulls out of the dive and fires its engines for escape velocity. The autonomous drones can't keep up, not that their weapons are any threat now that we're inside.

With little time, I stow Cassad in the airlock and race to the command deck. The G-Det is lit up, there are Coalition forces all over still engaged with the mini-fighters and there are more battleships in atmo now trying to destroy the *Njaro*. I'm getting comm inquiries by the dozens. But they're only after me because they're after everything in the air. They don't know I've got Cassad.

WarChild makes another course correction on her own before I can take control. The last two Nezerian cities are lifting off directly in our flight path. I strap in and augment the course, the remaining mini-fighters don't make through the next band of launch smoke but still manage to get *WarChild* with a few hits as I change course again and point us skyward.

All damn! The *Njaro* is so close now it fills the sky with its mass. Forgot how big that thing is. It's hull erupts with explosions as the different Coalition forces attack together but its size is too much. How did it get here…and who managed it? The Nezerian cities are still inside its collision course. Doesn't look like they have the speed to make it clear. The All…it's going to be bad. The few above haven't even made it clear yet. I jig *WarChild* through a tight course through the shrinking gap between the fleeing city levels and the falling *Njaro.*

Tight. Tight. Tight.

The top level of the Tower, the Administration Cap, plotted a bad course, they get clipped by the outer ring of the *Njaro* as they attempt to slip past. A brilliant explosion rips across it, and the Cap level starts to spin.

The air is filled with small fighter craft that were unable to get out of the way, debris from the city…skycars… citizens who failed to make it to a shelter…

I twist *WarChild's* course again, spinning up and past the Ataban city, where the trial was held, and …a quick dogleg to avoid the now falling Cap…and up and through the collapsing habitat rings of the *Njaro*.

And we're through!!

Buckin' New Regime! They made the same mistake the Cassads made; underestimating the resolve of their enemy. The Cassads wouldn't take the execution of their Alaafins son quietly. This could be the worst massacre since…well…since the New Regime took Cassad space. There's nothing I can do, only hope that those who can get out of the path, do. I point my ship towards black and cut all the feeds looking back.

WarChild pushes out of atmo with a shudder. The space in low orbit is as crowded; there are only minimal Coalition forces hanging back from the battle but that's still enough to give me problems getting out of here. Hails come in, at first individually, then by the dozens as my ship is I.D.ed.

"Arcadian ship, cut your engines and prepare to be boarded," comes from a Quaznian battle group.

"Arcadian ship, *WarChild*, heave to. Do not attempt to leave this system!" The Daliuns are out here too, but too far off to get to me before the Quaznians shoot my ship to atoms.

"Mercenary ship," it's the Brythons but not the big battle group, only one cruiser. The rest must be engaged with the *Njaro*. "Alter your course to ninety degrees right ascension, four hours high declination of New Beia. We will cover your escape."

They know I've got Cassad. I check the G-Det…

…they're outnumbered and out of position. Even if I could line *WarChild* up on that course they would be blown out of the air trying to cover me and my ship would follow not too long after. Instead I run up the engines to the red line and point us to the path of least resistance. If *WarChild* can just get up to speed…

The G-Det screams as we come under weapons fire. The Marajeshi have a ton a small attack craft out ahead of the Quaznians. G-Det tells me they're catching up but *WarChild's* rate of acceleration should get us away from them before they can bring enough fire to bear.

We break orbit and the game changes. Despite being only one cruiser, the Brython ship managed to slow the Quaznian group. Lucked out that the Coalition alliance is important enough to the Quaznian captains that they avoided engaging them. But it isn't the Quaznians that manage to get a solid weapons lock on me.

I swing the G-Det and zoom in on the three ships shooting in on an intercept course; Satrs...very dangerous assault ships, powerful engines, heavily armored and big guns. They're armed with energy and magnetic weapons that can do real and permanent damage to *WarChild* if I let them pound on me.

Buckin' Giak ships.

They're cutting me off from my escape route. It's either try and shoot past them and risk getting holed by those guns or swing back toward the Quaznians who've got serious numbers. I opt for the latter; the Quaznians'll take longer to disable me than the Giaks would.

"Back off," I check the ship registry on the Quaznian Capital ship. "...*Pjrul*, I'm authorized by the Coalition Council to exit New Beia space."

Not much of a chance that'll work. The Brython ship is still keeping pace with them but no longer in position to slow them down. Just a bit, I hedge our course in their direction then watch as the Giak Satrs accelerate in compensation.

My comms ping with hails. Both the Quaznians and the Giaks are ordering me to cut my engines. There's also a ton of cross comm traffic but I don't have time to check it. They're probably arguing over who gets to burn us down.

G-Det re-plots the intercept point after the course correction; the Giaks will get to me first. Can't let them get into weapons range! I push the engines past the redline, *WarChild* shudders around me. Shouldn'a egged them on during the trial.

I wiggle the course again. Intercept point with the Quaznians looms closer but the Giaks are really pouring on the speed now. G-Det identifies their weapons package and displays the fat cone of their effective range. The tip creeps toward my ship.

Two clicks past the redline now and I can hear the roar through the ship. The out-of-tune twin engines are pulling at each other instead of working together. Any other ship not made of cete armor would be ripped apart. As it is the engines will vibrate themselves into cracking. Then my ship, Cassad and I will be burned into so much subatomic dust by one of these Coalition pieces of fek.

Tactical pings with the weapons range warning but it's not the Satrs who've lined me up. The Quaznians have left the Bython ship behind and accelerated into effective range.

WARNING: ENEMY TACTICAL LOCK AQUIRED! PLASMA WEAPONS FIRE DETECTED.

The white pulses of light arc toward my ship and cut across my flight path. Instinctively I throw *WarChild* into an evasive maneuver to force the Quaznians to change course and lose their lock.

It works but my new heading has swung us right into the Giaks weapons cone. G-Det flashes the warning and I overcompensate; pushing us back toward the Quaznians. They open up again and this time *WarChild* is raked across the port housings.

The ship shakes with the impact but the cete-armor holds…better than I thought it would. There may be a path!

I change tactics and my course, diving toward the Quaznian

formation. The engines bang relentlessly with the torment I'm putting them through but, All bless them, they're still holding.

Tactical flashes and pings and screams as the Quaznian battle group establishes multiple weapons locks on us. How many hits can I take before they hobble *WarChild*? I drop the cete-armor shield over the forward canopy and the virtual display comes up so I can see the Quaznian ships converging on me in red and blue skeletal holographic detail. Tens of thousands of kilometers between us shrinks to thousands and then to hundreds. This is going to be bad.

The plasma pulses erupt from their formation, coming down on me like white rain fall. *WarChild* comes under the deluge, which is far worse now that we're closer to their weapons effective field. The virtual horizon hazes over as the sensors are overcome from the attack.

Should've taken that offer from Omega.

WARNING: HIGH ENERGY WEAPONS FIRE DETECTED.

Not the Quaznians…who? Who the buck else?

The plasma rain stops suddenly and the virtual horizon clears. Damn! I'm right in the middle of the Quaznian battle group and…

There's an explosion on my port side. I check the G-Det and see…what the buck? The Satrs have caught up to me and are flying in All damned cover formation! Instead of shredding *WarChild* their guns are opening up on the Quaznians.

Flying this close, maneuvering gets tough and I click the engines back down under red line. The roar of the discordant engines dies down and now I can hear the comms pinging.

I subvocalize and suddenly there's a bright indigo holo of a Stomper at my comm station. Because the comm adjusts for the size of my command deck the Giak doesn't appear to be much bigger than me so it's hard to tell but it could be the same commander who confronted me during the trial. Her body sways and shakes as her own ship is also under fire from the Quaznians. The holo of her barks an order to someone I can't see then turns and looks directly at me.

'Kevic." And the holo fades as they cut the transmission. Kevic? The comm stations offers no translation. But the Giaks stay in cover formation about *WarChild* until we're through the Quaznians.

The comm traffic increase exponentially but all of it is directed at the Giaks. G-Det shows me that several previously interested parties have cut off their pursuit. Only the Marajeshi and the Daliuns are still after us but they're both too far out of position to catch me before I make it out of New Beias gravity well.

The Giaks begin to fall back as well, only maintaining an angle of pursuit to keep the rest from making a run. What was that? Some attempt by the Giaks to get in good with the New Regime?

Not likely; my comms are old and don't translate the full spectrum of information that most communications nodes transmit. So when the Stomper appeared on my holo there were comm glitches in the pattern. Glitches that tell me that the Giak holo was probably a fake. Those were Giak ships but they weren't manned by Giaks.

Maybe… "kevic"? I've heard that before but where? …buck it.

With a groan I lean back into the Primary Control seat. New Beia's grav well drops off in about two hours, ships time. After that and a couple of jumps I should be able to get to one of the more open Median gates then find my way to Deggar.

I let out a very tired breath.

Almost done, Loren. Almost done.

And now; a sneak peek at the next Pack Loren novel; *DEGGAR*...

PACK LOREN:

DEGGAR

by

Howard Night

A DARK UNIVERSE NOVELLA

BARTER

The small window is hit with another coat of acid wash from the sea. The warden's office sits on the coastal side of Deggar prison peering out onto crystal clear but highly corrosive waters. The warden's called General Alt and although he commands a fearful respect from prisoner and guard alike I doubt the man was ever in any military. Word is, as a matter of fact, that he was once the most prized prisoner here. But that would have been before the regime change, before the Great House of Cassad fell.

The "General" is a big man, a calloused handed and hard muscled man. His face is pockmarked harshly on one side which is a sure sign of the grueling outside work details that problem prisoners are assigned to.

Leaning on his desk he glares at me with hard squinting eyes, taking in my measure and probably wondering where and how far he can push me. For long moments his eyes remained locked on the ghostly glowing triangular eyes staring back at him from the dark visor I'm wearing. He can't get my I.D. through the visor much less any idea if he's intimidating me. So he makes a show of looking me up and down while chewing on some foul smelling, backwater herb. First he stares hard into the holographic "ghost" eyes of the blacked out visor that covers my face from brow to upper lip. Then down past my hoofer hide flight jacket and its faded patches. He looks interested in my equipment belt and the big pockets of my machinist's pants but continues down without too much delay to my combat boots.

He snorts and spits the herb out into stained cup on his desk and immediately stuffs his mouth with another root. Most likely there are two beasts warring within him right now. One wants to dominate me… gain submission from me like some kind of pack animal but the other simply wants to celebrate having in his grasp, the last of the Cassads.

The General pulls both his massive fists off of his desk and clasps them behind his back stretching open the very regal service jacket that was too small for him by about a size. Just poking out at the collar I can see the tip of a scar that trails back under his shirt. All prisoners here are branded I remember.

Maybe he actually had been a prisoner…

Not that it matters to me. The only thing I'm worried about is my money. Not a pissing contest with some wannabe Supreme Commandant who obviously knows nothing at all about what it means to be a soldier.

"So…" his voice has the same dry rasp I'd been hearing since coming into standard communications range of this forsaken place. "… how'd you get him? Last I heard he was traveling with his personal guard."

"Tricks of the trade." I say, trying to keep the irritation out of my voice. Damn acid ocean sucks the moisture out of everything. I clear my throat wanting to move things along. "Let's deal."

He looks past me. "He doesn't look too good. The bounty stipulated he was not to be harmed."

Casually I glance over my shoulder. "He's fine." Khalid Cassad stands behind me in metal binders, flanked by Alts own security. Indeed the last of the Cassads looks a bit worse for wear; his royal attire was frayed and grimy but that had been mostly due the razor wire circus that was his trial. A bigger sham I had never seen or survived. But I had been forced to sit through it all and wait to deliver my mark here to Deggar. As much work as the different governments of the New Regime had put into to growing and usurping the known from the Cassads, they still had not managed to come together enough that they could trust each other with a prize as valuable as the last King. Getting him here had not been easy.

"How healthy does he have to be for 'styx end' anyway?" I point out.

The General laughs a long dry laugh. "Too right, boy, too right!" and then with a subtle glare that lets me know there's going to be trouble, he turns and looks out the acid proof window. "Damn shame how the trial ended."

He's referring to the attack on New Beia. The New Regime had been attacked at the trial during the verdict by what turned out to be the *Njaro*, the massive space city once in orbit around the Cassad home systems star. Someone hijacked the station just after I captured Cassad and used it in an insane suicide attack; they dropped the city station onto New Beia, killing millions.

"New Regime certainly took a hit," he says. He's not bringing this up for general small talk. What's his point? "Coalition's gonna take some time recovering from that debacle."

I don't say anything. I just watch him and let my visor keep track of the guards behind me.

"Fek like that might put them out of business."

Oh…he's implying that the deal he cut for Cassad might not be valid anymore. He's trying to lower the bounty.

"Seems to me," I say. "The way the New Regime pulled together, they're Coalition is stronger than ever."

He grimaces at that but doesn't look me in the eye, just continues to stare out that window. Then, "That's ten million New Reg credits and…"

"No." I state flatly. "The bounty was for fifty." This could be bad; he went way too low on the gouge. I expected him to try for half the money but not 80 buckin' percent!

"10." He spits a nasty gob onto the window and turns to stare into my visor with a clear challenge in his eye. "and be glad you'll get that much, boy."

I let a pulse beat pass. My heartbeat remains steady. Before chasing bounties I'd been an ACTUAL soldier.

"50." There's just as much challenge in my voice. Then I raise the small cylindrical device in my hand and point it over my shoulder. One click and the hologram of Cassad fades to nothingness. "Or you don't get your piece of Royalty."

available 2016!

Hey, I'm Howard Night.
I was born in the age of Star Wars, Star Trek and Marvel comics so of course as a kid I was into sci-fi and fantasy but my love didn't wear off as I got older, it grew.
I gobbled up Asimov and Tolkien, Claremont and Miller, and snacked late into the night on Night gallery and Wild West episodes.
As latch key kids my brother and I would rearrange the living room furniture to match the bridge of the Enterprise and ward off attacks from powerful alien invaders.
Even back then I felt the absence of people of color in the sci fi I loved. But that never stopped me from dreaming of being bitten by a radioactive spider or tracking replicants across cyberpunk streets.
Older, I began reimagining the sci-fi I loved with heroes that looked a lot more like the people around me.
Older still I began to wonder how sci-fi could be expressed from a perspective a little closer to home.
I'm a self-published author born and raised in Philadelphia. My first novel, The Serpent Cult, was set in an urban fantasy city much like Philly. Now, Pack Loren comes from a space opera world, Arcadia that could be a giant version of Mt. Airy.
Of course…there is no Arcadia.

I've been published in:
The CITY: A Cyberfunk Anthology,
Genesis Science Fiction Magazine,
Black Science Fiction Society anthology series:
Genesis (as Eugene Peterson) and Genesis II,
The Dark Universe space opera anthology,
and I've written movie and television reviews for the online magazine
O.T.H.E.R. SCI FI at
https://www.facebook.com/OTHERSCFI

Also available from author Howard Night:

"This is a suspenseful, edge of your seat journey that kept me turning pages all the way to the end. I want MORE—more of these characters and more of this story. Five thumbs up for The Serpent Cult and I'm anxiously awaiting the sequel!"

-Valjeanne Jeffers, author of IMMORTAL & THE SWITCH

Mountairy Rock...a modern city with an ancient soul. A city where goliath trees dwarf the skyscrapers, hidden packs of werewolves roam the rooftops, covert witches practice their crafts and a leviathan of a Demon secretly builds its own army of crazed worshipers.

Life had finally started to come together for Max Madigan. This was going to be the year that would see him finally earn his Doctorate, start his career and hopefully kick his long dormant love life back into gear.

But the New Year starts with a grisly massacre at Haley Museum. In its after math Max discovers the Stone

More than just a piece of debris, the path Max's life had been traveling has been irrevocably changed just by picking it up. Worse, the cult responsible for the murders now knows that it's in his possession. Their members are crazed, maniacal and in some cases; serpent eyed and fang toothed.

Fortunately the mysterious Stone seems to be in tune with his peril. It fills him with its power granting him the incredible strength, speed, and heightened senses of a feral animal. The mystical energy is just enough to keep Max half a step ahead of the cult.

But that power attracts enemies and allies alike; a flame haired vixen from the secretive Downhills and a mercurial witch have taken a keen interest in both the Stone and Max himself. They serve as guides to the side of Mountairy Rock that he's never seen warning him of its dangers, of the Serpent Cult... and of the Demon.

Though it's the members of the Cult that will fight, kill, and die if necessary, Max must ultimately deal with the Demon intent on possessing the Stone.

Beset on all sides by danger, the stage is set for the decisive face-off between the Demon and an exhausted and beaten Max in the back alleys of Mountairy Rock.

and

"The classic one-on-one, you-hunt-me, I-hunt-you duel is rendered in edge-of-your-seat style. And after all that, the ending still provides a jolt."

Charles Saunders, author of IMARO

In a world of utter despair, in a world, devoid of hope, in a world consumed by death and destruction, there is only one race left…to lose.

Also available from the DARK UNIVERSE…

The Dark Universe Anthology

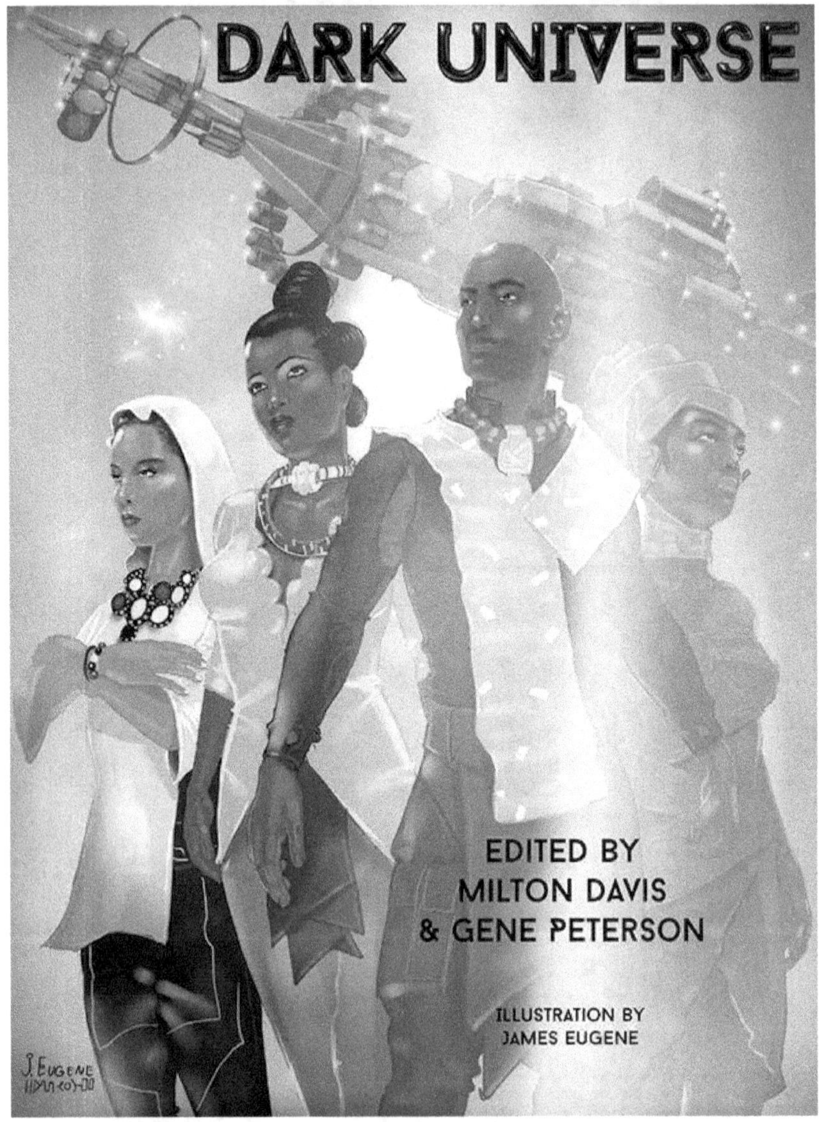

DARK UNIVERSE
EDITED BY
MILTON DAVIS
& GENE PETERSON
ILLUSTRATION BY
JAMES EUGENE

The known just got a whole lot darker…

The Mighty Cassad Empire has fallen and the known universe descends into chaos. The Coalition of Free Worlds, the NEW regime, now reigns but without the order established by the Cassads. Wars between worlds erupt, the mighty prey on the weak and power shifts with every passing half cycle.

Ose Cassad, the Alaafin of the Cassad empire, is executed on his home world by the New Regime leaving his son, Khalid, the heir to the Stool.

The young prince has launched his own offensive in an attempt to save the empire; a mission to the End of the Known. His goal is to stop the rising offensive of the Kur Dak; a people so remote and changed that the rest of the known consider them alien.

Even as he's leading his fleet the Coalition sets the known against him by placing an incredible bounty on his capture. They are intent on bringing him in and trying him for the thousand year tyranny of his family's empire.

Branded a war criminal and deserter by his own people, Pack Loren is a mercenary whose skills were forged in the Wars of the Blade. Life in the known can be hard for a man whose home world is dead but he has a ship, a gun and an idea in his head that he can capture the last king of the known.

A descendant of the First One Million and the granddaughter of a Cassad General, Protea was born to a level of power and privilege known only to a few. But such status in the Empire also comes with equal obligation and the Heir to the Stool demands that Protea honor those obligations in ways that she cannot abide. When she resists he holds her very world hostage. Now she is his weapon as he tries to bring his families empire back from the brink.

A wayward bird, an all-seeing widow and an illegal android…when top mind Amadi Zeli, Averator of the Cassad Empire, put a crew together for his ship, the Dubious, he was looking for those special qualities that would aid him in solving the greatest mysteries of man. But for such a mission, on the edge of the known universe, his chosen crew all had another quality in common he had not anticipated; they were all being hunted.

www.ingramcontent.com/pod-product-compliance
Lightning Source LLC
Chambersburg PA
CBHW070603130626
46556CB00001B/259

* 9 7 8 0 9 8 5 5 6 0 3 1 7 *